ROMAN
GAMES

BRUCE MACBAIN holds a BA in Classics from the University of
Chicago and a PhD. in Ancient History from the University
of Pennsylvania. He has taught Greek and Roman history at
Vanderbilt and Boston University. He lives with his wife in
Brookline, MA.

ROMAN GAMES

BRUCE MACBAIN

HEAD
ZEUS

First published in the United States of America in 2010
by Poisoned Pen Press.

First published in the UK in 2012 by Head of Zeus Ltd.

This paperback edition published in the UK in 2013
by Head of Zeus Ltd.

987654321

A CIP catalogue record for this book is available
from the British Library.

Paperback ISBN: 9781908800527
eBook ISBN: 9781908800961

Printed and bound by CPI Group (UK) Ltd,
Croydon CR0 4YY.

Head of Zeus Ltd.
Clerkenwell House
45–47 Clerkenwell Green
London EC1R 0HT

www.headofzeus.com

To Carol, with love and gratitude

...inopia rapax, metu saevus
Need made him rapacious,
Fear made him cruel.
  Suetonius, *Life of Domitian*

Lasciva est nobis pagina, vita proba
My ditties may be dirty,
But my life is oh, so pure!
  Martial, *Epigrams*

Dramatis Personae

The imperial household:
Domitian (Flavius Domitianus), emperor of Rome
Domitia Longina Augusta, the empress
Parthenius, the imperial grand chamberlain
Entellus, the imperial secretary
Earinus, the emperor's favorite slave boy
Petronius, the commandant of the Praetorian Guard
Domitilla, the emperor's niece
Clemens, the emperor's cousin and Domitilla's deceased husband
Stephanus, Domitilla's steward

Verpa's household:
Sextus Ingentius Verpa, a senator and informer
Lucius, Verpa's son
Turpia Scortilla, Verpa's concubine
Iarbas, Scortilla's dwarf
Pollux, Verpa's slave bodyguard
Ganymede, a slave pantomime dancer
Phyllis, a slave girl

Pliny's household and friends:
Pliny (Gaius Plinius Secundus), a senator and lawyer
Calpurnia, his wife
Martial (Marcus Valerius Martialis), a writer of satirical verses

Corellius Rufus, an elderly senator and Pliny's mentor
Soranus, Calpurnia's physician
Zosimus, Pliny's freedman secretary

Others:
Aurelius Fulvus, the city prefect
Valens, a centurion in the City Battalions
Alexandrinus, a priest of Anubis
Nectanebo (Diaulus), an undertaker
Amatia, a visitor from Gaul
Iatrides, Amatia's personal physician
Marcus Cocceius Nerva, an elderly senator
Papinius Statius, a poet favored at court
Atilius Regulus, Verpa's family lawyer

Chapter One

*The eleventh day before the Kalends of Germanicus
[formerly September].
The sixth hour of the day. The island of Pandateria in the Bay of Naples.*

A brassy sun beat down on the barren rock that for six weeks and four days had been Flavia Domitilla's prison. She hurried along the path that wound down from the house to the black volcanic beach and, squinting into the sun, searched the haze for sign of a fishing boat coming over from Pontia. But the youth was here before her and was already waiting at the water's edge. He gave a low whistle.

She glanced up over her shoulder to the white-washed cottage, far from the harbor, where she lived under the eye of her jailers. They dozed through the noonday heat. She reached into her bosom for the small packet wrapped in a square of silk cut from the hem of her gown. Her jailers would not allow her writing materials, but Flavia Domitilla had been very clever. She had trimmed scraps of papyrus from a volume of poetry which she had brought with her into exile, and by wetting the edges and pressing them together she had made two half-sheets large enough to print a message in tiny script using lamp black mixed with water for ink.

"The letter marked with an 'S'—this one, it curls like a snake, you see? Think of the 'sss' of a snake. Deliver it to Stephanus—sstephanus—my house-steward. Our villa is on the Via Appia at the third milestone. Ask for the house of Flavius Clemens, my husband, I mean—was my husband. After you've done that, then deliver the letter marked with a 'V' to Sextus…Ingentius…Verpa." She pronounced the name slowly to the youth, as though she were speaking to an idiot. "Look how the V is shaped like your hand when you raise it to say '*vale*' to your friends; the same sound—vale, Verpa. He lives in Rome, in a big house with red columns near the east end of the Circus Flaminius. Anyone can show you. Give it to no one but him, you understand?"

The boy nodded.

"And when you've delivered both letters, come back here and describe Verpa to me exactly so that I know you haven't cheated me and I will give you the other pearl earring."

She needn't have given up her pearl earrings, which were worth more than all the fish this boy could catch in a year. To help a cruelly imprisoned lady, to see Rome and go inside a rich man's house, the youth would have done it for nothing.

He extended a brown and muscular arm to take the packet from her. "This man Verpa, he's your kinsman? Your friend?"

"Not exactly. I need his help."

"My father wants to know how long I'll be away."

"Seven, eight days if you have to walk the whole way from Naples, but I expect you'll get a ride in some lady's coach, a good-looking boy like you."

He flashed her a white-toothed smile: "If the lady's as beautiful as you, I won't mind."

"Off with you."

She turned and went up the path again, thinking it not the least of her miseries that the grand-daughter of the Deified Vespasian and the niece of Emperor Domitian must suffer the impudence of a peasant. As beautiful as you? Her mirror told her how this furnace of an island was already ravaging her beauty. Fear etched its mark upon her too. Fear of withering and dying here, forgotten and alone. Fear that the emperor, who had ordered her husband strangled, might turn his wrath on their helpless children, too. Did he have them now? What would that monster not sink to?

Ingentius Verpa, the informer, had denounced her and her husband to Domitian on charges of "atheism" and following Jewish practices. Atheism meant refusing to worship the gods of the official state religion, with the emperor and his deified forebears among them. And an attraction to Judaism was tantamount to sedition. Even after the crushing of the revolt, hatred of the Romans still smoldered in Judaea. Not even kindred blood—she, Clemens, and the emperor were all of the Flavian clan—had sufficed to save them. After all, an emperor who believes himself to be a god is bound to resent atheism!

She sat down in the shade of her doorway and the goats came up to nuzzle her. She wasn't as brave as the other God-fearers. She was ready to bargain for her freedom and her children's lives with the one thing of any value she still had. And Verpa would help her because there was profit in it. If she must betray her friends, she thought, where else should she turn for help but to her enemy?

She fell on her knees then and prayed to the One God to forgive her for what she—a weak and sinful daughter of Eve—was about to do.

◇◇◇

The seventh day before the Kalends of Germanicus.
The eleventh hour of the day. Rome.

> *…I despise you. But if I must betray my friends where else shall I turn for help but to my enemy?*

Verpa set the letter down, barked at a slave to bring him chilled wine, wiped his lips with a thick hand and wiped the hand on his thigh. Though the sun had sunk below the housetops, still the heat was insufferable; the fountains that leapt and splashed in his spacious garden did nothing to relieve it. He took a sip of wine and returned to the letter.

> *…I dare not write directly to the emperor. Too many eyes see his correspondence. Go to our house. Stephanus expects you and will show you where to dig. Take the horoscope that you will find under a paving stone in the garden. It predicts that my husband will sit on the imperial throne. What a cruel joke! Clemens rests with the Patriarchs now, better than any earthly throne.*
>
> *There was a second horoscope—I don't know who has it, though I could guess—that predicts the date of the emperor's death, not many weeks from now. I don't doubt that the plotters by now have chosen another candidate for the throne.*
>
> *Bring my husband's horoscope to the emperor with this letter. It will convince him that I am not lying. But tell him I will give him the other names only in return for my freedom, my children, and my property.*
>
> *Do not try to deceive me, Verpa—I will answer no communication that doesn't bear his seal. I've no doubt he will reward you for your trouble; he pays his informers well, as who should know better than you? Farewell.*

Verpa allowed himself a smile of astonishment. It was seldom that he felt himself at a loss, but this—this had taken him completely by surprise. All the time he was preparing to denounce them for atheism, the two of them had been involved in a plot to assassinate the emperor and replace him with his cousin Clemens! It was easy to imagine how the plotters must have flattered Clemens, the last surviving male member of the dynasty, and he, that amiable sheep, had allowed himself to be persuaded despite the warnings of his hard-headed wife.

And who were these other conspirators that Domitilla was now so anxious to betray? Verpa had not spent thirty years as a Roman senator, courtier, and spy for four emperors without forming some shrewd opinions as to who some of them, at least, were. And what should he do with this information? His civic duty? Warn the emperor? No doubt he would be rewarded. But was there not perhaps a greater reward to be had if he played a different game?

◇◇◇

Since the execution of his master and the banishment of his mistress, Stephanus, the house-steward, had taken to carrying his left arm in a sling, telling people that he had broken it in a riding accident. The sling concealed a narrow-bladed dagger. Now, with his right arm, he held a lamp over the three Syrian toughs as they grunted, putting their weight on the pry bar to move the stone. Verpa, hovering behind them, mopped his glistening face and cursed at them to hurry. The lamplight threw their shadows huge against the columns of the portico. Finally, the stone came loose, and Verpa shouldered the men aside, reaching for the oilskin packet that lay beneath it. Even a hand as steady as his shook with excitement. He was holding a fortune.

After they had gone and Stephanus was alone in the dark, deserted villa, he unslung his arm, massaging the stiffness out of it, and ran his thumb along the edge of his dagger. He thought about what he should do.

Oddly enough, while Ingentius Verpa was digging in the traitor's garden, somebody was digging in his own. The lady Turpia Scortilla, his mate of seventeen years, crouched in a shadowy corner, trowel in hand, excavating a hole in the ivy bed that bordered the wall. It only needed to be a small hole to hold the object that she intended to bury—a tablet of lead, covered with incised letters and wrapped around an iron spike. She had paid the witch a great deal of money for this thing; to possess it was a capital offense.

As she tamped the earth over it and pulled the ivy tendrils back into place, the clouds parted and a full moon cast its rays upon her. Isis, who is also Diana and Hecate, blesses me, she thought, and her heart beat harder. In a whisper she recited the words of the curse:

"I entrust this spell to you,
Pluto and Proserpina,
Ereschigal and Adonis,
And Hermes-Thoth Phokensepsou Erektathou
Misonktaik,
And Anubis the powerful, who holds the keys of Hades,
And to you divine demons of the earth.
Do not disregard me, but rouse yourselves for me.
Destroy Sextus Ingentius Verpa—
Bind him, blind him, kill him.
Pierce his heart, O gods.
Pierce his liver, O gods.
Pierce his lungs, O gods.
I conjure you by Barbartham Cheloumbra
And by Abrasax
And by Iao Pakeptoth.
Let him not live another day!"

The lady Turpia Scortilla struggled to her feet and walked unsteadily into the house.

Ten days after he had left, the handsome youth returned. Flavia Domitilla flew down to the beach to meet him.

"Did you find him—Verpa?"

But the youth would rather tell of his adventures: he had gone to the Circus, but there were no races that day, but then he had gone to the Colosseum and watched men die amid the jeers of the crowd, and afterwards he had eyed the whores who plied their trade under the arches there.

"Answer me!"

His expression turned serious. "I found him. He's a big man with a fringe of white hair, thick lips, a jaw that juts out like a boulder on a hillside. Muscle underneath the fat."

"That's him!"

"Not a nice man. I would have to be desperate, Lady, before I asked that man for a favor."

She half-smiled; no words were needed.

"He pinched me and tried to make me go into his bedroom, the youth continued, "but when I wouldn't he hit me and threw me down the stairs. His slaves stood by and did nothing except for one old fellow with a broken nose and crumpled ears, who picked me up and helped me out the door."

"I'm sorry."

The youth shrugged. "It's nothing."

"But did he give you a message for me?"

The boy looked down. Flavia Domitilla asked him again, feeling a sudden coldness in her belly. It was plain that he did not want to answer, but she dragged it out of him.

"He said he hoped the climate on Pandateria agrees with you."

"Ahh!" She sank down on the stones. "That filth! He has abandoned me! O God of Abraham!" And she wept with her hair hanging over her face.

The sound of her wailing brought two of her jailers bounding down the path toward them, drawing their swords as they ran.

The youth leapt into his boat, rowed quickly away, and never went back again.

Chapter Two

The third day before the Nones of Germanicus.
The first hour of the day.

Rome. The great city woke up as early as any country village.
The sun was not yet above the house tops and already the streets
rang with the chatter of half a dozen languages, the rumble of
carts, the cries of hawkers, the shouts of schoolteachers in their
curb-side classrooms bawling at sleepy pupils. Why then was
Master still in his bed? His dutiful clients already crowded his
atrium to wish him a good morning and receive their hand-outs:
the obligatory morning *salutatio*. Elsewhere in the house, slaves
sponged glittering mosaic floors with a clatter of buckets, polished red-veined marble walls till they shone like mirrors, and
dusted the countless statues that populated the wide corridors
of this princely mansion.

But the four bedroom slaves—each ready to perform his
assigned part in the morning ritual of getting Master up, shaved,
fed, and dressed—stood hesitating before his door. Old Pollux,
the night-guardian of the bed chamber, touched the bronze
handle, drew back his hand, knocked again, and listened. A
doubtful look came over his battered face. "Fetch Master's son,"
he ordered the young slave who carried the razor and mirror. The
boy dashed off down the hall and around the corner to young
master Lucius' bedroom.

Presently, Lucius appeared, his eyes swollen with sleep and in no good humor. Shouldering the others aside, he gave the door one smart rap, then pushed it open and stepped inside with Pollux and the others at his heels.

The single narrow window was a rectangle of pearl gray in the dark wall, and one guttering lamp hanging from its stand threw an uncertain circle of light over the bed. There a motionless shape, dark with blood, lay face down in a tangle of sheets.

Lucius sucked in his breath, leaned close over his father's body, touched it with a finger. Then, in a swift instant, he bolted from the room and down the staircase to the ground floor and through a colonnade to the atrium. "Someone has murdered my father! You," he shouted at one of the astonished clients, "run to the city prefect's office. The rest of you, man the doors and windows. Quickly! The killer may still be in the house."

With expressions of horror, the obsequious clients raised their hands to heaven and demanded angrily of each other who could have committed such an atrocity on this great and good man, their patron?

To the slaves gathered round the corpse upstairs, the sight of their dead master stirred a mixture of emotions. Joy that their tormentor was dead; but then dawning terror. They raced down the stairs after Lucius, shrieking their innocence.

By this time other slaves and freedmen were running from distant parts of the house to see what was the matter. A woman, overcome by shock, backed out of Verpa's bedroom door screaming, and all of them together set up a wail. The slaves understood what danger they were in. They were as good as dead.

In another mansion, across the city, the same obligatory morning ritual was in progress.

Gaius Plinius Secundus, Roman senator, lion of the court of probate, currently acting vice-prefect of the city, arose well-rested from his bed and took his breakfast: the bread dipped, not drowned, in wine, the pear neatly sectioned, a few figs, and all arranged on the tray with his napkin folded just so, the way he liked it.

This small repast over, a slave buckled on his red leather senatorial shoes while another, an elderly man of dignified bearing, commenced to wrap him in a dazzling, purple-striped toga, not releasing him until he was satisfied that every fold was perfect. This was the man's single job and he performed it with great state. Even on a sweltering September morning like this one, the ridiculous garment was mandatory for Romans at the salutatio. So the *mos maiorum*, the way of the ancestors, commanded: those ancient, grim shepherd-warriors who could think of no more fitting badge of citizenship than to wrap themselves in a woolen blanket from neck to ankle and damn the weather. Already, his clients gathered, in the atrium, were itching and sweating in their own togas, and all, patron and clients alike, would have to endure this for an hour.

What an inexpressibly tedious chore, thought Pliny to himself, not for the first time, as one by one the family freedmen together with a clamorous multitude of flatterers, place-seekers, seedy literary gentlemen, and the merely hungry, bustled forward with hearty looks to kiss his hand and receive their food basket and a few coins.

As though from a great distance, Pliny heard himself murmuring inanities: "What a fine young fellow! Do you go to school?" He smiled benignly on a squirming boy thrust at him by an eager father.

A chore, but *dignitas* demanded it. A man of his position must have clients thronging his atrium, and clients must have patrons to defend them in the courts, whisper in a magistrate's ear, commission a poem, dower a homely daughter. The morning salutatio was one of the duties pertaining to rank, and Pliny was a man who took his rank and his duty seriously. And every so often, he reminded himself, there came along some promising young man from his native district, just setting his foot on the path to advancement, who deserved the counsel, wealth, and connections that an up-and-coming senator like Pliny could offer.

Though he ached to stand up and massage his neck, Pliny stifled a yawn and kept his stately pose, fondly conscious of the eyes that admired him from behind the door curtain—the dear girl, so curious, so shy. He squared his shoulders and looked magisterial.

At last, the clock slave called the second hour of the day and the crowd began to shuffle out. He watched their backs retreating through the vestibule and out into the street. Fewer clients nowadays, he reflected, sought their patron's advice or his blessing on their endeavors as they once had done in the old republican days. Now they came mostly for the handout, the money that was just enough to keep food in their bellies for another day. They would all be back again tomorrow, and the whole tedious degrading routine gone through again. At least, with the Senate and courts in recess, he would not need to be accompanied by a horde of them throughout his day. What a relief!

As the door closed behind the last of them, a plump young girl emerged from the side chamber where she had been hiding. She looked up at him with a grave and gentle gaze, full of love and admiration. With her own hands she unwound his sweat-soaked toga and draped a light linen cloak over his shoulders. Pliny held her round chin between his fingers and gave her a tender, almost fatherly, kiss on the forehead.

But this fond moment was interrupted by a female slave bursting into the atrium, baskets of vegetables spilling from her arms. "It's all over the market, Master," the woman gasped. "Senator Verpa's been murdered! Hacked to bloody pieces, they say. Troopers from the City Battalions are there already and have the slaves under guard. Thanks to the son, they say, not a single one got away…" She stopped to catch her breath.

There followed a moment of stunned silence while Pliny's slaves stood stock still and exchanged fleeting looks. The girl turned wide eyes on Pliny. "Husband, what does it mean? Are we…?"

He checked her with a stern look. "Now Calpurnia, you're not to think about it at all. There's simply nothing to be afraid of. Do you hear me, my dear? That's better. Helen, take your mistress into the garden and fetch her kitten or her sparrow or something, you know what to do. Go along, my darling, and put this completely out of your mind, completely out of your mind. You know you mustn't excite yourself, not now."

"Gaius, I'm your wife, I've a right…"

But he leveled his gaze at her, and the girl reluctantly allowed herself to be led away by her nurse. Calpurnia Fabata was fourteen years old, less than half her husband's age. And she was pregnant with their first child. Pliny watched her with anxious concern. A pregnancy could be difficult in one so young. Her morning sickness had now stretched into the sixth month, and her doctor insisted that excitement and mental stress must be avoided. In an age when Romans of his class had to be bribed by the government to procreate, Pliny longed for children.

Swift-footed rumor raced through the city. By mid-morning there was no one in Rome who hadn't heard of Verpa's murder. And, as always happens, exaggeration flourished. The isolated murder of one master, and a notoriously cruel one at that—he was once said to have thrown a miscreant slave into a pool of carnivorous eels—had now swelled to the first act in a bloody slave insurrection. Romans, reminding each other that fully one-third of the city's population was of servile origin, felt stirrings of panic.

By midafternoon the wilder reports had begun to subside. Nonetheless, the killing of even one master by his slaves chilled Roman hearts. Living in a sea of slaves—slaves to dress them, feed them, bathe them, brush their teeth, wake them, put them to bed, carry them, read to them, teach them, amuse them, sleep with them, even remember their friends' names for them—Romans had a queasy fear of them. A man had no secrets from his slaves. They were everywhere in the house, silent shadows, seeing, hearing things that might interest a tyrannical emperor and cost their master his life.

And whenever a slave, driven beyond endurance, turned on his master, Romans responded with hysterical savagery, for this was every slave owner's nightmare. The Law was explicit. All the slaves in the house must be punished alike. Could one slave alone plot his master's death without letting a word slip to the others? Could he procure the weapon, creep unnoticed past the night-guard, open the door to the chamber, carry in a light, do the deed, and make off all in total silence and secrecy? Impossible. Every slave in the house, it must be assumed, knew what was afoot and could have reported it. To put it simply, no slave was innocent of his master's death, and the whole *familia* without distinction must be executed. "Are not some punished unjustly?" asked a few. "What of it? Unless we keep them in constant fear, we are at their mercy."

Even the mild Pliny, who had never raised his hand or spoken a harsh word to a slave in all his decorous life, could not suppress a shudder.

Chapter Three

The day before the Nones of Germanicus.
The ninth hour of the day.

The bronze gates of the palace swung shut behind them with a clash of metal. A moment later the figure of Parthenius, the imperial chamberlain, preceded by a cloud of scent, strode toward them with arms outspread. Vast sheets of colored silk draped his whale's body, rings glittered on his fingers and thumbs, the crisp curls of his hair appeared to be sculpted in silver. He performed, as well as his belly permitted, a low bow.

"What a pleasure to welcome all of you, my lords and ladies," the chamberlain panted. "A rare evening is in store for you. If you will follow me, please."

The guests made the minimal reply that etiquette demanded. Roman senators despised these imperial freedmen. Spawned in the gutters of Antioch and Alexandria and sold as children into the emperor's service, they wielded more real power than any senator did. Parthenius, for example, oversaw the emperor's domestic arrangements, woke him in the morning, and all but tucked him in at night. At dinner, in the bath, even in the latrine, some said, he never left the emperor's side. A good word from Parthenius was worth much gold.

Preceded by this great man, the dinner guests filed into the Hall of Audience. The heat of the streets never penetrated here. Pliny shivered in the marbled chill and felt goose bumps on his arms. The hall was empty now that the day's business was done, but visitors were always taken this way for a good reason: the vast space was designed to awe. In this stupendous vaulted cavern a man was no more than an insect. Pliny had not been here for some months, and so it was with surprise that he noted a new feature. Disks of moonstone as big around as shields and polished like mirrors had been attached with brackets to the walls and columns wherever one looked. For what purpose, he could not imagine.

From the great hall, their way lay through a splendid formal garden in whose center a sunken fountain shot jets of water high above their heads. Peacocks strutted past them on the path.

"Chamberlain, have you forgotten where the emperor's banquet hall is?" Several of the guests had stopped where the path divided and regarded Parthenius with amused contempt.

"Our Lord and God," he answered, breathing heavily, "prefers a more intimate room tonight, as we are so small a party. Come this way, please."

Obediently they went through a door and down a succession of sloping corridors that turned and twisted until they had lost all sense of direction. And it seemed as if at every turn the corridor grew dimmer, dustier, quieter. Conversation died until there was only the shuffle of sandals and the wheezing and puffing of their guide to relieve the silence.

"And just down these steps, my lords and ladies…" A flight of worn stone steps descended into a well of darkness. No, this was all wrong. There was no dining room in the bowels of the palace. The guests bunched together, turned round and found their retreat blocked by a dozen Praetorians who had come up silently behind them. Women turned to their husbands with wild, questioning looks. Pliny caught the city prefect's eye, but his superior's face, controlled through years of practice, told him nothing.

"Before you, honored friends, gapes the Portal of Hades, the bourn from whence no man returns. Your Lord and God commands you to join him tonight in the realm of Pluto, his brother god." Parthenius delivered this speech with the voice and gestures of an actor on the stage. Pliny breathed a silent prayer of thanks that he had not brought Calpurnia, though she had begged and pouted.

The Praetorians took a menacing step forward, hands resting on the hilts of their swords. Among the guests, hearts froze but faces remained under control. It was crucial not to show fear, not to betray the smallest doubt about the emperor's good will. A frightened man was a guilty man.

"I'll lead the way," Atilius Regulus called out. "Hercules wasn't afraid to visit Hades, and I think I'm as good a man as he!" The rest of them took up his light-hearted tone as best they could. There was simply nothing else to do.

"I pray I don't meet my first husband down there," cackled Arulena Rustica, the much-married wife of a general.

"I think I'll just stay there until my creditors go away" cried the gourmand Gavius Apicius, who had squandered a king's ransom on oysters.

Their lips twisted in desperate hilarity, the guests descended, half-stumbling, into the black pit. One elderly senator turned and tried to claw his way up again, but was borne down by the weight of the others. At the foot of the stairs, moved by invisible hands, a door swung inward on screeching hinges

"Nice dog, Cerberus!" joked someone, but there was no laughter.

They were plunged into darkness. Suddenly Pliny could not breathe, and the blood pounded in his temples. Whichever way he turned, other bodies pressed against him. He had no idea where the stairs were. The air stank of burnt charcoal. It was obvious they were in the furnace room which, in wintertime provided currents of hot air to warm the floors above.

Then a line of tiny lights appeared in the blackness. As Pliny watched spellbound, the lights advanced in a double column, drew nearer, divided and formed a circle around the huddled guests. When they were just an arm's length away, he saw in astonishment that each was a candle held by a little boy, who was entirely naked and black.

"Your name, master?" whispered a little candle-bearer. The accent was of the Roman streets, not Africa—the child's color was painted on.

Pliny croaked a reply. In the crepuscular glow of the gathered candles, rows of chairs could just be made out, and beside each a dark object of some sort, standing about waist high. The child took his hand and led him to a chair. The candle dipped and gave its light to an oil lamp on a stand, the sort of lamp that hangs in tombs. Then pointing to the slab-shaped thing beside the chair, the child commanded Pliny in a piping voice to read his fate. All around him other demon-children were doing likewise and other guests were helplessly obeying. Pliny heard their gasps and stifled cries and a rising commotion of angry and frightened voices. He examined the thing, touched it. It was a plank in the shape of a gravestone and on it was carved *his* name.

From somewhere a double-flute began to play a funeral dirge and the naked boys, gliding like phantoms, performed a weird circle dance, weaving patterns in and out with their glowing candles. Now black-clad servants appeared, carrying tables with trays on them which they set before each place. Pliny peered at his. Black dishes containing black fruits and flowers—offerings to the dead. When a hand touched his shoulder he nearly leapt straight out of his chair. But it was the city prefect. "Ready to do your duty," Fulvus whispered into his ear, and then moved away.

Now, over the shrilling of the flute, a disembodied voice began to chant Homer's dismal verses which describe the pitiful, squeaking shades of the dead. There was no mistaking that voice. Frightened whispers hissed around him.

"Tell him, Publius, for the sake of the children!"

"It's a trick, shut up!"

"Tell him!"

Other voices: "We adore your image every day at sunrise, Caesar!"

"We shut our doors to our son and his republican friends."

"We rejoiced when the criminals, Senecio and Priscus, were put to death."

"And when you drove the rabble of philosophers from the city."

"O, Lord and God, spare us," a woman beside Pliny sobbed. "We never hid the traitor, Musonius, in our house, never! Torture our slaves, they'll tell you who…"

Her husband clapped his hand over her mouth, but not before Pliny recognized her voice. He recognized them all, and in that instant, realizing why he was here, he groaned with shame. More guests leapt to their feet, upsetting the lamp stands and "tombstones" with a clatter, and all trying to be heard at once. They were innocent. They swore it on their children's heads. But they knew who his secret enemies were, if he would only spare their lives…!

Then one voice made itself heard above all the others. "Hush, all of you! Silence, I say! Caesar, this excellent joke is worthy of your divine wit. Why, our friends who are not here tonight will feel themselves slighted when we tell them what fun we've had! But I fear some of your guests, and particularly the ladies, are taking it entirely too seriously. It would be unkind to encourage them further. I, for one, am hungry and want my dinner." The speech ended with a forced laugh.

Old Cocceius Nerva, thought Pliny. An ornament of the Senate for more than forty years. Smooth, adaptable, a friend of the dynasty or, at least, not an enemy. He had never, before tonight, been remarkable for courage, but this was a brave thing he was doing.

There followed a tense silence which lasted until Pliny thought he could not bear it another moment, and then a trap door opened above them, letting in a shaft of light, and the distinguished lords and ladies, the flower of Rome's aristocracy, made an unseemly dash for the stairs.

Above ground, the Praetorians were gone and Parthenius, smiling blandly, congratulated them all on their return from dead. But his hooded eyes said something else. Pliny stole a look at his companions. Women, bewigged and bejeweled, tried to repair tear-streaked makeup. The men avoided each other's eyes, but all gazed at the tall, stooped figure of Nerva, their savior.

As though nothing were amiss, Parthenius, clasping his hands and smiling wetly, led them back the way they had come to the entrance to "Jupiter's Banquet Hall" for the real dinner. Here, servants in white livery removed their shoes and led them in groups to their tables. Pliny noted that he, the city prefect and the informer Regulus, their companion of the evening, were each placed at a different table—to continue eavesdropping, of course. Pliny felt sick to his stomach and prayed that his face did not give him away. Had things come to this? A dynasty that had started off so fair? He would march into the prefect's office tomorrow at daybreak and resign his post.

It had been only that morning, coming on the heels of the excitement over Verpa, that a message had arrived from the Prefecture.

"To Gaius Plinius Secundus, greetings from Aurelius Fulvus. Your presence is commanded at the palace at the ninth hour for dinner. Wives are particularly invited." Pliny raised an eyebrow at this; as a rule, the emperor had little use for senatorial wives. "We will meet on the steps and go in together. Be prompt. Farewell."

Curt and faintly unpleasant, as usual. Pliny disliked his superior. Some months ago he had been plucked from his civil law practice and asked to assist the Prefecture in clearing away a great backlog of criminal cases. Not long afterward, one of the deputy prefects, a man tortured by ulcers, committed suicide, inconveniencing everyone, and Pliny was moved into his position. Only for a few days, he was assured, but days had stretched into weeks with no end in sight. It was another feather in his cap, no doubt, but the job was irksome.

The sun was still high and the heat oppressive as his litter-bearers had snaked along the teeming streets, holding him high above the filth. The narrow streets of Rome were clogged with thousands of visitors streaming into the city to enjoy the revels that would occupy the next fifteen days: tomorrow the *Ludi Romani*, the Roman Games, began.

The palace sprawled over half the Palatine Hill, rising up "like seven mountains piled one atop the other, reaching to the sky," said a flattering poet. It was divided into a public and a domestic wing. In the former, the *Domus Flavia,* toiled a thousand imperial slaves and freedmen—the clerks, scribes, and accountants whose drudgery made the vast Roman Empire run, while in the latter, the *Domus Augustana,* other slaves, sleek and perfumed, performed more intimate services for their "Lord and God."

The building was entirely Domitian's creation; he had supervised the design of it down to the smallest detail. His father and elder brother in their lifetimes had both been content with far more modest quarters.

When they had arrived that evening at the breathtaking sweep of steps that led up to the monumental gates, Pliny had been astonished to see among the company several known critics of the regime. Could reconciliation be in the wind? He had heard no such rumors, but the thought gave him pleasure.

Catching sight of his chief, Pliny had made his way toward him. The city prefect, a sallow, long-jawed man, gripped his forearm with false bonhomie and intentional pain. Aurelius Fulvus had been a stalwart of the regime for years. Raised to senatorial rank by Vespasian as a reward for his family's loyalty in the civil war, he now held this powerful and lucrative office which was far beyond his modest intellect and sluggish nature. By his side was Atilius Regulus—senator, lawyer, informer—a man Pliny despised. Was he on the prefect's payroll too? Regulus threw a friendly arm around Pliny and brushed his cheek with his lips.

"I regret that the Lady Calpurnia…" Pliny had begun.

"Yes, yes, never mind," said Fulvus, "We didn't bring ours either." He drew the two of them close and whispered over the hubbub. "We are not here tonight to enjoy ourselves. Our instructions are to look sharp and listen well. Those were Our Lord and God's precise words." *Lord and God.* How easily the phrase rolled off Fulvus' tongue.

"And for what precisely are we listening?" Pliny had asked, but at that moment, the tall gates of gilded bronze had swung open and the elegant mob swarmed up the steps between a double line of Praetorian Guardsmen in their white tunics and scarlet cloaks.

...Yes, he would resign his post. This embarrassing charade was the last straw. He was a Roman senator, not a common spy.

"You are all looking well, my friends. Hale and strong. No need for any of you to fear Hades!" Domitianus Caesar, Conqueror of Germany, Conqueror of Dacia, *Pontifex Maximus*, Consul, Lord and God, regarded them all with a tight smile. Like his father Vespasian before him, the emperor was thick-bodied, big-shouldered, and bull-necked. He had managed to enter the hall ahead of them through some secret passageway, no doubt, and was already reclining beside his wife on the imperial couch, raised upon its dais. An exuberant laurel wreath failed to conceal his thinning hair. When some of the guests began laboriously to kneel, Parthenius assured them that the emperor did not wish to stand on ceremony tonight and the prostration could be omitted.

"My only thought," Domitian continued, "was to honor Pluto on the night before we honor his more genial brother, Jupiter."

Vigorous nods of approval. Fixed smiles.

"Cocceius Nerva, I believe, is hungry? Am I right, Nerva, it was you, wasn't it, who said so?"

"I am perishing of hunger, Caesar." In fact, Nerva was a martyr to indigestion and seldom took anything but porridge.

"Perishing! Well, we shouldn't allow that. Best eat your fill tonight, my friend, for who knows what tomorrow may bring, as some poet has no doubt said."

The air crackled with malice.

Trying his best *not* to overhear any of the conversation around him, Pliny's eyes strayed to the imperial couple. Domitian was a man of forty-five who had once been thought handsome. Now baldness and a paunch had ruined his looks. Beneath dense black brows, quick, mistrustful eyes peered out.

Behind him, as always, stood his cup-bearer and bed-mate, Earinus, a young boy of exceptional beauty except that his head was grotesquely small. As the boy leaned over to refill his master's goblet, Domitian reached under his red tunic—the youth always wore red—and ran his hand up the inside of his smooth leg. Earinus smiled. The empress, however, did not. Domitia Longina Augusta, stared stonily ahead of her, putting not a morsel of food to her lips. A man of breeding does not fondle his pet boy in his wife's presence.

She was a proud woman, the daughter of Nero's best general. She had inherited her father's strength of character, but, sad to say, his looks as well. She was as tall as a man, with a square jaw and prominent nose. Her face was thickly coated with powder of white lead—some said, to hide the bruises made by her husband's fists.

It was not only with boys that he humiliated her. If one believed the palace "smoke," Domitian had committed incest with Julia, his niece, a pale and delicate girl, and then forced her to have a near fatal abortion.

At a signal from Parthenius, waiters—Ethiopians, Egyptians, Syrians, Greeks, all of them beautiful young boys—came round with the appetizer course on trays of solid gold. On offer were baked dormice rolled in honey and poppy seed, Lucrine oysters, pickled eggs, and snails fattened on milk.

Course succeeded course without pause: sow's womb stuffed with herbs and surrounded by the teats boiled in milk, lamprey eels from the straits of Messina, roast boar, mullet, hams ingeniously carved in the shape of pigeons, an enormous lobster garnished with asparagus, goose livers with truffles, and sea urchins. For drink there was Falernian wine, strained through snow. The beautiful boys refilled the crystal goblets as fast as they were emptied. Other slaves hovered about the guests, ready with silver ewers of rosewater to pour on greasy fingers and to offer their long hair with which to dry them.

Pliny was offended in his philosopher's soul by these grotesque displays. He took just a little of each dish and drank abstemiously, as ever. He doubted whether anyone had much of an appetite left after what they'd been through. Still, his table fellows outdid each other in praising the fare, heaped up their plates, and belched enthusiastically.

Meanwhile, to entertain them, dwarfs dressed in miniature suits of Greek armor fought bare-breasted Amazons. The guests did their best to look entertained but their laughter was too gay, their smiles tense and wary. The only safe topic for dinner table conversation was tomorrow's great sacrifice to be followed by days of theater and chariot racing.

As the dessert course of imported fruit and honeyed wine came round, the emperor rapped for silence. "Papinius Statius," he called out, gesturing to the couch alongside him, "one of the few living poets worth hearing, is with us tonight. Though he is weighed down by years, he has obliged me by coming up to Rome to attend the Games and immortalize them in verse. I have asked him to recite to us from a work in progress."

This was received with dutiful murmurs of thanks. The emperor's love of poetry was genuine; he rewarded poets lavishly and provided copies of their works to the public libraries.

Statius, a frail old man with wispy white hair, got shakily to his feet. His bearing was patrician. He gravely acknowledged the emperor and empress, calling them "our own Jupiter and Juno." In a quavering voice he read portions of an epic poem on which he was engaged and, soon running out of strength, sank down on his couch again. The guests applauded warmly, especially Pliny, who dabbled at poetry himself. Domitian, in a voice noticeably thick with wine, praised the old fellow's years of loyalty and service to the Flavian House. "Where will I find your like again, Statius. Nothing but your poetry gives me pleasure any more." It seemed sincerely meant. A mood almost of warmth had been created by Statius' presence, but it wasn't to last long.

The emperor's tone changed in an instant. "I have lost a close friend today," he said in a somber voice. "A pillar of the government. A colleague of yours, Senators. I heard of his death this morning with a sense of shock and"—he selected a succulent mushroom—"outrage."

"Oh, irreparable loss," murmured Regulus with feeling. Others felt differently. Lackey of the regime, enemy of his own class, one of Domitian's most notorious and best paid informers, compared with whom Regulus was a mere tyro, who else but Ingentius Verpa? No one had dared to speak his name all evening, though his murder was uppermost in everyone's mind. Now the emperor himself was going to confront them with it.

"It's said he was killed by a slave," Domitian looked hard into their faces. "Perhaps. Such things have happened. And yet there may be something deeper at work here. Atheism. *Atheism!* Verpa had uncovered its poison in the bosom of my own family. And, though it saddened me, I punished it as it deserved. Now, I swear to you, Senators, I do not take this lightly. Aurelius Fulvus is going to give his immediate attention to the case—we have already spoken about it—and I promise you, punishment will be swift."

This was answered with loud "hear, hears" from the guests, whose sentiments, this time, were genuine. No one lamented Verpa, nor did any of them have much of an opinion about this atheism, which seemed to exercise the emperor so much. Still, Verpa was a Roman senator and a slave owner like themselves. That was enough.

"…swift…" the emperor's words trailed off and he sank back on his couch. He held out his cup to Earinus for more wine. Momentarily his eyes closed. Pliny was struck suddenly by how tired he looked.

The soirée, it seemed, was over. At a gesture from Parthenius, the dining room doors swung open and the servants crowded in carrying the guests' outdoor shoes. Pliny stood up with the others.

"You and I will remain a moment," Fulvus whispered close beside him.

With a curt gesture Domitian dismissed his wife. "You! You ate nothing tonight," he shouted at her departing back. "Did you think your food was poisoned? I don't need poison to deal with you."

"Earinus, leave us." He addressed his pet in a gentler tone. "Parthenius, get rid of those donkeys." He meant the slaves, who were making a racket with the plates. They fled.

"And will you be needing me further, Master?" the chamberlain murmured.

"Need you? *Mehercule*, what would I do without you!" Parthenius accepted this tribute with bowed head.

Domitian strode to the side of the room, where silk tapestries hung between the columns. He pulled each one aside and looked behind it.

"They spy on me, you know," apparently meaning the slaves." They're being paid to do it. They think they can evade me, a god! But I'll catch them out!"

"Shall I have them killed, Ruler of the Universe?" Parthenius asked mildly.

The Ruler of the Universe sat down on a vacant stool and squeezed his temples with his fingertips. "As you think best." The voice was flat and lifeless. "Now, Fulvus," he turned his gaze on the prefect, "make your report. I could hear the shouts myself, I put no stock in them. I trust you heard the whispers. Who among them is plotting my death?"

"No, Caesar, impossible!" This was Parthenius again, an expression of horror on his face.

"What, then, am I mad?" Domitian rounded on him. "An emperor is the most unfortunate of men, because no one believes that his life's in danger until he loses it!"

Pliny felt as though an elephant's foot was on his chest. He struggled to draw a breath, then blurted out, "I heard nothing, Caesar, nothing at all. Not a word. Nothing…"

"I think you've made yourself quite clear, Gaius Plinius," said Fulvus with a touch of sarcasm. "I too heard nothing distinct, Caesar. If it had not been for Nerva…"

"Nerva," Domitian said very softly. "We will have to do something about Cocceius Nerva."

"And the unfortunate matter of Senator Verpa?" Fulvus said. "I've had a detachment of troopers in the house since early this morning. What more do you wish done?"

"What do I wish?" Domitian gave him a ferocious look. "If I can't protect my senators from being murdered in their beds,

I shall have no allies at all among 'em. I suppose the slaves did it. I want them all tried and burnt alive as soon as the Games are over and the courts are in session again. Fifteen days from tomorrow. Plenty of time."

"More than enough, Caesar," the prefect replied, "if these were fifteen ordinary days. But it is my job also to maintain public order while the city is packed with visitors. Crowds must be managed, drunkenness and petty crimes repressed. Add to that the number of, ah, clandestine operations that you have entrusted to me. All this with only four thousand men. I can't be everywhere at once."

"Are you getting old, Aurelius Fulvus? Is it time I replaced you?"

"Please, Lord of the World, allow me to explain." His voice cringed though his body remained upright. "If I were to take on the investigation personally, would it not seem to make too much of Verpa's death? On the other hand, we don't want to assign it to a mere tribune or centurion. I had thought to put a member of my staff in charge of it. A proven man, a man with many friends in the Senate chamber. In short, my acting deputy, Pliny—that is, with your approval, of course."

Pliny, who had let his attention wander, began at once to stammer. "But, Prefect, I am a probate lawyer, not a policeman! In fact, I have made up my mind to return to my practice."

"You've said nothing to me of resigning," the prefect said in a menacing tone. "Will you oppose yourself to my recommendation and Our Lord's wish?"

"Why, no, I…"

Domitian gripped Pliny's shoulder with a hand that could have crushed an apple and brought his face close—that face with its eagle's beak, jutting chin, thick neck. The red-rimmed eyes searched his. "It is my wish. I have been…" he searched for the word, "preoccupied lately or I would have spoken to you sooner, my dear Pliny. You know your late uncle served my father with the utmost loyalty and discretion for many years. I've already helped your career along, haven't I? Without a word from me you'd still be waiting for your praetorship with the rest of the provincial newcomers."

"I know, Caesar, and I'm most…"

"Grateful? Of course you are. Then show your gratitude now."

"Certainly, Caesar, it's only…"

"You have your uncle's temperament, you know. Scrupulous, meticulous, careful. And your private life is irreproachable, that counts for a great deal with me. I only wish I had more senators like you instead of those 'philosophers,' as they like to call themselves. I admire philosophy, and so do you. But those people, they use it as a cloak for treason! I know you agree with me."

Pliny abandoned all attempts at speech and merely nodded. The emperor's grip still held him fast.

"I knew I could count on you. Now then, you need only attend the procession and sacrifices tomorrow morning and then again on the Nones. The rest of your time you will devote to this matter. Understood? And now go home to your lovely child-bride. I envy you. You see the dragon I married!" Domitian let out an unpleasant laugh. "Come and kiss me, Gaius Plinius." Domitian offered his cheek, a mark of signal favor.

Pliny and the city prefect emerged into the sultry September night. The sun had set hours ago and, except for a lamp glowing from a window here and there, darkness covered the great city like a lid on a pot. The two men stood talking at the foot of the steps while their litter slaves stretched and shook themselves.

"This business tonight in the furnace room. You must have known," Pliny said, trying not to show his anger.

"Not in every particular," Fulvus answered easily.

"But inviting the wives!"

"Much more likely than their husbands to let something spill. Now let us have done with complaining and turn to the matter of Verpa."

"You might at least have prepared me for that! I'm a probate lawyer. I'm not used to dealing with criminals—at least, not this sort of criminal."

Fulvus waved off the note of indignation. "Nothing could be simpler. Don't worry the thing to death like one of your convoluted inheritance cases. Just have a look around the place tomorrow, take depositions from the son and the woman Scortilla—she's a bit of a whore, I'm told. Do you know her? No? What chaste ears you have. Question the slaves, of course. Oh, don't look so queasy, they won't need much tickling. Someone will talk, they always do."

"The slaves are being confined in the house?"

"Yes, well the Tullianum is full up at the moment with more important prisoners awaiting a—ah—final disposition of their cases, if you get my meaning."

Pliny knew what he meant.

"So, no place else to put them. Anyway, then all you have to do is sit down and write an impassioned speech condemning them. All in a day's work for a lawyer, I would have thought. And the emperor and I will be most grateful to you. Now, I've assigned you a centurion—manners a bit rough, but a good man—and five troopers from the City Battalions, all I can spare, I'm afraid. As for the slaves, I've ordered them collared and shackled in their sleeping quarters, and that's where they'll stay until we execute them. Why can't this great city of ours build a proper prison?" He raised his arms to heaven. "Well, goodnight, my friend. Best to your wife."

As they mounted their litters, Fulvus called back, "Full dress uniform tomorrow. Mustn't let the Praetorians outshine us."

Chapter Four

Late that night Pliny peeped into his wife's bedroom. It was hot and she had thrown off the covers. She lay on her back, her chestnut hair spread out on the pillow, the swelling curve of her belly a gray outline against the pale lamplight. Old Helen slept on a cot at the foot of the bed.

He made scarcely a sound but Calpurnia awoke and sat up in the bed. "Dearest, forgive me…" She took pride in always waiting up for him.

"Don't be silly. Helen was right to make you go to bed."

"Was it a fine dinner? I wish I could have gone."

"I am inexpressibly happy that you did not. Go back to sleep like a good girl. We'll talk in the morning." He kissed her forehead and felt a surge of tenderness run through him.

In his own bed in the adjoining room Pliny tossed fitfully. One could have said, before tonight, that if ever a man was pleased with himself, comfortable with his certainties, satisfied with his circumstances, and confident of his future, it was he.

Now doubts assailed him. He had attended dinners at the palace before but nothing like tonight's grotesquerie. Was the emperor going mad as some in the Senate whispered? And if so, then where did duty lie? Could a good man serve a bad emperor and keep his own hands clean? Pliny was on the horns of a dilemma. He was a good man. But he was also an ambitious one, and he could not put out of his mind the emperor's words to him: a chance to emulate his uncle, that paragon of learning, virtue, and dedication.

He tossed and turned, but sleep would not come. He counted the hours until dawn, when he must rise and present himself for the opening ceremony of the Roman Games, a festival that occupied two weeks in the middle of September—not September—"Germanicus," he must remember to say! For many senators and lawyers, with the cessation of public business, the Games, which only the priests were strictly required to attend, meant a fifteen-day vacation from the sweltering cesspit of Rome to their estates in the hills. But no such respite for him this year. And all because this wretched Verpa had got himself killed.

Pliny had known the man only by sight and reputation. The world of senatorial society was large enough that he could avoid meeting people he found disagreeable, and Verpa had never shown any interest in meeting him, the gods be thanked! The man had been a notorious informer all the way back to Nero's reign.

Informers were a cancer on the Roman Senate. Every emperor began his reign by denouncing the evil, but sooner or later succumbed to the temptation of listening to the vicious innuendo spread by the informer against his fellow senators and their families. Condemnation was certain, and the informer divided the victim's property with the emperor.

Verpa had begun by denouncing a woman of senatorial family for treason because a slave saw her undressing before the emperor's image, and, on another occasion, he condemned a man for carrying a coin with Domitian's portrait into a privy. But he had outdone himself when he denounced Clemens, the emperor's own cousin, and his wife, Domitilla, on a charge of atheism and performing Jewish practices. Verpa had brought this charge openly in the Senate. Pliny had been there to hear him. It was indeed a shocking revelation, but Verpa had incontrovertible evidence to back it up, and the emperor went nearly insane with anger. Clemens was swiftly strangled and his wife banished for life to an island. Sextus Ingentius Verpa was riding high; that is, until someone butchered him in the night. Tomorrow Pliny must poke a stick into this anthill and turn it over. The thought of it revolted him.

When at last he drifted off to sleep, naked black children invaded his dreams, hanging on his arms and legs, dragging him somewhere he did not want to go.

Pliny was not the only one whose night was filled with terrors. Domitianus Caesar, Lord and God, emperor and high priest of Rome, sat alone in his bed chamber—his refuge, his inner sanctum, where few ever penetrated. Because he feared the dark, tiers of lamps made the room almost as bright as day. A bluebottle struggled between his thumb and forefinger, waving its small legs. He raised a needle-sharp stylus and ran it through. More flies buzzed inside a baited jar, waiting execution.

When he was a boy, ignored, despised by everyone, Domitian would while away whole days brooding over hurts and resentments. Lately he had begun to do it again. The Helmsman of the World had sunk into a misery of fear.

Parthenius scratched at the door and eased it open—the nightly ritual of bringing the emperor his wine and a few choice tidbits left over from dinner on a silver tray.

"Master, I congratulate you on tonight's performance. Who but your divinity could have conceived such a stratagem?"

"I!" Domitian swept his arm across the tray, sending flask and dishes clattering to the floor. The boy with the small head, Earinus, who had been asleep in the corner, sat up and blinked.

"My plan? You fat turd, this was your plan! Frighten the senators into betraying themselves, you said, with all that childish mumbo-jumbo. Well, you see how well we succeeded. One word from Nerva quelled it in an instant, and we learned nothing. Instead of exposing them, these philosophers and republicans and atheists, we only drive them deeper underground. You know what happened to Epaphroditus, your predecessor. He gave me bad advice. He was younger and smarter than you are, Parthenius. I loved him." Domitian smiled; his teeth caught the candle light and glittered like knives.

Parthenius, his several chins quivering, stooped to gather the dishes. He had raised self-abasement to an art. "Cocceius Nerva could be removed, Master. It only takes a word."

"And seven more will spring up in his place. I'm fighting a hydra. They all hate me."

"No matter, you saw their fear, Lord of the World. Recall the words of Caligula, 'Let them hate, as long as they fear.'"

"Yes, and look what happened to him, you donkey!" The Lord of the World squinched his tired eyes, then opened them again.

Parthenius' smile never faltered, though the pain in his belly was excruciating.

"Don't stand there, grinning like an ape, pour me more wine, and put a drop of laudanum in it. You know I don't—don't sleep well lately."

"Of course, Master." Parthenius extended a pudgy hand with the goblet. "Will you require anything else tonight?"

"Ah, what would I do without you, my friend. Who else can I trust? Come here, kiss me."

The chamberlain bent awkwardly to comply, and Domitian struck him across the mouth with his open hand. "Get away, you disgust me, you're too fat."

Parthenius, his face a frozen mask, bowed himself out the door and sagged against the corridor wall. With a perfumed handkerchief from his sleeve he dabbed at the blood trickling from the corner of his mouth. He remembered that Epaphroditus had been summoned one night to Domitian's bedroom. The emperor had made love with him, had dined with him, sent him away with every sign of affection, and the next day signed an order for the man's crucifixion. Parthenius sighed as the spasm of pain passed off. He smoothed his gown, took a deep breath, and went unsteadily down the hall.

Ever since Augustus Caesar had made himself Rome's first emperor a century ago, it was the freedmen of the imperial household who made the wheels of government turn. Senators and magistrates, for all their wealth and pretensions, were really no more than the ornamental detritus of the vanished Republic, honored in inverse proportion to their relevance, or terrorized, depending on the emperor's whim.

But the imperial freedmen, too, lived lives of constant dread. Without family, without inherited wealth or status, they were all caught in the hollow of the emperor's hand. One misstep and it was back to the gutter, if they were lucky. Parthenius had a wife and a small son, born without the taint of slavery, who might make him proud one day if the chamberlain could stay alive long enough. And, if Fortune favored him, he hadn't long to wait until there would be an end to fear and humiliation, to the stomach aches and the bile rising in his throat. He shook himself and straightened his shoulders. After tonight's events he and the others needed to talk.

"It wasn't you, was it, Stephanus?" the empress said. "With your dagger?"

They sat on delicate-legged chairs around a rosewood table inlaid with ivory. Each had come stealthily along a different corridor to Parthenius' office in the working wing of the palace. It had taken time to arrange. It would be dawn soon. Entellus was there. He was the freedman who received petitions to the emperor; his favor was worth a fortune. Titus Petronius, the commandant of the Praetorian Guard, recently appointed and already insecure in his post. Stephanus, still with his left arm in the sling. He was fiercely loyal to Domitilla and her family and ready for anything. And finally the empress, herself, who hated Domitian perhaps more than any of them. They all deferred to her.

Stephanus was a lean, olive-dark man of about forty, with greasy black hair. He shrugged noncommittally. "You wouldn't expect me to admit to murdering a Roman senator, a low-born fellow like me?"

"Well, if it wasn't you who stabbed him, then who in the name of thundering Jove was it?" This was Petronius, the Guard commandant, blustering as usual.

"And does his death solve our problem or compound it?" asked Entellus in his quiet, precise way. The man of letters. "We must assume that Domitilla's letter and her husband's imperial horoscope are still in Verpa's house somewhere. What if someone else finds them? Someone more loyal to the emperor than Verpa was—this fellow Pliny for instance? He'll have the run of the place."

"Oh, I wouldn't worry about him," Parthenius said. "A pettifogging lawyer drafted into a police job that he clearly has no relish for.

"You should've seen his face when Fulvus proposed him. Still I'm concerned for the Purissima. We've had no news of her yesterday or today through the usual channel. What is she thinking of? I was against this in the first place…"

The empress raised a finger and Parthenius instantly shut his mouth. "That woman will decide for herself what's best to do. She always does. We will leave it to her."

"Of course, empress, as you say."

"And now, my friends," said the empress, "we had best go to our beds. Tomorrow will be a long day."

◇◇◇

While Pliny tossed in his bed and Domitian brooded in his; while others worried and fretted, Lucius Ingentius Verpa, son of the late Sextus, eased open the door to the family *tablinum*. Feeling his way in the dark, he located the lamp stand beside his father's desk and struck a spark. By the lamp's wan light he pawed through a thick sheaf of papers that lay scattered on the desk. Tossing these aside, he scooped up another batch from the table by the wall, and riffled through them. If only he knew what he was looking for! But he would recognize the papers when he found them; his father had waved them under his nose. The recollection of that scene churned his stomach. What could have made his father so mightily pleased with himself?

With heaps of papers and scrolls still unexamined, Lucius sank down on his father's chair and, as he did, heard the scuffle of footsteps by the door. He dashed across the room but found no one. But it could have been only one person: Turpia Scortilla. I'll see her dead before I'll let her have them! He thought of chasing her, allowed his imagination to play with the thought of beating her face in. Not a good idea—not yet. Doggedly he returned to his search.

Chapter Five

The Nones of Germanicus. Day one of the Roman Games.
The second hour of the day.

In the early morning haze a holiday crowd was already gathering in the Forum Romanum, elbowing the homeless who huddled there nightly.

In Pliny's mansion on the fashionable Esquiline Hill, the atrium was empty of clients; no time for them today. Instead, slaves tugged and pulled at the buckles of his cuirass while he sucked in his stomach, obedient to the prefect's orders to appear in full fig. A civilian to his fingertips, Pliny hadn't worn the loathsome thing in a dozen years and knew that he looked ridiculous encased in those sculpted bronze muscles. When he had served his military tribunate as an army accountant he had never drawn his sword in anger. He finally had to banish Calpurnia from the room when her praise of his dashing figure became too much to bear.

The Roman Games, inaugurated five centuries earlier, were the most ancient festival in the sacred calendar. Amid clouds of incense and the wailing of flutes the procession wound its stately way through the Forum and up the steep slope to the top of the Capitoline Hill and the triple temple of Jupiter, Juno, and Minerva. Near the head, Pliny, puffing and sweating in thirty pounds of burnished bronze, struggled to keep step with his chief and the other prefects, vice prefects, magistrates, and ex-magistrates of the Populus Romanus who trooped behind the imperial family. Following these worthies marched, or in some cases danced, the priestly colleges: the college of Pontifices, whose chief was the emperor himself; the Fifteen Sacrificers, who interpreted the Sibylline Oracles; the Seven Banqueters; the Bird-Watchers; the Brethren of the Soil; the Leaping Priests of Mars, brandishing their spears; the Etruscan Gut-Gazers; and the Vestal Virgins, the keepers of the sacred flame, their faces shrouded by their long veils.

But Pliny's eye took in more than the pageantry and gaiety. The parade route was lined with red-plumed Praetorian Guardsmen, their oval shields decorated with moons and stars and scorpions. And beyond them, he knew, the city prefect's plainclothesmen circulated in the crowd, ears stretched to catch any treasonous word.

Behind the priests marched the five hundred or so members of the Senate, Pliny's friends and colleagues, grave as statues, in purple-striped togas and golden laurel wreaths. And last of all came the pageant's star performers: a dozen splendid, unblemished white oxen, hung with garlands, horns gilded, going placidly to their deaths.

A more cynical mind than Pliny's might have drawn an uncomfortable parallel between oxen and senators. Were the latter not gilded victims too, reserved for a later slaughter? Such thoughts may have lurked behind some of those grave faces, but not his. Senator Gaius Plinius Secundus had by now nearly succeeded in putting last night's bizarre episode out of his mind like a bad dream.

Cynicism was simply not in Pliny's nature. He was an honest man, who never lied to anyone but himself. He needed to believe that his emperor was worthy of him, and to maintain this article of faith he could excuse much. It was lack of funds that made Domitian greedy and fear of assassination that made him cruel. Add to that the crowd of flatterers and informers who brought out the worst in him, and one could understand how a good emperor had gradually gone bad. Then what should decent men do? With so many bad men to serve the emperor ill, all the more reason why good men should serve him well. And as for those senators who insisted upon throwing their lives away in futile acts of defiance, what good had they done themselves or anyone else at the end of the day?

From the top of the Capitolium, where the procession halted, the whole glorious city lay spread out before him. The greatest city in the history of the world, built by blood and iron, but equally by a native sense of propriety, dignity, and reverence for tradition. Occasions like this always brought a catch to Pliny's throat, a bursting pride in the majesty of Rome that was subtly blended with pleasant expectations for his own future—a consulship some day, then governor of a province. Sprung from a line of sober and virtuous northern Italians, Pliny was the first in his family to reach the Senate, and already he had received assurances of the emperor's favor. And soon dear Calpurnia would give him an heir, a little senator to follow after, and there would be more… The cries of the *lictors* for silence woke him from his reverie. The temple of Jupiter Best and Greatest rose on gleaming white pillars sixty feet high, topped by a golden roof that flashed in the rising sun. At its foot stood the great altar, a massive block of carved marble, blackened by centuries' accumulation of burnt offerings.

And now the first ox was led to the altar while a priest intoned archaic prayers in the emperor's ear and he, with his toga pulled up over his head, repeated them in a ringing voice: "…*wherefore, that thou mayest enlarge the dominion of the Roman People, the Quirites, and favor, nurture and strengthen the legions of the Roman People, the Quirites, and preserve, protect and defend the constitution of the Roman People, the Quirites…*"

A single omitted word, a mere slip of the tongue, would compel them to stop the ceremony and start again from the beginning. Meanwhile, flute players with bulging cheeks shrilled on their instruments to prevent any ill-omened word from being overheard. A burly *victimarius,* naked to the waist, swung his hammer, striking the animal between the eyes, then swiftly its neck was stretched over the altar and its throat cut so that the severed jugular spewed hot blood onto the stone. Then the belly was slit open and the Gut-Gazers performed their ancient charade, frowning over the animal's steaming liver, turning it this way and that, pulling apart the lobes, noting the striations—a map of the heavens written in flesh—searching for the smallest disqualifying blemish. They pronounced it acceptable and the next animal was led up.

Beast followed beast until soon the altar was a dripping mess and round it the officiants stood ankle deep in slippery pools of blood, each animal spilling about two gallons on the ground.

If this was how the ancestral religion worshipped the high gods, there was little here to excite the ordinary man or woman in the Roman street, whose grandparents, very likely, had been brought here in chains from the swamps of Germany or the sewers of Antioch, and few of them bothered to attend. Their religion was something else entirely, a grab-bag of popular deities: Isis, Cybele, Atargitis, and a dozen others, who promised ecstasy, secret knowledge, and a blessed hereafter to their devotees. Their priests and priestesses could be seen on any street corner, jumping up and down in some outlandish eastern garb, clashing cymbals, wailing, some even slashing their arms with scimitars. To a conservative like Pliny these cults were contemptible, disturbing, even frightening—the more so because people of his own class, people who should know better, had begun lately to dabble in them. The Flavian dynasty, it was well known, was devoted to Egyptian Isis. The present emperor's father, the otherwise sensible Vespasian, had actually performed faith healings in her name, and the young Domitian, at a dangerous moment in the civil war, had been smuggled to safety disguised as one of her priests.

By mid-morning the last animal had been dispatched. A portion of each was burnt on the altar and tasted by the priests. The fat-rich smoke rose up and drifted over the city. The remaining carcasses were already being carted off to the city's butcher shops for sale as ordinary food. The Roman Games would continue, however, for another fourteen days, beginning with a round of stage plays in all the theaters and concluding with five days of chariot races in the Circus Maximus. During this time public business came to a standstill. The law courts did not meet and therefore no verdict could be handed down in the Verpa case.

The Verpa case, thought Pliny with an inward groan. He must begin his investigation, such as it was, today. The prefect's orders. As the crowd dispersed, Pliny summoned his bearers. First, lunch and a mid-day nap.

At home his slaves unbuckled his helmet, his boots, and his cuirass. He shrugged the thing off gratefully, letting his belly expand with a sigh. He felt as though he hadn't drawn a deep breath in three hours. His tunic was sticking to him. A slave hurried up with a basin of cool water and a sponge. There wasn't time for a proper bath.

Calpurnia had felt nauseous again in the morning. He was happy to see her feeling better now. He called for a light meal and watered wine for them both and, while he ate, answered her endless questions distractedly.

Because something was bothering him. Not Verpa. But something to do with the ceremony. It had occurred to him on the way home. He had not had a clear view of the altar during the sacrifice and hadn't really been paying attention. But had he counted wrong? Wasn't someone missing who should have been there? He dismissed the thought from his mind. He had more pressing things to think about.

Chapter Six

Earlier the same day.

Marcus Valerius Martialis awoke before dawn from long and necessitous habit, yawned heavily, and heaved his bulk out of bed. He was a big man, barrel-chested, coarse-featured, with a broad forehead, which, as soon as he stirred, began to throb horribly, the result of too much bad wine and too little sleep.

His breakfast, a cup of watered vinegar and a lump of hard cheese, delayed him only a moment. He splashed water on his face, combed his thick head of curly, salt-and-pepper hair, and rubbed a bit of pumice over his teeth. His toilet complete, he tipped the chamber pot out the window, flung on his threadbare toga, and was out the door. The whole process had not taken the tenth part of an hour.

Martial inhabited a one-room flat on the third floor of a ruinous seven-story *insula* on the Quirinal Hill, near the Temple of Flora. In pitch darkness, he descended the sagging steps. That the stairwell stank of urine, charcoal, and rancid oil, he scarcely noticed.

Outside, there were other mice—Martial thought of himself and his fellows as mice—scurrying along the dark streets toward the proud houses of their patrons. Such was the life of a humble client, and Martial, after a moment's thought, turned his steps to the house of one Paulus, who lived on the fashionable Esquiline Hill, a strenuous walk away. As he walked, he thrust his large head forward as if against an invisible wind. It was his characteristic gait and suggested a personality that combined extroversion, aggression, and a dogged determination to show a brave face to a world that undervalued him.

By the time he arrived, his toga was wet with sweat and he was in a foul mood. And then to be told by the exquisite door-slave that Master was not holding a salutatio this morning!

Merda! thought Martial. He's probably dancing attendance on some patron of his own. Oh, the ignominy of being a slave's slave!

Cursing all the way, he barely arrived in time to receive a measly handout of twenty-five coppers from Arruntius Stella, another patron, who happened to dwell in the same region of the city. With this pittance in his purse and the sun rising over the crest of the hill, Martial set about his day; a day that would end by changing his life in ways that even his rich imagination could not have pictured.

Making his way down the Argiletum toward the Forum Romanum, he stopped at a sidewalk barbershop and took his place on the bench of waiting customers.

Martial was a swarthy and hirsute man, covered cheek, chest, and leg with coarse black hair, like the true Spaniard he was; and this in a city where men and women of fashion regularly depilated themselves. After two or three days without a shave you could have painted an eye on his forehead and passed him off for Cyclops. Women, who were accustomed to smooth-skinned men, were sometimes contrarily attracted to the hairiness of him, but to sleek young boys, whom he much preferred, his body seemed a kind of insult to their own, and they shied away from him, though he pursued them tirelessly.

The barber greeted him with a toothy smile. The man had a tolerably good hand; he didn't slash more than one or two throats a week. Yet at that particular moment he was attempting to plaster a rather nasty cut with spider's web soaked in oil and vinegar.

The principal business of a sidewalk barbershop, however, was gossip. To the snip-snap of the iron shears, to the rasp of the razor and the occasional yelp of pain, a desultory commentary on the week's events went on among the bystanders. Not that one ever spoke carelessly. Even poor people had learned to be guarded. It was well known that plainclothesmen of the Prefecture hung about in taverns, and in the baths and basilicas listening for rumors, for the careless joke, the murmur of complaint.

The chief topic, even two days after the event, was still the Verpa affair. It was not only senators who felt themselves vitally interested in the outcome of that case; anything that touched upon slaves was bound to engage the Roman proletariat, a great many of whom were of slave descent. Martial, who had spent the last several days shut up in his garret, writing feverishly and, when inspiration flagged, drinking himself into a stupor, was very likely the only man in Rome who had heard nothing about it, and so he listened intently to the handful of facts and the basketful of speculation that was going the rounds.

Warding off the barber's attempt to perfume his hair—for how could he ridicule scented dandies in his poems if he smelt like one himself?—Martial paid and went on his way.

By now the sun was climbing the sky and the streets were filling with holiday-makers. Tendrils of smoke rising from the Capitolium carried the aroma of burnt flesh out over the city. Passing a street-corner urinal, he unlimbered a *mentula* of noble proportions and directed his stream into the foaming contents. It would be collected by the fullers and contribute to the process by which togas were whitened. While he pissed long and thoughtfully, a small crowd of onlookers gathered round.

"That's Martial," whispered one to another, "the one that writes the dirty poems."

A glow of pride suffused him. He was known everywhere!

Strolling farther down the Argiletum, he found himself at Atrectus' bookstore, one of his favorite haunts. Its doorposts from top to bottom bore advertisements of the poets whose works were for sale. Inside, pigeon holes containing the tightly rolled scrolls of authors, living and dead, lined the walls. And in one of them, tagged with a price of five silver *denarii*, was his latest volume of epigrams—biting, satirical, abusive, indecent.

Would anyone read them if they weren't? And people did read them. Still, he reflected bitterly, the imperial patronage that he longed for eluded him.

Exchanging pleasantries with the proprietor, he made to leave, only to find his way blocked by a small army of clients on the door step, the entourage, he guessed immediately, of Publius Papinius Statius, most favored of the emperor's court poets. The two men detested each other.

The frail Statius, his skeletal form swathed in a thick and glistening toga, his white hair meticulously coifed, was just descending from his litter.

Martial, seeing no escape, greeted him with a wolfish grin. "*Salve,* Publius Papinius. You've been away from Rome so long I thought you were dead. Imagine my disappointment."

The clients hummed like angry bees.

But Statius returned him a benevolent smile. "My dear Martial! What a delight! Our Lord and God invited me up for the holidays. I recited a new work of mine at a dinner he gave just last night. I must confess, I was gratified by his warm praise of it. And how are you? Still a poor man? Your toga's quite worn out." His lean fingers stroked it.

"Not as worn out as your *culus.*"

Statius was unruffled. "Let me make you a present of a new one."

"No thanks. People will ask what I had to do to you to get it."

Statius' composure was beginning to crack just a little. "That tongue of yours will land you in trouble one day, my foul-mouthed friend."

"What's your tongue been getting into lately, some old hag's crack?"

"Guttersnipe!" Statius snarled. "I know what eats at you night and day. Put it out of your mind. Our Lord and God is offended by your indecency. Send as many poems up to the palace as you like. I assure you they're taken out with the trash. And your crude attempts at flattery make us all laugh."

The old man's hands were shaking, red spots were burned on each cheek. Martial was in hardly better condition.

"Out of my way! Must you block the road with this army of toadies?"

Statius, his voice thick with sarcasm, commanded, "Make way, make way there for Martial, Prince of Poets!"

"And so I am!" cried Martial as he shouldered his way through the crowd, feeling all their eyes on his back. It was a weak exit and he knew it. If he had been in a bad mood before, he was in a worse one now.

The Forum Romanum was by now packed with people, mostly out-of-towners, waiting to see the emperor, priests, and senators descend from the Capitolium. In front of the Rostra, a flurry of excitement broke out where a ragged street-corner haranguer, one of the Cynic breed, no doubt, was being hustled away by troopers of the City Battalions. The emperor's relentless war against philosophers continued.

Martial mingled with the jostling crowd, while keeping a hand tight on his purse to ward off pickpockets, though indeed there wasn't much in his purse but cobwebs. He searched the sea of faces for Diadumenus.

Diadumenus was fifteen years old, had skin like alabaster, long golden hair, and buttocks, round, white and smooth, that no woman's could equal. And he was heartless. Martial longed for the dewy kisses which he granted just often enough to keep the poet forever in pursuit. How he ached for the boy! Hopeless to look for him in this mob. Anyway, he was probably still asleep in some rich man's bed, his curls spread out prettily upon the pillow. Parades didn't interest Diadumenus much.

The crowd dispersed, the hungry to the butcher shops, where beef would be cheap and plentiful today, the rest to the magnificent open-air theaters for a day of entertainment. Actors were celebrities almost on a par with charioteers and gladiators, and Romans were eager connoisseurs of the art. Each boasted his own noisy claque of supporters. For those who couldn't afford the price of a ticket there were still the street-corner buskers, block parties, and neighborhood processions. Domitian had banned the cruder forms of pantomime, the sexy, scurrilous burlesques that had so often led to rioting and sedition. Still, the comedies and farces provided ribaldry enough for most tastes.

Martial debated with his grumbling stomach, but decided at last for the theater. That would occupy his day, he'd eat a sausage or two during the intermission, and then it would be time to head for the baths and the serious business of hunting up a dinner invitation.

Chapter Seven

"Name and unit, centurion?" Brusque tone, Pliny admonished himself. Assert your authority at once.

"Titus Ursius Valens, sir." The officer sketched a salute. "Twelfth Cohort, City Battalions." He was a bristle-headed, big-boned man and stood a head taller than Pliny. "And your name would be, sir, if I might ask?"

The tone was faintly insolent—the professional policeman suffering the meddling amateur. Pliny ignored the question.

Gaius Plinius Secundus was thirty-five years old but had the smooth, boyish face of a much younger man. It was not a handsome face but a pleasant one: pink cheeks and mild blue eyes. His family hailed from the Lake Como region, where Celtic blood mingled with the Italian. It accounted for his rosy complexion and the light brown hair that lay in soft curls across his forehead and neck. He worried that his appearance lacked the *gravitas* of a Roman senator and so he frowned whenever he wanted to impress. He was frowning now. "Where are your men posted, centurion?"

"Two upstairs guarding the slaves, sir. Two more at the front and back doors, one more for relief."

"Quarters comfortable enough? You may be here for several days."

Valens smiled crookedly. "Compared to the camp, sir? This is a holiday."

The City Battalions, under the command of Aurelius Fulvus, the prefect, shared a camp with the Praetorian Guard on the outskirts of Rome. Rivalry between the two forces was intense; insults and fistfights were a common occurrence. The five thousand Praetorians, pampered and well-paid, were the emperor's household troops. The troopers of the City Battalions, on the other hand, were the poor relations—understaffed, underpaid, with little chance of promotion. But it was they, nonetheless, who did the hard work of policing this great, teeming beehive of a city with its million inhabitants, half a dozen languages, festering slums, and casual brutality, to the extent that it could be policed at all.

"Hardly a holiday," Pliny said, maintaining his scowl. "We've serious business to do here."

"Quite so, sir." Again, the mocking tone.

"And where's the new master, what's his name, Lucius?"

"Sleeping late, sir. I've sent one of the lads to rouse him. With the slaves all locked up, the house has stopped running."

"And where have you put them?"

"We've crammed 'em into two large rooms upstairs. Forty-six all told, about equally male and female with some kids. The prefect has ordered them all shackled and collared, just to be on the safe side. If they all decided to make a break for it we aren't enough to hold 'em."

"Hardly likely, Centurion." Pliny found this business of chaining distasteful, but he couldn't countermand Fulvus' order. While they waited for Lucius to appear, Pliny looked around the atrium. It was twice the size of his own and ornamented everywhere with symbols of the cult of Isis. One whole wall offered a crowded panorama of imaginary Nile scenes done in exquisite mosaic: reed boats plied the river, crocodiles yawned, palm trees swayed, throngs of happy worshipers crowded little temples. Elsewhere in the room stood statues of Queen Isis holding her *sistrum* and water jug, and bearded Serapis, her consort, and jackal-headed Anubis.

It was no surprise, Pliny reflected, that Verpa and his family had become enthusiastic devotees of the cult which the emperor himself favored. All of it mere fawning imitation probably. As far as he knew, Verpa didn't have a spiritual bone in his body. Of Lucius and Scortilla he was uncertain.

Lotus flowers floated in the *impluvium* and a couple of fat carp could be seen gulping at the surface. There was no sign of the carnivorous lampreys which, it was rumored, Verpa fed his unlucky slaves to. Still, one never knew. The man had a sinister reputation.

"What about Verpa's papers? I'd better have a look around the tablinum."

"Already done, sir. Two men from the prefect's office were here at the crack of dawn and left with a bushel basket of stuff."

"I see." But he didn't see. If the investigation had been given to him, why were things being done behind his back?

At that moment Lucius Ingentius Verpa shuffled into their presence, sleepy-eyed and unshaven. He looked like a man who had spent the night drinking and dicing, which, in fact, he had. The last of his friends had shuffled off at day break and he had thrown himself on his bed still in his clothes. He was in no mood to be awakened at this ungodly hour, whatever it was.

Pliny guessed he was in his late twenties and thought he could see the father's dissoluteness in him but nothing of the old man's thrusting, bullying energy. He took an instant dislike to him.

It seemed to be reciprocated. Lucius glared in open hostility and acknowledged Pliny with a sullen nod. As custom required, they gripped forearms; Lucius' grip was as weak as a girl's. There followed an uncomfortable silence.

"Yes, well," said Pliny finally, "let's have a look at the body."

"Not possible," Lucius said. "It's gone to the embalmer's. There's to be a funeral according to the rites of Isis—mummification and all that rigmarole. Scortilla's idea, not mine."

"I see. Well I'll have a look at the bedroom anyway." He resumed his frown of authority. "Come along, centurion. You've seen the room already, I suppose."

"Oh, yes sir." Valens' eyes glinted with amusement. "All the lads have seen it."

With a shrug, Lucius led them through a series of public chambers off the atrium which brought them to the east wing of the house and a grand staircase that led to an upper story. Along the way they passed columns and walls in every hue of the rainbow. Fine old mosaics covered the floors, and painted vistas seemed to make the walls dissolve. Verpa had amassed Corinthian bronze vases and massive candelabra, marble statuettes on onyx pedestals, and bric-a-brac of jasper and agate. Here priceless citrus-wood tables stood on spindly ivory legs, there water tinkled in silver fountains.

Pliny, whose own house was not nearly so grand, was impressed in spite of himself. The stairway led up to a second story gallery that ran the length of the house, its tessellated floor glittering like glass.

"That's my room ahead, if you care to know." Lucius halted at the top of the steps. "Go left, my father's room is at the end there."

"Five, six doors down. Who occupies those rooms?"

"No one, at the moment. They're for guests. Sometimes my friends sleep over if they're too drunk to find their way home."

"Did any of your friends happen to sleep over the night before last?"

"Maybe—I mean, no, no one."

Pliny lifted a quizzical eyebrow. "And the room below his?"

"His room overlooks the back corner of the garden. Below it is a shed for garden tools and whatnot. No one sleeps there."

They stood in the doorway and Pliny took in the scene at a glance: a small desk and chair, a lamp-stand and a gilded chamber pot with handles in the shape of urinating Cupids; and Verpa's bed, its costly Babylonian coverlet tangled and spattered with blood. All at once an unexpected thrill of excitement shot through him. The thing began suddenly to seem real to him. Here a man had died, butchered by a resentful slave, a castoff lover or perhaps some other enemy.

"Of course, without our slaves there's no one to clean," Lucius said in a petulant tone.

"Uncommonly large for a bedroom, isn't it."

"The family that built the house bedded a dozen slaves here. My father felt that was far too generous. One only needs to squeeze slaves closer together to get them in smaller quarters.

Pliny seemed to recall that this mansion in the Vicus Pallacinae had formerly belonged to a senator whom Verpa had denounced years ago for dabbling in philosophy. It was a beautiful house, far the grandest in a neighborhood of grand houses, and the emperor gave it to him as his reward. Informing on one's colleagues paid well.

"My father took this room as his private, ah, lair, if that's the right word," Lucius continued. "He wanted someplace that was more secluded than the downstairs bedrooms. He was a secretive man who craved privacy—not easy to achieve in the houses we Romans live in. The rest of us have seldom had occasion to enter it. As you see, he decorated it to suit his taste."

Until now, no one had called attention to the room's most striking feature—the murals. On every wall, horse-tailed Satyrs with bulging eyes and huge curving penises performed sexual acts in every imaginable position with naked women, their hair loose, their mouths open in shrieks of ecstasy. The figures were life-sized, painted by an undoubted master of anatomy, color, and modeling.

Pliny, like any Roman, was not easily shocked. Sex was celebrated everywhere in the city; you could see similar things in the public baths. Still, his Northern conservatism was pricked. His parents' house had allowed no such stuff as this. "Great gods, it looks more like a brothel than a gentleman's bedroom." All this to stir the man's flagging libido or, more likely, to instruct the younger slave girls in what was expected of them. What shameful sights these walls must have seen.

Valens grinned. No doubt he and "the lads" found frequent occasion to come up here. Lucius stared straight ahead and said nothing.

Pliny hastened on, "Lucius Ingentius, tell me in your own words what happened that night."

The young man shrugged—shrugging seemed to signal the way he dealt with the world—and explained how he and a few slaves had burst in at dawn when Verpa failed to answer their knock and found him naked, on his stomach, one leg curled under him, the other extended straight, his back and buttocks shredded with bloody slash marks. The body was cool to the touch and already stiffening.

"And there was no one else in the room when you entered?"

"No one."

"And no one heard a struggle, a cry for help?"

Lucius hunched his shoulders again, "I was out most of the night. Scortilla's room is downstairs."

"What about the slaves?"

"I've already questioned them, sir," Valens struck in. "None of them admits to hearing anything."

"And none of them ran away?"

"No, they're all here," Lucius said.

"Interesting. How did your father get along with them."

Lucius looked doubtful. "He was a strict master, but hardly the monster people made him out. Not loved. But this? I don't know."

"And where do the slaves sleep?"

"There are two other big rooms at the other end of the house. Most of them sleep there."

"Under guard?"

"They're counted every night, but not locked in."

"You said most of them sleep there."

"A few privileged ones sleep elsewhere."

"And they are?"

"The night staff, the door slaves, the clock slave. Oh, and Iarbas the dwarf. He's Scortilla's pet and plays the clown in her pantomime troupe. He sleeps with her."

"Her own troupe?"

Lucius had the grace to look faintly embarrassed. "I know, frowned on in these virtuous days, but her tastes are old-fashioned. Harmless, really—bit of slapstick, rude songs, boy ballet dancers."

"Quite," Pliny interrupted. "And so she and your father never slept…"

"Together? No, not for years."

"Did any other slaves have the freedom of the house at night?"

"Phyllis, one of the slave girls, generally slept with my father, she was his current favorite. And there's Ganymede, the *cinaedus* in our troupe."

"And where does he sleep?"

There was a half-smile on the young man's lips. "Ganymede sleeps wherever he likes."

"Hmm. Well, I will question them all in due course. None of them sounds like a likely suspect. But your father didn't have Phyllis to bed that night, or anyone else?"

"No, he didn't. It was his custom when he had important business to transact the next day not to squander his vital force in lovemaking."

"And what business would that have been?"

"I've no idea. But he seemed agitated at dinner and drank more than usual. Something was in the wind."

"Sir." Valens had been circling the room, doubtless with the object of appreciating the muralist's extraordinary technique. "Look at this here. We never noticed this before." He was pointing at what appeared to be a charcoal sketch of some kind high up on the wall beside the bed: three semicircles one above the other, the largest one at the bottom bracketing the other two. A vertical slash drawn through their centers connected them and protruded a little way above and below them.

"By the gods," whispered Lucius, squinting up at it. "Jews! My father prosecuted them, you know, and their friends, the ones who call themselves God-fearers."

Pliny cast him a questioning look.

"What, you don't know about the God-fearers? Romans, people of our own class, mind you, who attend the lectures of the rabbis where they listen to a lot of nonsense about how their books contain wisdom the equal of Plato or Pythagoras. They worship a god with no image, if you can imagine it, and not only that but he's worse-tempered than Zeus with a hang-over, spouting rules about this, that and the other. But they eat it up. I had to sit through hours of it, pretending to be one of them, and it all went over my head, I assure you. The only thing that was clear to me is that they're traitors. But that's how we caught Clemens and Domitilla. It was my father's idea."

What a long speech suddenly from this reticent young man, Pliny thought. "But what does that have to do with this scrawl on the wall?"

"I know what this is a drawing of," Lucius replied. "And so do you, vice prefect, think about it."

"*Mehercule*, he's right!" Valens exclaimed. "On the Arch of Titus, sir. That bloody huge seven-branched candlestick from the temple in Jerusalem."

Of course! He'd seen it a hundred times. Every Roman knew those bas-reliefs that depicted the triumph of the emperor Titus, Domitian's lamented elder brother, over the Jews. All the treasures of the temple had been paraded through the streets of Rome more than a quarter century ago and commemorated in carved and painted stone on the triumphal arch that Titus built near the Forum.

"Sir?" Valens scratched his jaw. "If I might make a suggestion, sir."

"Yes, what?"

"Ask about the murder weapon."

"Right, of course, centurion. I was just going to." In fact, it hadn't occurred to him. He was no policeman, damn it!

"I have it," said Lucius. "We found it on the floor by the bed. I took it to my room, I'll get it."

Lucius returned moments later with the dagger and held the hilt toward Pliny, who took it in his hand. It was a heavy piece with a wicked-looking curved blade incised with symbols in a foreign script. Black flakes of Verpa's blood clung in them.

"A Jewish *sica,*" said Valens. "An uncle of mine worked for tax farmers in Judea before the revolt. The Zealot terrorists used to slash Roman throats with these."

"You're a font of information, centurion."

"Thank you, sir."

"Here, you'd best take charge of it. It's our only evidence so far." He handed it to the centurion. Turning back to Lucius, he asked, "Are there any Jews in this house?"

The young man looked at his feet. "Well, yes, one among the slaves that I know of. But really, I don't think…"

"And who is that?"

"Old Pollux, a former boxer, who guards—guarded—my father's door at night."

"Then, I think we'd better speak with him."

Chapter Eight

Valens stepped out and returned a moment later with Pollux and a second soldier to guard him, even though the man was shackled hand and foot. Ignoring Lucius, he gazed steadily at Pliny. There was nothing servile in his manner. Valens lifted the man's tunic with the point of his sword, exposing his nakedness.

"Well, the old boy's a Jew, all right."

Pollux stood as still as a statue but Pliny saw his jaw muscles quiver. Valens was no weakling but this man could have broken him in half.

"Leave the man alone, centurion," Pliny snapped. "There's no call for that."

He reminded Pliny of a Greek statue he had once seen of a boxer, not in triumph but in defeat: battered, scarred, sad-eyed and infinitely weary. This fellow could have posed for it. He looked to be in his late fifties, his hair and beard grizzled. His shoulders were huge, his big-knuckled hands hung at his sides, gnarled from years of being wrapped in the cruel iron-studded thongs that boxers fought with.

"How did your father come to own this man?" Pliny asked Lucius.

"He served in Judaea during the revolt; legate of the Fifth Macedonica under Vespasian. Pollux here was a Zealot fighter. Thousands of them were crucified, others sent to the mines. My father brought him home, trained him as a boxer, and used to hire him out for private shows. He's been in our familia since before I was born. After some years he begged to stop fighting, lost his heart for it I suppose. My father made him his bedroom slave instead."

"Why would your father entrust his life to a former rebel?

"Why do some people keep pet panthers? It's the kind of man my father was."

"You speak Latin, man?" Pliny addressed Pollux.

The slave inclined his head ever so slightly.

"The night your master was killed when did you take up your post?"

"Always at the fifth hour."

"And was your master already in the room?"

The slave nodded.

"Speak when I ask you a question!" Pliny felt unaccustomed anger rising in his chest. This turbulent race with their single god who refused to live peaceably within the Empire like everyone else. Surely, they deserved what had happened to them.

"He was inside," answered Pollux.

Valens snarled at him, "You'll address the vice prefect as 'sir.'"

"And you were outside the door all night," Pliny continued, "and yet you heard nothing?"

"Nothing." A pause. "Sir."

"I can have you tortured, you know." But there were slaves, Pliny knew, who would go to the rack before they would betray their master, and one look into that brutal, battle-scarred face told him that Pollux would not yield to torture, at least not to any degree of torture that Pliny had the stomach to inflict. Anger gave way to a feeling of helplessness.

"Take him back, centurion. I'll question him again later."

He turned back to Lucius. "What's your opinion of Pollux's loyalty?"

Lucius gave his characteristic gesture of indifference. "My father saved the fellow from crucifixion and promised him his freedom one day in return for good service. And as far as I know, that's what he got."

"Until now, that is," said Valens. "I'll have the truth out of that brute in short order—"

"What are you saying?" Pliny turned on him. "That Pollux came in here, butchered his master, drew the candlestick on the wall, dropped the dagger by the bed—all making it plain that this was an act of *Jewish* vengeance—and then went back and calmly took up his post again outside the door until morning?" At last he'd scored a point against this overbearing soldier. Valens frowned at the floor and said nothing.

There was a hint of a smile on Lucius' lips.

Pliny turned back to the young man. "Is there anything else here we've overlooked? Think carefully. Any other way into this room besides the door?"

"Well, the window, but I hardly think… Wait, though, the shutters were open. Yes, I'm sure they were. And that wasn't my father's habit, even on the hottest nights. He dreaded night vapors."

The single window was barely a foot wide by two feet high. This part of the house was raised on a tier of columns, topped by a course of overhanging eaves that surrounded the garden at the rear. Pliny crossed to the window and peered out. Ivy grew thick around the window frame.

"We'll go down to the garden, centurion."

They all trooped downstairs and looked up at Verpa's bedroom. Strands of ivy spiraled up the columns producing a striking and pleasing effect, but they could see plainly at the base of the column nearest Verpa's window that the tendrils were torn and loose, used as handholds.

Valens scratched his jaw. "Seems an impossible climb, sir, getting around that overhang and up to the window. And what man of normal size could have squeezed through it? It was clearly designed to give the slaves who were kept there a little air, but no means of escaping."

"Maybe a trained assassin…," Lucius said, looking thoughtful. "Not impossible. I've heard from my father what those Judean Zealots were like. And if Pollux was his accomplice? I mean, telling him which window, signaling when the time was right, and then guarding the door in case anyone came by?

Pliny was silent for a moment. It sounded fantastic, yet who could say that Jewish assassins hadn't made their way to Rome, where the filth of all the world eventually collected.

A thought occurred to him. "Are there other Jews in the familia?"

"Don't know, really. We've got slaves from everywhere."

"There's one way to find out, sir," said Valens, eager to regain his authority. "None of them will sacrifice to our gods. Why don't we put them to the test? I mean, if you agree, sir."

"Oh, I don't think…" Lucius began, but Pliny cut him off. "No, my centurion's right—again." Pliny was beginning to feel distinctly annoyed at this competent officer. "We may as well know the worst. What images of the gods have you?"

"Dozens, look anywhere in the house. We've an altar too, quite nicely carved."

"Show my men. Bring one of every deity out into the garden, we'll do it there. And have you an image of Our Lord and God?"

Lucius replied that they kept a small bust of the emperor in the *lararium* together with their household gods so that they could venerate it everyday.

"Put it with the others and fetch wine and incense. In the meantime, centurion, show me to the slave quarters."

A rank stench of bodily waste, sweat and terror assaulted Pliny when the door was unbolted. And this, after only two days of confinement. What would it be like after fifteen—if any of the slaves were still alive by then? With a wail of shrieking protestations they cried out that they knew nothing of any plot to murder Master. On their lives, they would have told if they did. And why would anyone do such a thing to Master? Good, kind Master.

Here was the blood and bones of the household, Pliny reflected. They were Levantines, Nubians, Dacians, and Germans. They were litter bearers, torch bearers, bodyguards, and private bully-boys; doorkeepers, footmen, and messengers;

valets, butlers and barbers; lady's maids, dressers, bath women, hair curlers, and masseuses; scullions, chefs, pastry cooks, waiters, cup bearers, and tasters; keepers of the silver, the unguents, the pearls; short-hand writers, hour callers, name rememberers, bed partners of both sexes, musicians, mimes, dancers, and reciters of poetry. Among them also were children, for Verpa permitted his slaves to cohabit on payment of a fee. Pliny saw backs and shoulders seamed with the marks of old floggings and more than one face branded like a felon's to serve as a warning to the rest. And now, by order of the city prefect, all wore iron collars on which were inscribed the words, *"I'm running away—seize me."* The collars were linked together with chains.

Valens banged his staff against the door jamb and bawled at them to shut their yaps.

When there was some semblance of quiet, Pliny spoke to them, while breathing as little of the fetid air as he could. "I am going to ask you to do something very easy, to sacrifice to the gods and our emperor, only that. No one will be tortured, I promise you. We have reason to think that there may be one, or a small number, of depraved madmen among you, devotees of a vicious cult. If that turns out to be true, then maybe, I can promise nothing yet, maybe the rest of you can be saved."

Pliny heard with genuine surprise these words come from his lips. Like anyone with a smattering of Greek philosophy, he knew that slavery was against nature. There was no difference between a freeman and a slave except a cruel twist of fate. But as far as Roman law was concerned, the slave was not a man at all but a "speaking tool," possessing no rights. Pliny wasn't sure quite when it had occurred to him that his purpose here was to save these men and women from an unjust death. It certainly had not been in his mind two mornings ago when news of the crime had alarmed the city. Valens looked at his superior, incredulous that anyone would talk to slaves this way, while the slaves resumed shrieking their innocence.

The garden was quite lovely: boxwood hedges, tall elms, and fruit trees; stone benches round a pool where fountains splashed.

Here a miscellany of divine images had been assembled. There was, besides the head of Domitian Lord and God, a bronze figurine of Hercules, a lovely marble Diana, a bust of Jupiter, a statuette of Isis, and the inevitable statue of Priapus, godling of vegetation and sex, who leered mischievously here as in every Roman garden.

The slaves were brought out in batches of ten, shoved along by the troopers, with swords drawn, who cursed at them and struck them with the flat of their blades. Eager to prove their piety, they stumbled forward one by one, dropped incense and wine on the altar fire and mouthed a prayer at Pliny's dictation.

Finally it was the turn of Pollux, whom Pliny had saved for last, and four others who clung to the man: an older woman, his mate, said Lucius, and two young women and a boy. All of them tried to shelter behind the boxer's broad back. There was fear in their eyes. Pollux's lips moved soundlessly. If it was a prayer, it was not directed at those lifeless statues arrayed before them. Like a statue himself, his ugly face unmoving as a mask, Pollux stood before the altar and did nothing with the incense and wine cup handed to him. For a long moment there was dead silence save for the chirping of song birds in the trees.

Then, before Pliny could stop him, Lucius dashed forward and struck the slave in the face with all his strength. Pollux, who had been hit by tougher men than Lucius in his time, did not flinch but continued to look straight ahead of him. His fellow slaves stood by, stunned to silence. Then, one after another, they began to murmur: "Atheist, traitor, you'll get us all killed!"

One of the young women broke and ran forward to the altar, crying "Please, Masters, I'll burn the incense!" But Pollux caught her by the arm and pulled her back. "Sister, be brave, in the name of the True God." In an agony of doubt, the girl looked from the altar to Pollux's face and back again. The older woman came and put her arms around her and drew her back into their circle. The murmurs of the other slaves rose to angry, menacing shouts. The City Troopers cast nervous looks at their centurion.

"Murderer of my father!" screamed Lucius. "Heat irons. I'll have the truth out of him!"

Pliny felt the situation slipping out of control. "I give the orders here," he warned Lucius. "Stand back."

The young man looked mutinous.

Stepping close to Pollux, Pliny said in a low voice, "You have put yourself and these others in grave danger. I give you one day to think it over." The boxer only stared back impassively.

"Centurion, take them back to their quarters," Pliny ordered, "and double the guard." And to Lucius he confided, "I am encouraged that the poison seems to have spread to only a few. I wish I could release the rest of your slaves now but I haven't the authority. They will have to remain under guard until the Games are over and a trial before the prefect can be conducted. No doubt, you have other slaves in your country estates. By all means bring them in. And now," he said, "I am leaving." The urge to be gone from this place was suddenly overwhelming.

Lucius expressed sullen thanks.

"But sir," Valens interrupted. "The lady of the house, Turpia Scortilla. Shouldn't you have a word with her?"

"*Mehercule*," cried Pliny in exasperation, "haven't I done enough here today?"

"It's procedure, sir. She might just know something." He used the tone of voice one would in speaking to a dull child.

Pliny let out a sigh. "Conduct me to the lady, then."

Standing guard outside her chamber door, the dwarf Iarbas tried to block their way, hopping from one flat foot to the other and mouthing insults at them. He was the most extraordinary creature that Pliny had ever seen: a black dwarf, fat-headed, with tiny mole's eyes, a big belly, and short, muscular legs. Golden torques and armlets gleamed against his dusky skin. On his shoulder perched a monkey, equally bejeweled, and making savage grimaces at them with yellow, pointed teeth. Valens pushed man and beast roughly aside. "We tried locking this one up with the others," he explained, "but the lady was so distressed we let him loose. Seems harmless enough, the ugly little imp."

"Harmless?" As soon as he laid eyes on him, an image sprang to Pliny's mind of the dwarf scrambling monkey-like up the column and through the narrow window of Verpa's bedroom. And who but Scortilla would have sent him on that mission?

The lady lay propped on her bed, bone thin and bone white, the tendons in her neck standing out like ropes, her towering red wig askew. But it was her eyes that held him. He thought back to this morning's sacrifice on the Capitolium—the look in the ox's eye when the victimarius stunned it with a blow of his hammer. Turpia Scortilla had that same stunned, glassy-eyed look. And the dead whiteness of her face wasn't just the effect of cosmetics.

"Madam, I…"

At the sight of him she shrank back against her pillow, nearly dislodging her wig, the back of one thin hand pressed to her mouth. Iarbas ran around them and clambered up on the bed beside her. She clutched his wooly head to her breast. The woman looked terrified. Why?

This was not the moment to confront her head-on. Pliny forced a smile. "Come now, I've only a few questions for you, nothing to be alarmed at." Had she heard a disturbance that night? When had she gone to bed? Had Iarbas spent the night with her? Had Verpa seemed worried at all? Had he hinted at anything in the preceding days?

But to all these questions she only shook her head and clutched the dwarf tighter. In desperation, Pliny addressed the dwarf directly, but got in reply only a string of uncouth syllables. Finally, he gave it up. "I will return another time, Lady, and hope to see you in a better frame of mind."

They closed the door softly on her and returned to the atrium. Pliny was unbearably weary of the whole thing: the odious Verpa and his unpleasant family in their ostentatious house, the pathos of the slaves, the centurion's smirking superiority. This was no job for him. "Now I really must be going," he said firmly.

"Sir."

"What?" He nearly shouted at Valens.

"Perhaps just a word with the door-slaves of the front and back door? They may have seen something."

"Yes, yes." Pliny was in a state now. "Bring them here."

The two men, who a little earlier had been among those who had proudly sacrificed to the gods in the garden, fell on their knees before Pliny as though he were a god himself.

"Just think hard now and tell the truth," he assured them, "and all will go well with you. Now, did either of you see anyone lurking about the house on the night your master was killed? Anyone strange to the neighborhood?"

The slave of the back door shook his head. But yes, said the slave of the front door. There had been someone. Someone who had stood across the street for an hour or more from sundown until it grew too dark to see. Describe him? Well, about average size, neither young nor old, dark-haired, nothing special. One thing though. He carried his left arm in a sling.

Chapter Nine

By the time he left Verpa's house, it was nearing the ninth hour of the day, and the sun was creeping down the sky. The heat was still oppressive, as it had been for days. Pliny longed for the baths. Cool water, a bit of modest exercise, a rub-down, uncomplicated camaraderie with a few casual acquaintances, the blessed anonymity of nakedness, or so he thought. He directed his bearers to take him to the Baths of Titus. But the City Prefecture was on his way and conscientiousness got the better of him. He would stop and make his report first.

The Prefecture was a sprawling labyrinth of offices, archives and courtrooms connected by dim corridors where clerks and secretaries, minor officials and armed troopers bustled to and fro on hurried errands. Pliny hated the place. He passed rooms where lines of weary petitioners waited patiently to speak with clerks who ignored them. In other rooms, secretaries shuffled through stacks of files and dossiers. Was his own name, he wondered, on one of them? There were still other rooms, rooms in the cellars with iron doors and brick walls. He preferred not to think about what went on there. He pressed on.

In the antechamber of the city prefect's office, he asked for Aurelius Fulvus and was told that the chief had gone for the day. He was turning to leave when he heard loud laughter coming from the inner chamber. Suddenly angry, he brushed past the secretary and marched in.

The prefect was sprawled in a chair with a cup in his hand. Some other men, whom Pliny didn't know, sat around him. All of them were flushed with wine. Fulvus looked up as Pliny entered. He seemed to have some trouble focusing his eyes.

"Yes? I gave orders not to be—oh, it's you, ah, Gaius Plinius. Yes, well, what brings you here? Ah, sit down, won't you?" He gestured vaguely with the wine cup, spilling half the contents, but there were no empty chairs in the room. "Orfitus, get up and let my vice prefect sit."

Pliny replied stiffly that he preferred to stand.

"As you like. And so, this is about…?

"The Verpa case."

"The…ah, yes, of course." Fulvus made a visible effort to compose his long-jawed face. "And so what have you concluded? The wretched slaves, of course. It always is."

"In this case not, sir. Or, not the majority of them. Everything points to a Jewish assassin who crept in through a window aided by a slave in the household."

"Jews you say? By Thundering Jove!" Fulvus slapped the chair arm with a ruby-ringed hand. "Our Lord and God *will* be pleased! And how many are there?"

"Only five. One man, three women, and a boy."

"Nonsense! Bound to be more. You keep at it, then. Don't stop short. See what else you can nose out. The emperor likes you, you know. You can make a name for yourself with this case."

"If that is your wish, sir. My hope is that the other slaves, the ones who aren't atheists, can be exonerated. I'm ready to vouch for them myself if need be."

"What?" Fulvus looked up in astonishment. So did his friends. "Exonerate? Slaves? Yes, well, something to think about. Now, is that all, my dear Pliny?

Pliny made no move to leave. "I mean it, sir. They had nothing to do with this murder."

"You've made yourself quite clear. I said, we'll see. Just you do your job." Irritation rose in his voice. He turned his face away.

"Orfitus, fill my cup like a good fellow. Good day, vice prefect. Look in again, won't you, when you have more to report."

As he left the building, Pliny's stomach was churning. He was not ordinarily an excitable man, or so he believed. He had chosen a dull profession—or it had chosen him—because it imposed a wall of paper between himself and the sweaty emotions of real people. If he were investigating a charge of unjustified disinheritance or the distribution of assets among the offspring of a man who had been married four times; if he had been faced with a suspicious codicil or a questionable signature—here Pliny felt himself capable and sure-footed. He was not a stupid man. But this! Bloody daggers, sexual perversion, murderous fanatics, secret symbols scrawled on walls, a louche and slippery *filius familias,* a concubine catatonic with fright. He felt like a man standing on a pitching deck, grasping vainly for a handhold.

The crowd streamed out of the Theater of Marcellus and Martial patted his grumbling stomach. It was a long, hot walk to the Baths of Titus, but that was his hunting ground. He wouldn't leave without a dinner invitation from some rich booby. He had lived more than thirty years in Rome since emigrating from Spain, a young man full of hope and poetry. In all that time he hadn't had to stand in a bread line yet, although he had come close more than once.

Outside the baths, hucksters, street performers, and food-stalls filled a broad courtyard. Inside rose a vast, echoing fairyland of brilliant mosaics, high coffered ceilings, wide windows that flooded the spacious rooms with afternoon sunlight; and everywhere, priceless works of art, though here, as elsewhere in the city, the new golden statues of Domitian the God effaced all else. Martial paid his copper coin and went in.

The Baths of Titus, built by Domitian's elder brother during his brief reign, was only the latest of the great imperial *thermae* provided by emperors to the Roman people at enormous expense. The shouts of happy citizens disporting themselves, men and women together, filled the vast echoing complex. There was method to this philanthropy. It had not taken the emperors long to learn the profound truth that people who are warm and wet do not, as a general rule, riot in the streets. In this democracy of nudity even the poorest Roman could, for an hour every day, imagine himself to be a little king; could forget for a moment that elsewhere a real king, in a real palace, held the power of life and death over him.

Martial undressed in one of the large changing rooms and stowed his things in an open cubicle. Other bathers posted slaves to guard their belongings; Martial had nothing worth stealing.

Beyond, all was bare flesh. Here respectable citizen and cruising libertine, rich man and poor man, male and female met as equals.

Martial went first to the *caldarium* to luxuriate in the steam. Adjacent to the steam room lay the exercise court, from where the poet, who never exercised himself, could hear the grunts and groans of men swinging lead weights, of ball players tossing a medicine ball in a three-cornered game of catch, of wrestlers and runners. On his other hand, were the massage rooms. From here echoed the slap of hands on oiled shoulders and the shrill voice of the hair-plucker, calling his trade.

When he was red as a mullet, Martial went on to the *tepidarium* and from there into the *frigidarium,* where he dove into the cold pool with a great splash and a boy's happy shout, and swam vigorously for a minute or two.

The baths cultivated the mind as well as the body. Beside the swimming pools and gymnasia, there were libraries, art galleries, and a large and beautiful recitation hall, where people, back in their clothes again, could beguile the hours, listening to a play or a poetry reading. Hither, in his threadbare tunic, went Martial.

Instantly a circle gathered round him, already chuckling. He was among friends. He knew their names, knew their foibles, knew they'd take insults from him that they wouldn't have taken from anyone else. He whirled from one to another, leering, mugging, improvising.

He flung a hairy arm about the stooped shoulders of an elderly man. "Caecilianus!"

"Now you've shut your wife up tight,
(A woman as homely as she is!)
Fututores besiege her by day and by night,
Got any more bright ideas?"

He moved on to an aging prostitute, who plied her trade in the baths, and, wrinkling his nose, declaimed—

"Why won't I kiss you? Philaenis, you ask.
You're one-eyed, you're red-faced, and bald.
To undertake so vile a task,
Why, let some *fellator* be called!"

He pranced over to a heavy woman with pendulous breasts and clapped his hands with delight—

"Dasius sells tickets here,
No brighter boy than he!
Big-titted Spatale just tried to come in,
And Dasius charged her for three!"

He pounced upon a portly man with curled and scented hair and, waggling a reproving finger under his nose, improvised—

"Your slave boy's *mentula* is tired and sore,
And, Naevolus, so is your *culus*.
We reckon what he has been using you for,
O Naevolus, don't try to fool us."

Poor Naevolus looked like he wanted to escape. Martial released him and tip-toed over to another, his hand cupped behind his ear.

"Flaccus, listen, d'you hear
The sound of hundreds clapping?
It must be Maro strolling near,
His great *mentula* flapping."

This brought a lot of laughter; the well-equipped Maro was a familiar sight.

Martial was warming to his work, starting to enjoy himself—and then in one swift instant he found himself abandoned. Pliny had just been spotted near the door.

The most populous city on earth was still in many ways only an overgrown village, where nothing stays secret for long. The prefect's troopers stationed at Verpa's house had told friends, who had told other friends, and so on, until all Rome by now knew that Gaius Plinius Secundus was handling the Verpa case. He was instantly mobbed.

Martial knew him by sight; had heard him holding forth in the Basilica Julia where the Chancery Court sat and any passerby might stop and listen. He had put him down as just another brass-throated haranguer with the soul of an accountant.

There being nothing else for it, Martial was forced to follow his audience, only to hear the vice prefect protesting that he had no comment, and would they kindly let go of him! Spying Martial in the crowd, Pliny shouted over the hubbub, "I fear I've spoiled your recital, and most amusing it was."

"Not your fault, sir." Martial shouldered his way to Pliny's side and held out his right hand. Never to quarrel with a potential meal was the chief rule of his life. "Marcus Valerius Martialis at your service."

"I know your name. Who in Rome doesn't? How can I make it up to you?"

"Well," the poet favored him with his most winning smile—he could be charm itself when he wanted to. "It is approaching dinner time, and I find myself actually unengaged…"

"Say no more. Literary men are always welcome at my table. I'm on the Esquiline near the Lake of Orpheus. Ask anyone in the neighborhood for directions. I'm going home soon. Come in an hour. *Vale.*"

As Pliny passed through the exercise yard, some rowdy young men were making a nuisance of themselves, kicking a ball around in a circle, running and making diving catches, accompanied by much shouting and laughter. Suddenly the laughter died in their throats. One of them had kicked the ball high up over the heads of his companions and they watched in horror as it struck the gilded body of the Lord and God, towering on its pedestal over the exercise yard. Instantly they scattered, trying to lose themselves in the crowd. But some weren't quick enough. An older man tackled one, held onto him by the ankle, crying, "Here, I've got the traitor!" From the edge of the crowd grim-faced troopers closed in on the terrified boy.

Pliny didn't stay to watch the outcome. He felt a coldness in his belly.

Chapter Ten

The tenth hour of the day.

The sun was dipping behind the housetops as Martial, dressed in his one presentable dining-out suit, set out from his tenement on the Quirinal along cobblestone streets still littered with the detritus of the morning's festivities. His way lay across the Viminal, and up the steep slope of the Esquiline. At his heels trotted a sad-looking little boy who carried his napkin. The poet couldn't afford to keep a slave, but hired one sometimes for appearance's sake. Martial was hungry, starving in fact, but the evening held no further enticements for him. Dinner with this earnest, unimaginative lawyer and his equally dull friends would be something to suffer through. But that was how impecunious poets survived.

A slave met him at the doorway, removed his shoes and gave him dining slippers to wear, and conducted him into the *triclinium,* where his host rose to greet him.

To his surprise, Martial found himself the only guest. "We dine intimately tonight," said Pliny, "just my wife and my freedmen. Simple fare. No roast piglet stuffed with thrushes, no honeyed dormice, no sows' udders. A 'philosopher's meal' is my style."

Martial, who relished sows' udders, did his best to hide his disappointment.

"I feed my freedmen and my humblest guests the same food and wine I consume myself," Pliny burbled, "I make no distinctions of class."

"Admirable," murmured the poet, wishing that Pliny fed his freedmen on mullet and Lucrine oysters.

"Recline here by me in the place of honor. I've long wanted to meet you, in fact. I'm a bit of a poet myself actually. Oh, I don't publish. Just for my own amusement."

The slaves brought honeyed wine and Pliny poured the customary libation to the *Lares* and *Penates.*

Martial gave him an appraising look. "You don't include the emperor's bust among your household gods?"

Pliny's hand froze for an instant. Without looking at the poet, he said, "Do you?" Then they measured each other with their eyes. "Of course, I worship him—" they both said at once. Then both stopped. Then both smiled. It was a delicate, dangerous moment. Either one of them might have been a spy. "We must serve the emperor we have," said Pliny carefully.

"Indeed we must," said Martial. The moment passed. It would be all right.

While slaves carried in the first course, Pliny introduced his freedmen; there were three of them reclining on one couch. "This is Zosimus," he indicated a thin, serious young man in his twenties. "He is my secretary and my most gifted Greek reader, and my trusted friend. And this is—but, ah, here she comes now!"

Leaning on her nurse's arm, the heavily pregnant girl came into the room and eased herself onto the dining couch beside her husband.

Well, here's a tasty morsel, thought Martial. Though his preference ran mostly to the other thing, the poet was an admirer of feminine beauty. He noted her lustrous dark eyes and her swelling breasts.

For her part, Calpurnia didn't know what to make of this shaggy bear of a man with his flashing teeth and rolling eye. He was certainly unlike any other of her husband's friends, being rather what she imagined an aging pirate might look like. She struggled with her shyness and risked a smile. "I am pleased to meet any friend of my husband's. Are you new to our city?"

Though you would not have guessed it from his poems, Martial had a charming manner with women. He made her a low bow, then laughed. "I come from gold-bearing Tagus, from high-girt Bilbilis and the banks of rugged Salo, in short, from Spain. I came to Rome to seek fame and fortune as a writer, and Rome has grizzled my locks." He raked his fingers through his hair. "The noise, the distractions drive me wild, and yet I can't break away. The city gets in your blood. And though I am read all over Rome, nay, all over the Empire, it brings me no money. Fortune still eludes me."

"You wish to be known at court, my friend?" Pliny broke in.

"That is my desire, sir." The poet put on his serious face. "I've sent trunksful of verse up to the palace. I've praised the worthy Parthenius, I even dedicated half a dozen poems to little Earinus, though I blush to admit it."

"You know your language is rather, ah, indelicate for the ears of this chaste court."

"I've been told so once already today by that old fart Statius," the poet replied. "However, I've lately written a whole book of poems praising the emperor, and all without a single word that would make your maiden aunt squirm. But I need someone to actually put it in his hands, don't you see? I halfway believe that Statius intercepts my offerings."

"Papinius Statius," said Pliny stiffly, "happens to be a very dear friend of mine. I assure you, your suspicions are absurd. Nevertheless, when this Verpa business is over I'll see what I can do for you."

"I would be forever grateful, *Patrone.*"

"Now, now, no such word as that between us. You must consider me a friend."

The first course was served and cleared away. During the interval Pliny urged his young wife to recite for them. "I mean if you're feeling up to it, my dear. It's her pregnancy," he said in an aside to Martial, "she's under doctor's orders not to tire herself. Still, if you would…" He gazed at her hopefully. "I mentioned I write verses. Calpurnia sets them to music and accompanies herself on the lyre, with no schooling from a music teacher, but with affection, which is the best possible teacher."

Martial steeled himself. Clearly, the pompous man was dying to show off his verses and show off his child wife too.

The verses were pedestrian, but she was charming. She sang in a light, girlish voice while her fingers plucked complex patterns on the strings, and all the while her husband beamed at her with indescribable complacency.

"Bravo!" Martial clapped his hands when she had finished. "Why, mistress, put *my* verses to music and you'll make my fortune for me!"

She blushed. "My talent is small, sir, but it is at your service. Tell me, what meters do you employ? For the lyre I find that iambic trimeter works best, although the dactylic, of course—"

"Calpurnia?" Pliny 's face was a picture of baffled embarrassment.

"Why, husband, what is the matter?" She raised an innocent eyebrow. "I must ask him, mustn't I?" Martial caught a gleam of amusement in her eye and an answering one from the freedman, Zosimus across the table. Well, well, thought Martial, this young lady has been taking lessons, and not only from Cupid. And now she's teasing him. Here's a girl with more spirit than she's given credit for.

They spent the next few minutes discussing Latin lyric meters and the poet was impressed, both by her knowledge and by her tact in drawing her husband back into the conversation and smoothing his ruffled feathers. Meanwhile more dishes were brought out—filling, if not exciting. Presently Calpurnia stifled a yawn and excused herself.

"You chose wisely, my friend," said Martial when she was gone, and meant it. "She's charming. I've been in half the bedrooms in Rome, but I've no one to go home to tonight. It's no life for a man my age."

"She is devoted to me, the dear thing." Pliny was moist-eyed. "She memorizes my courtroom speeches, you know; even sleeps with a sheaf of them beside her on the bed when I have to be away from home."

"No, really?" said Martial. He had to bite his lip to keep from laughing. "But when you're lucky enough to be *in* the bed, she's not, ah, too modest, I hope."

"Oh, goodness no," Pliny assured him. Lately, of course, because of the fear of a miscarriage, they had been abstaining. Pliny had a more ardent nature than many would have suspected and he was beginning to feel quite definitely deprived.

Leaving the subject of his host's marital bliss, Martial ventured, "This murder case you're on…"

"*Mehercule*," Pliny burst out with feeling, "I don't know why this business has been thrust upon me. The babe unborn has as much knowledge of crime detection as I do. I'm no more a policeman than you are."

"But it is of some interest," the poet replied. "What little I've gathered from the barber shop gossip. What have you learned so far?"

Pliny described his morning's investigation.

"Jewish assassins," said the poet. "And you believe it?"

"Well, I mean to say, the evidence all points that way. I only hope I can save the other slaves."

"You actually care about them, don't you? It does you credit. I once composed an epitaph in verse for a little slave girl who died on our estate back home. A dear little thing. I'm not all winks and nudges, you know."

Pliny affirmed that he was glad to hear it.

The poet made a temple of his fingers and rested his chin on them. "You knew Verpa, of course."

"Only slightly, and his wretched family not at all. Lucius seems to be a typical young man of our age, that is to say good for nothing. And as for the lady, she is either a mad woman or she's afraid of something. Her behavior this morning was extraordinary."

"You don't say. Well, I can tell you that our Lucius has been living far beyond his allowance; gambled and whored it all away—reminds me of myself when I was his age. I've learned that half a dozen usurers are pursuing him and have threatened to cut off his credit or even complain to his father if he doesn't pay up."

"That's an old story in our city," Pliny sighed. "A son with a living father possesses nothing of his own, can't sell anything to raise money, can't legally borrow money, but they all do anyway. And then they wait for father to die."

"And sometimes, if father is tiresomely long-lived, they don't wait," Martial concluded the thought. "I'm told he begged his father to free him from *patria potestas* or, at least, raise his allowance, and the old man refused. Now, of course, that's all changed. Lucius is his own man at last." Martial paused and moistened his throat with more wine, enjoying the attention of Pliny and the freedmen, whose eyes were riveted on him. "And as for Turpia Scortilla, her case is more interesting. Did you know she's not his wife?"

"What are you saying, she's only a *concubina?*"

"Exactly. Her father was a stable hand for the Greens, she grew up in the Circus, started out as a bare-back rider and acrobat, if you can believe it. Yes, quite an athlete, our Scortilla: handstands on a galloping horse during the intermissions between races. From there she worked her way up to high-class courtesan. She was some courtier's girlfriend, and burrowed her way into the palace, where she made herself a fixture and eventually a nuisance. She drank too much and made scenes. A nasty piece of work altogether. And she and Domitilla didn't get on at all. Which is interesting, isn't it, in light of that lady's recent condemnation for atheism. Anyway, Scortilla wanted the wealth and status a senator could provide, and Verpa, who was recently divorced, fancied her. She was beautiful once, in a brittle sort of way, and she got her hooks into him. Of course, the Julian Laws don't permit a senator to marry a woman with a background like hers, so she settled for being his concubine."

"But I gather," said Pliny, "that they haven't been intimate for years. Why didn't Verpa break it off when she no longer pleased him?"

"Probably because she knows all his secrets. She's not an absolutely stupid woman, and she amuses herself with the slaves just as he does. Those eight strapping German litter bearers of hers? It's said that they carry her all day and she carries them all night. Say, that's rather neat, isn't it? I must make a verse of that."

"My good man," Pliny said in a tone that approached awe. "How on earth do you know all this?"

"Scandal is my stock in trade," Martial smiled modestly. "Everything is meat for a satirist, and 'smoke,' my friend, is everywhere if you have a nose for it. I swim in waters where you would not dip your toe, if I may mix my metaphors."

"And so you think…"

"I don't think anything. Probably it was this Jewish brute after all. But I would like to hear more as you carry on your investigation. It's food for a satirist. Perhaps occasionally over one of your excellent dinners we might exchange thoughts?"

"Why, I should like nothing better, my dear Martial. You're a gift from the gods! With your assistance I *will* get to the bottom of this business. Shall we say tomorrow at this hour?"

"I'm honored by your confidence, sir." The poet heaved an inward sigh of relief and vowed an offering to Bacchus. That was dinner taken care of for the next few days!

The tenth hour of the night.

In a corner of the temple compound in the Campus Martius, almost under the shadow of the great Isis temple itself, a passerby might observe a shop sign with a painting of the mummified Osiris, brother-husband of the Queen of Heaven. Within the cluttered workshop, the curious visitor would notice a cage with an elderly ibis, its beak tucked under its shabby wing, a stuffed crocodile, a pair of somnolent cobras, a bale of linen, a nested pile of caskets, and jars containing various unguents. The odor of camphor, resin, and myrrh hung like a fog in the small workroom. But Nectanebo used none of these in his work. Their only purpose was to impress the temple trade, who were directed to his establishment by Alexandrinus, the priest of Anubis, in return for a share of his fees. Quite a satisfactory arrangement really. And this was only the beginning, for Alexandrinus had plans to enlarge the embalming works and Nectanebo intended to be a part of that. He had latched onto a good thing. Until lately, Roman worshippers of Isis had cremated their dead like everyone else, but in just the year since he'd set up shop, with the backing of the temple, Nectanebo's exotic services were beginning to catch on.

Of course, it was all a sham. The ancient ritual of mummification was supposed to take half a dozen men seventy days to complete—you could read that in Herodotus. But nobody these days had time for that. Nectanebo had been given a mere five days to prepare the body of the murdered devotee. Well, they couldn't expect miracles, then, could they? Scoop out the guts, stuff in a lot of sawdust and rags soaked in cheap oil, shovel on some salt, wind the wrappings, none too carefully, and nail a lid on the casket. By the time the smell got too bad the thing would be safely in its tomb. Of course, in this unseasonable heat they'd been having lately…

Nectanebo was lean as a bone and had the waxy skin of a man who seldom saw daylight. His kohl-rimmed eyes narrowed, he bent his shaven head close over the corpse. He had rolled it over on its back on the stone draining slab and was preparing to slice open the abdomen. He pursed his lips, puzzled. For him this was the reward. He had been hired by Alexandrinus because he knew how to keep his mouth shut about certain things that went on in the temple, but he was a doctor by training, not an undertaker. He had closed up shop early yesterday, as soon as he'd returned from Verpa's house, and had done nothing but dissect since then: peeling away layers of fat, tracing veins and tendons, probing the puckered knife wounds that covered the man's back. There was something very odd there; he didn't know what to make of it. And now this. His nose twitched with excitement.

"Here, what's this, then?" he spoke aloud to the sleepy little slave who sat beside him and whose job, performed with a minimum of effort, was to wave a horse-hair whisk at the cloud of buzzing flies that hovered over them. Holding the lamp closer, Nectanebo peered and poked at the little, livid bump which was already turning from purple to black. "By the beard of Ptah, most peculiar." It looked for all the world like a nasty bee sting. Nectanebo frowned in thought. "Now, how in the world does a man get a bee sting in a place like that?"

Beyond Nectanebo's workshop the columns of the great temple rose up black against the midnight blue of the sky. Before the temple stretched a broad courtyard flanked by porticos of lotus-stalk columns under whose eaves inert figures lay curled on papyrus mats, men and women indiscriminately. One could hear the collective sigh of their breathing. Now and then, one would moan or stir in his sleep. Serpents glided silently among them, tongues flicking out, touching eyelids, bringing dreams. Incense hung heavy in the moist night air.

The only illumination was the pale glow of oil lamps set upon the ground by each sleeper's head. The priests of the temple kept watch throughout the night, some resting on stools, others bending over the recumbent figures, those who were restless, whose dreams wouldn't come—touching, whispering incantations, assuring them that the compassionate Mistress of the Universe and her consort were with them and would heal them of their gout, their headache, their infertility. Attending were the priests of Isis, of Serapis, of Thoth; and the priest of Anubis—Alexandrinus—his head covered by the towering jackal mask, long-snouted and sharp-eared, painted black on one side and gold on the other. Through small eye-holes in the long neck he peered into the darkness.

Then one of the sleepers—she hadn't really been asleep at all—arose and came silently toward him, holding her lamp before her. Quickly Alexandrinus led her around the back of the temple and through a small door into a private cell. He turned to her, raising his arms to shoulder height, palms outward. "Praise the Queen of Heaven," he said. The voice was deep, the accent Egyptian, whether honestly come by or not. The voice of a god.

"Praise the Daughter of the Stars," repeated Turpia Scortilla and threw herself against his broad chest. He could feel her trembling.

"Not wise for you to come here."

"It worked! My Lord, it worked! Eight nights passed after I buried the tablet, I didn't sleep a single one, lying in my bed, listening, not daring to hope. Then the night before last they came—Ereschigal, Phokensepsou, Cheloumbra, and Abrasax. They came! Flying through his window. I heard the beating of their wings, and then slashing and ripping with their talons. I saw the marks on his body the next day and nearly fainted. I haven't stirred from my room since then until tonight. But I had to see you, to tell you. It's all happening exactly as you told me—"

"*I* told you?" he broke in sharply. "I told you nothing. It is the divine that speaks through me. Never say *I* told you."

"Yes, my Lord." She lowered her head. "We—we haven't done wrong, have we?"

He stroked her hair. "Isis is Queen of Hades as well as Queen of Heaven. All means to an end are within her compass."

"But I'm frightened. The penalty for magic is death. The police are camped in our house, some inspector came around. I wouldn't speak to him, but what if he comes back?"

"These police are stupid men. Calm yourself. The next step is the will. When is the reading?"

"Lucius wants it the day after tomorrow."

"Then there isn't much time. Verpa wrote what you suggested to him?"

She nodded. "A hundred thousand."

"Now I'm going to teach you how to lift a seal. It's a simple trick, some book maker's glue mixed with chalk, it hardens quickly. Lift it off and you have a perfect mold. The rest will be simple."

"Oh, Goddess help me. I'm afraid. I don't think I can go through with this. My nerves…"

"You can. The demons have done what you commanded, the rest you must do yourself. Anubis will hold your hand, as

I do now." He pulled her to him. Not gently. An animal growl rose deep in his throat, he pushed her on her knees on the cold stones, although he knew it hurt her, and pulled up her *stola*. Her spine was like a string of knucklebones, her buttocks thin, her hips razor-boned. He mounted her from behind, the dog-headed god himself in all his power and ferocity. He howled and barked through the megaphone of the mask, and she arched her back and cried out as he thrust—the god inside her!

After she had gathered herself and gone, Alexandrinus took up his place again in the courtyard of the sleepers. Human life, he considered, is ruled by the tyrants Hope and Fear. If you employ them skillfully, you can do very well for yourself. Turpia Scortilla was not the first overripe matron, drunk with faith, who had crawled on her knees to Queen Isis only to be lifted up by him.

Nectanebo, standing in the doorway of his workshop for a breath of fresh air, was thoughtful. Whatever he had seen was none of his business.

Chapter Eleven

The eighth day before the Ides of Germanicus. Day two of the Games.
The second hour of the day.

With great satisfaction, Lucius Ingentius Verpa watched the last of his clients bow themselves out of his atrium. *His* clients. *His* atrium. Now he was *paterfamilias* here. He looked around with distaste at the Nile mosaic and the Egyptian bric-a-brac that filled the room. That would all have to go, whether Scortilla liked it or not. He was master here now and there would be some changes made.

The *salutatio* had not been an entire success. He had soon grown bored trying to make sense of the clients' petitions and finally ordered them all out. Of course, they were all scum—parasites and legacy hunters hoping for a share in the old man's estate. And just as soon as the undertaker returned the body, they could proceed with the lying in state, break the seal of the will, and find out exactly what the estate amounted to. Then there was the matter of those papers, the ones his father had waved under his nose, hinting at their great value, taunting him with them. What were they? *Where* were they? That first night after his father's death, he had ransacked the *tablinum* looking for them, and surprised Scortilla in the dark, obviously on the same errand. Since then, with troopers all over the house, it wasn't safe to be seen searching; that would only arouse the curiosity of that meddling vice prefect.

These thoughts were interrupted by the arrival of the man himself. Lucius looked at him sourly. "Am I to look forward to these visits on a daily basis, Gaius Plinius?"

"No more than I do, I assure you. I've come to interview Pollux again, with your permission, of course."

"My permission seems to weigh little against the authority of the city prefect. You've turned my house into an army camp. The soldiers are into everything, I'm hardly master here. Do what you like by all means." Lucius waved his arm and let it drop.

Pliny ignored the insolent tone. "And Turpia Scortilla? I hope she is better disposed this morning?"

"She's out of her room, if that's what you mean. Not that you'll find her very helpful. She begins drinking as soon as her eyes are open."

"Yes, well then, I'll start with Pollux."

The slaves who languished in the stifling dormitory looked and smelled worse than they had the day before. Two more weeks of confinement and there would not be many left to execute. He looked from one face to another—pinched with hunger, glassy-eyed with fatigue and fear. Something odd about them today, too. Yesterday they had greeted him with screams. Why were they so quiet now?

"Pollux, step forward!" bawled Valens, the centurion. But no one stirred.

With a sudden premonition, Pliny plunged into their midst. He found the broken bodies of Pollux and the four others who had not sacrificed in a tangled heap in the far corner of the dormitory, throttled with their chains, their heads savagely battered.

"Carry them out," he shouted at Valens, and bolted for the door with his hand over his mouth. He had seen his share of dead bodies in the arena, still death up close always shocked him.

The troopers dragged the corpses into the corridor, each one leaving a smear of blood on the stone floor.

"Centurion, here's another one," called one of the men inside, and presently a sixth body was laid beside the other five, a boy of about thirteen, slim and dark, with fine features and silky skin.

Lucius appeared suddenly at Pliny's elbow. "Here, what's all this? They're dead!" He looked like he wanted to run.

"You know nothing about this?

"Of course I don't! What are you suggesting?"

An idea was beginning to form itself in Pliny's mind. Had Lucius and Pollux been in this together, and had it now been necessary to silence Pollux? But how could he have carried it off? The two sentries who stood watch outside the dormitory were questioned with Valens glowering over them, but they swore they had seen and heard nothing during the night. Wasn't it more plausible, after all, that the other slaves had turned on the Jews out of rage and in hopes of appearing loyal to their masters? It must have been swift and sudden. Pollux was a trained fighter, after all. But among the slaves were eight matched litter bearers, fierce-looking men spawned in some German swamp. If the victims were taken by surprise in the dark, it would have been over in a moment. What about this boy, though?

"His name was Hylas," Lucius offered. "One of my father's recent purchases. Kept him all for himself, too. Quite a tender morsel, I imagine."

"But he wasn't an atheist," said Pliny. "He sacrificed yesterday, didn't he?"

Lucius nodded.

"And he's not a Jew either, sir," Valens observed. The boy's tunic was up around his waist, his tender nakedness exposed. It was also apparent that, while the other slaves were beaten and bloodied as well as strangled, Hylas had only been strangled. His throat was bruised but he was otherwise unmarked.

There were too many mysteries here, and Pliny was a man impatient of mysteries. Why hadn't he questioned Pollux harder yesterday? Wills, contracts, account books were his meat, not this foul business. He squeezed the bridge of his nose between thumb and finger. He would insist that Aurelius Fulvus take him off the case.

"Centurion, question the slaves. I want to know who killed Pollux. Flog them, if you have to." Was this him speaking, who had never ordered a slave flogged in his life?

Valens looked happy to obey. He saluted and turned away. Then turned back again. "Sir, there's another thing, too."

Whatever it was, Pliny didn't want to hear it. But the centurion pressed on. "There's another person in the house. A lady. She keeps to her room, we only came across her yesterday when some of the lads were, you know, exploring. Nobody had mentioned her to us."

"What! Where?"

"At the end of the corridor there, near Verpa's room."

Pliny shot a questioning look at Lucius.

She was some house guest, the young man explained. He didn't know anything about her really except that she seemed sickly. He'd hardly seen her since she arrived. Didn't catch her name. What with everything else, he'd forgotten all about her.

Pliny sighed. He hadn't learned much so far. He supposed it couldn't hurt to have a word with this woman.

He tapped on the indicated door. Hearing a faint answer within, he opened it but hesitated on the threshold. She lay on a couch in the shuttered room, covered with a blanket although it was very hot. "Please come in, you aren't disturbing me. I am Amatia," she said in answer to his unspoken question. "And you are…?" The voice was low-pitched, warm, though with undertones of weariness in it. She threw off the cover and sat up as he entered. A short woman, pleasantly stout.

Pliny introduced himself and explained the reason for his presence in the house. When he mentioned Verpa her eyes seemed to widen momentarily. "I'm told you were here when the murder occurred. You didn't perhaps hear anything that night, madam?"

She shook her head, no. Pliny came closer and searched face. It was a serious, sensitive face. He guessed her age at five or fifty, though she might have been younger. Clearly, illness had aged her: there were deep furrows of strain around the mouth. Her skin was translucent, without a touch of powder, and her graying hair was parted severely in the middle and pulled back from her forehead in a style that had gone out of fashion a generation ago. In face, she reminded Pliny of his mother, who had died when he was a boy. He began falteringly, "How long have you been in this house, madam?

"Six days."

"And may I ask who you are?"

"I am Amatia, a widow from Lugdunum in Gaul."

He waited, but no more was forthcoming. It seemed he would have to draw every answer out of her. "A long way away, Lugdunum. And may I ask what has brought you to Rome?"

"If you must know, I have traveled here to become an initiate of beloved Queen Isis and seek a cure for my hysteria. Doctors say that the womb is an animal with no fixed home. In my case it climbs up to my chest. The symptoms are unbearable. I can't breathe or speak. I lose control of my limbs, I faint."

"Dear me. Is there no cure?"

"My physician makes me inhale sulfur and other evil-smelling things to drive the womb down to its proper place, but the effect is only temporary. And so, at last, I have turned to religion. The goddess appeared to me in a dream, beautiful in her mantle of shifting colors, and exhaling breath like the spices of Arabia. She told me what I must do and promised to heal me. We must believe in our dreams, mustn't we?"

"Oh, to be sure," said Pliny, who didn't.

"I came with my physician, Iatrides, half a dozen slaves, and a strongbox full of money for the initiation fee. When we disembarked at Ostia, the slaves robbed us of everything and ran off, leaving us alone and penniless."

Pliny gave a sympathetic shake of his head. It was all too common a story.

"Iatrides and I went to the temple of Serapis in Ostia and asked for help. They arranged for us to stay here with Ingentius Verpa, who is a notable devotee, until I can make other arrangements.

Scortilla has been kind enough to send one of her servants to Lugdunum to contact my son-in-law and arrange for more money to be sent. But now with this murder, I…I'm afraid. I don't know what to do, and I don't know where Iatrides has gone off to either." Her voice faltered. She clutched her chest and her breath came hard.

"I'm sure he'll turn up. I will have my men make inquiries. In the meantime, my house is at your disposal, ma'am."

"It's very kind of you. But an invalid is a burden, sir. Are you sure?" She searched his face.

"I insist upon it. It's quite impossible for you to stay here another night."

"Then I accept gratefully."

"Here, let me help you up. Valens!" Pliny yelled down the hall. "I need you. We're taking this woman to my house."

The centurion and two of his men carried Amatia, couch and all, into the vestibule while another followed behind with a bag containing her few possessions. Pliny's litter bearers ran up to assist.

Lucius watched them silently, not appearing to care whether the woman stayed or went.

And then Turpia Scortilla appeared, accompanied by Iarbas and his monkey. She took a step forward, swayed on her feet, and put a hand on a column to steady herself. If Amatia looked ill, Scortilla looked worse. This was the first time Pliny had had a good look at her in full daylight. He strained to see the young bareback rider in this ravaged body. The red slash of mouth in the chalk-white face, the straining tendons of the neck, the blue-veined hands.

"You're not leaving? But we took you in, I offered you my friendship, I wanted us to be…" Her eyes seemed to plead.

"I'm sorry, Turpia Scortilla. This gentleman has offered… Under the circumstances…" She looked away.

Scortilla turned on Pliny, her voice shrill. "You've no right!"

"Lady, calm yourself." Pliny held up his hands to ward her off. He was honestly a little frightened of her. "I remind you that Verpa's murderer has yet to be identified. It simply isn't safe."

"You *policeman.*" She spat out the word. "Think you can do whatever you like. We'll see."

Amatia raised herself on an elbow. "My condolences on your tragedy, lady, and my gratitude for your hospitality. We will see each other at the temple?"

Scortilla shot a venomous look at both of them, turned and walked away with a lurching, stiff-legged gait. The dwarf held on to her dress, and the monkey on his shoulder looked back and grimaced, showing all its sharp little teeth.

Lucius stood in the doorway and watched them until they were out of sight.

◇◇◇

The eighth hour of the day.

Pliny had wondered at his own impulsiveness in inviting this strange woman into his home. But as soon as he saw her and his darling Calpurnia together, he knew he had made the right decision. There was an instantaneous bond between the two women. Amatia almost seemed to have been sent by some benevolent goddess to be the mother that Calpurnia scarcely remembered.

His wife proudly displayed her swelling abdomen and asked, "How many children have you, Lady?"

"Please, call me Amatia. Five—all daughters, if you can believe it."

Everyone at the dinner table that evening exclaimed over this prodigy of fertility.

"I will have a son," said Calpurnia, setting her mouth firmly. "For my husband."

Pliny gazed at his wife anxiously. "The dear girl has had a difficult time," he confessed. "She has a doctor of course, a good man. Soranus, recently arrived from Ephesus. A specialist in women's complaints. Still, he can't be here all the time. Anything you could do to instruct her, calm her fears, ma'am..."

"Dear Pliny, I will treat her like one of my own." The two women reclined side by side on the dining couch. Amatia took the girl's hand and squeezed it. "I only hope I won't impose on your hospitality too long."

Pliny waved this aside. "Lugdunum is weeks away. In the meantime, this is your home."

"Yes, please," said Calpurnia.

Amatia smiled and nodded graciously.

At that moment, Martial burst into the dining room. His face was flushed with wine, a garland sat askew on his shaggy head, and he smelled of scent. Clearly he was coming from a day's drinking with his fellow poets and their hangers-on. Pliny gave him an indulgent smile. "You're just in time for the braised leeks."

"Ah, the braised leeks!" the poet rubbed his hands together in what he hoped was a convincing display of anticipation.

Introductions were made. Amatia appraised the newcomer with observant eyes. "I am only a provincial countrywoman," she said. "Forgive me if your fame has not reached us. What sort of poems do you write?"

"Yes, well," Pliny broke in hastily "Perhaps this is not the time."

"But it is, my friend," Martial said, reaching into the fold of his cloak and bringing out a small scroll." If I may, this is a gift for your charming wife. Our conversation last night put me in mind of it. Years ago in Spain, during one particularly bitter winter, a little slave girl of ours, Erotion was her name—I told you about her—well, she took sick and died just six days short of her sixth birthday. I was fond of her—well, we all were. I wrote an elegy for her. Would you favor me by setting it to music, Calpurnia?"

She took the scroll from his hand, unrolled it, and read it aloud. When she came to the end there was silence around the table and Pliny looked at his guest as though seeing him for the first time.

"It's beautiful, sir." She regarded him gravely and repeated the last line. *"Gently cover her tender bones, ye rugged earth, for she trod so light on thee."* She rewound the scroll and tucked it in her bosom. "I will do my best with it, and thank you."

Suddenly the poet was embarrassed—an unaccustomed emotion for him. To cover it, he lifted his cup and drank deeply.

"Yes, well," he blustered, "didn't mean to interrupt things." He turned instead to the older woman. "Amatia, this Verpa business, then. I confess I'm curious. How did you come to be in that dubious household?"

Amatia repeated her story, adding that Scortilla seemed especially glad to receive her, actually flattered that her home was recommended by the temple authorities. "She seemed lonely, troubled."

"Most unpleasant woman," Pliny broke in. "The whole damned family. Imagine those priests sending this unsuspecting lady to that house. What an unworldly lot they must be."

"Which brings us," said Martial, suddenly sober, "to the mystery."

But Amatia had little to tell. She had taken a sleeping draught that night and heard nothing, although her room was not far from Verpa's. She was awakened by the uproar the next morning when his body was discovered. She came out into the hall to see what the matter was and peeked into Verpa's room where everyone was milling around and shouting. She had just a glimpse of the horrible, bloody scene and felt an attack of hysteria coming on. She retreated to her room, feeling breathless and faint, and had stayed there until the soldiers discovered her.

"And your physician took himself off somewhere and never came back?" said Pliny. "On the same day that Verpa died? Curious. More than curious, in fact. Did he say where he was going?" She shook her head. "Well, the city is full of dangers for the unwary. Give me his description and I'll convey it to the prefect's office. If he's come to harm, we'll learn of it sooner or later. In the meantime, I'll ask Soranus to have a look at you the next time he comes to examine my wife."

"Oh, no, please," she protested. "I mean, I'm used to Iatrides. He must come back soon."

"Well, as you wish."

Martial asked what impression she had formed of the family during the days she was there.

His question seemed to make her uncomfortable. "I mustn't speak ill of my benefactors, fellow-worshipers of the goddess," she answered, "but, well, I suppose it wasn't a very happy family. I began to regret that I had agreed to stay there. So much shouting. I tried not to listen, but you couldn't avoid it."

"Shouting between…?"

"Verpa and his son, mostly. They had several rows. Lucius complained about not being given enough spending money. He called his father ungrateful. There was some talk about atheistic Jews which I didn't understand. Then another time they argued about one of the slave girls, Phyllis, I think, and on that occasion the father actually threatened to kill his son if he caught him with her again."

"Hmm. And Scortilla?" Pliny asked.

"She just seemed, I don't know how to describe it, preoccupied, jumping at the slightest noise. She hardly spoke to either of them as far as I could tell."

There was a thoughtful silence all around until finally, Amatia asked, "What will you do now, Pliny? Is the case closed? I suppose there's no doubt the slaves did it."

"Husband," Calpurnia asked, "what will they do to the slaves?"

Pliny had no desire to tell her, but she persisted. "Some will be dressed in shirts covered with pitch and burned alive. Others will be thrown to the lions in the arena." The girl gave a shudder.

Zosimus, Pliny's secretary, who had said little all evening, looked straight ahead, not a muscle in his face betraying his feelings. Zosimus had been born a slave in this house and, although he had been educated, cherished, cared for when he was sick, and finally rewarded with freedom, he vibrated with a sympathy for the enslaved that none of these others would ever understand.

"It is the *mos maiorum,* child," Amatia explained, touching Calpurnia's arm.

"You are a traditionalist, dear lady," Pliny said. "I admire that in you, so rare these days. And yet one's human feelings rebel…"

"Oh, yes of course," she murmured.

"But, to answer your question, the case is not closed. Not until I know for a certainty who killed Ingentius Verpa."

That night Pliny lay in bed, waiting for sleep to come, and thinking how pleasant it was that Calpurnia, his darling Calpurnia, had a new friend.

Chapter Twelve

The seventh day before the Ides of Germanicus.
Day three of the Games.
The first hour of the day.

The usual crop of drowsy-eyed clients filled Pliny's atrium. With one significant addition—Martial. Pliny had half expected this, but didn't relish it. He had hoped to have the poet as a genial acquaintance, even a helpful assistant in the Verpa affair, but not as a client. But by attending the *salutatio*, Martial was proposing himself for that status, and Pliny didn't see how he could refuse. In a moment of careless generosity, he'd brought it on himself. Now, as the poet's patron, he had obligations toward him. If the *mos maiorum* still meant anything at all, he would have to use what small political capital he possessed to get his poems read by the emperor. This meant fawning on the chamberlain, Parthenius—a thought which filled him with disgust. Well, all that was for another day. He had too much else on his plate at the moment.

When the others shuffled out, clutching their daily handouts of food and coin, Martial made no move to leave. It was an awkward moment for both men. But before either could speak, a strange voice sounded from the back of the room. Pliny, looking up, saw that two men whom he did not recognize lingered near the door. One, the shorter of the two, decently dressed in a Greek cloak; the other tall, shabby, long-bearded, and very old. They approached, the short man taking the lead, bowing as he came.

"I am Evaristus, bishop of Rome," the man said. "My companion is Ioannes of Patmos. He is a visitor to our city. We are Christians." He said it as easily as one might say, *We are rug merchants.* He was a man of middle age, olive-skinned, with gray starting in his beard. He searched Pliny's face with intense black eyes.

Pliny returned a blank look. "Christians," he said, trying to remember in what connection he had heard the word before. "You are their high priest?"

"One of them," Evaristus gave a deprecating smile.

"And your business with me?"

"Today our brothers Pollux and the young man Arminius, and our sisters Modestina, Artemisia, and Graciliana are sitting at the feet of God. They will live forever, hallelujah. But I have come to beg for their bodies, to bury them according to our rite."

"This is a police matter, I can't allow it."

But Martial interrupted with an unpleasant laugh. "Immortal are they? What, merely by dying? Seems a cheap and easy way to achieve immortality. Any gladiator can do it. The Isis priests, so I hear, make you pay through the nose and spend months in initiations."

The bishop seemed to notice him for the first time. His black eyes flashed. "You are that poet, I believe."

"I am delighted to hear my fame has spread so far."

"Oh yes, I know your works: the language of the gutter employed with the skill of an artist for the solitary purpose of drawing blood. The women, whores when they aren't bald, toothless and eyeless; the men, gluttons, hypocrites and perverts." Martial opened his mouth but the bishop silenced him with a dismissive flick of the hand. "I know what you're going to say: you attack the vice, not the person; your verse is lascivious while you yourself are chaste. But I tell you, God sees through that false rhetoric."

"Rhetoric! What does a drag-tail fellow like you know about rhetoric?" Martial sputtered.

"I was a professor of it for twenty years before my eyes were opened." It was said with more than a trace of pride.

And, for once in his life, the poet found himself without a riposte.

While the two men stared each other down, Pliny was recalling a public reading he had attended some years earlier, given by the historian Cornelius Tacitus: How these Christians were every bit as atheistical as the Jews, from whom their sect had sprung, though now they claimed to hate the Jews. Like everything filthy and degrading, Tacitus had said, they eventually found their way to Rome. Nero accused them of starting the great fire that had nearly destroyed the city some thirty years ago, and executed some of them with particular savagery—so much so that they excited a degree of public sympathy. It was the common belief, nevertheless, that they engaged in orgies and sacrificed children to their god and even ate them. Probably an exaggeration, but who could say, since they practiced their rites in secret.

Then another thought struck him.

"Fellow, bishop, whatever you call yourself, answer me one question. Is the seven-branched candelabrum a symbol of your cult?"

"Certainly not! That is for the ones who reject Our Lord, who misunderstand their own prophecies. Our symbol of recognition is a fish."

"Then Pollux and the others you named are not Jews?"

"Not since they chose the true path to salvation. I converted Pollux myself some years ago, and from that day onward he never struck a man."

"You mentioned four others besides Pollux. We found a sixth body, a boy of twelve or thirteen, Hylas he was called. Is he not one of yours?"

Evaristus shook his head. "He is not known to me."

Pliny motioned Martial to come closer and they exchanged a few whispered words. If Pollux was, in fact, one of these Christians, then perhaps the sketch of the candelabrum and the Jewish dagger had been planted as clues to implicate him by someone who *thought* he was still a Jew. And who would that someone be? Lucius leapt to mind; he certainly had the motive. But the question remained, how was it done? Who had come through that open window, if not a Jewish assassin? And how could Pollux not have heard sounds of the struggle? And then why was the boy Hylas killed by the other slaves if he was neither a Jew nor a Christian? Whatever theory he had had about the case before was now shipwrecked. He would have to begin all over again. There were too many puzzles, and Pliny, whose whole professional life dealt with certainties, with documents and numbers, hated puzzles. He discharged his annoyance at Evaristus.

"They say you are atheists and haters of mankind. You gather secretly like rats in the sewers. You do not sacrifice to our emperor. If even half what they say about you is true, you deserve to be punished. What gives you the nerve to come here and ask me for a favor?"

The bishop returned his angry gaze with eyes as bright as steel; there was no fear in them. "We are men of peace, we obey the laws and those who are set over us. We pray for the emperor, though not to him. We mean no harm to anyone. I say to you, Senator, save yourself, be born again in Christ Jesus—"

"Macro!" Pliny shouted to his door keeper. "Escort these men out."

Until then, the bishop's companion, the cadaverous, bearded ancient in his threadbare cloak, had stood silently by, giving no sign that he understood what was being said. Macro's firm hand on his shoulder set him off. Without warning, he flung his scrawny arms wide and burst into shrill Greek. "Fallen, fallen is Babylon the great. Babylon, the harlot of the seven hills. Alas, alas for the great city that was clothed in fine linen and purple and scarlet. Alas that in a single hour she should be laid waste…" He stared with all his eyes, seeing something that was invisible to the rest of them. While his breath came short and sharp between his teeth, he poured out a torrent of words.

Bishop Evaristus, for the first time showing fear, looked this way and that. "The vision comes upon him sometimes, unfortunate timing, please excuse us…" He tried, with Macro, to push Ioannes toward the door but the holy man was not to be silenced. The Greek was so rapid, the man gasping in the throes of his vision, Pliny could only understand bits of it—a woman riding on a scarlet beast with seven heads and ten horns—the seven heads were the seven hills of Rome and the woman was drunk on the blood of God's people—foul and malignant sores on those who wore the mark of the beast and worshipped its image, plainly the emperor himself—the seas, the rivers, and springs were turning to blood and every living thing dying—now the kingdom of the beast, plunged in darkness and men gnawing their tongues in agony—tormented in sulfurous flames...

"Enough!" Pliny sprang from his chair. "Monsters! Out of my house!"

When they were gone, the old man's voice echoing down the street, Martial groped for a stool and sank on to it. There was a moment of shocked silence while the two men looked at each other.

"What on earth was that about?" breathed Pliny.

Martial shook his head. "Sounds treasonous to me."

"Well, that's not our concern right now."

"Yes, but d'you think one of them could be Verpa's killer? Blame it on the Jews?"

"I doubt it. Why bother if we're all going to go up in flames soon anyway?"

The sound of a girl weeping came from behind the half-open door of one of the side chambers.

"Calpurnia!" Pliny ran to her at once and clasped her in his arms. No telling how much she had understood but the girl seemed scared out of her wits. A moment later, Amatia appeared from her bedroom, her face still puffy with sleep. Between them they got Calpurnia to a couch.

Martial watched discreetly from the sidelines. When some calm had been restored he asked Pliny if he was going back to Verpa's house today.

"I'm staying with my wife. Tomorrow the will is going to be read. I will attend that. Wills, at least, are something I understand. Come with me if you like."

The poet bowed himself out.

Chapter Thirteen

*The sixth day before the Ides of Germanicus. Day four of the Games.
The fourth hour of the day.*

For the third time in four days Pliny reluctantly mounted his
litter and was carried above the jostling crowds, the choking
dust and stinks of the city. The foot traffic eddied around his
conveyance, a small boat riding a turbulent stream. The heat
already felt like the exhalation from a potter's oven.

His way took him down the slope of the Esquiline, past the
Colosseum and the Temple of Venus and Rome, along the Via
Sacra and on into the Forum Romanum. On his left he passed,
with a throb of longing, the noble Basilica Julia, the two-storied
colonnaded building which occupied nearly the whole north side
of the Forum. His view of it sadly was obscured by an immense
bronze equestrian statue of Domitian, which towered over the
surrounding buildings. But this was his arena, the scene of his
triumphs since the day he had argued his first inheritance case
there at the age of eighteen. In its vast interior the law courts
met in open view of passers-by, and when he pleaded a case,
audiences would desert the other orators to gather round him!
Over the years, he had made a name for himself and done quite
well off his fees. How he wished that this interminable month,
not yet a third over, would end, allowing him to get back to his
proper vocation.

Leaving the Forum behind, he was carried along the Clivus Argentarius, skirting the north flank of the Citadel, and coming out in the Vicus Pallacinae, near the east end of the Circus Flaminius.

As he swayed comfortably on the broad shoulders of his bearers, Pliny let his mind drift. He realized with a twinge of guilt that all during the morning *salutatio* he had scarcely heard a word anyone had said, including himself, so preoccupied was he with this wretched case. (Martial had sent a note, saying he'd had a late night and begged to be excused.)

Should he consider now that the Jewish business was a blind, intended to throw him off the track? And, if so, by whom? By Lucius? Or even Scortilla? Or, both of them? He knew so little. A man like Verpa would have had hundreds of enemies who wished him dead, any one of whom might have found a way to accomplish it. But how? A room with one high, narrow window and one door guarded by a man who, in spite of being a slave and a former Judean rebel, struck Pliny as truthful. And who was now revealed to have been a different sort of atheist altogether.

At any rate, today's task was to interrogate those few slaves who had had the run of the house that night, something he should have done in the first place. That and listen to the reading of the will. Perhaps there would be a clue there.

His bearers, by this time, could have found their way blindfolded to the imposing porphyry-columned entrance to Verpa's house. They set him down before the bronze-studded double doors which, today, were decorated with dark acanthus wreathes and bows of cypress, proclaiming that the deceased's lying-in-state had begun.

The great man lay encoffined in a vast gilded mummy case resting on a black-draped catafalque which occupied the center of the atrium. The head of the case was painted with a likeness of Verpa's face which, despite the artist's best intentions, did not completely disguise the hard jaw line, the pugnacious nose, the heavy-lidded eyes. The actual burial was scheduled for four days hence. Were those alien gods, Pliny wondered, who stood ready to receive his spirit on the banks of the Styx, or wherever it was Egyptians went—were they quite prepared for what they were getting in this pretty package?

The atrium was mobbed. The rich, the envious, the senator and the freedman; the pinch-faced legacy hunter and the humble, hopeful sycophant; the clergy of Isis, bone-thin, brown and bald; the matrons, painted and coiffed, and many decked out with jeweled scarab beetles or other Egyptian gewgaws. In the midst of these, receiving their fawning condolences, was Turpia Scortilla. For the occasion she wore a new wig, tier upon tier of massed blond curls for which a dozen German captives must have given up their hair. She held to her thin bosom Iarbas' monkey, who rejoiced in a new collar of lapis lazuli and gold. It leapt out of her arms at Pliny's approach and disappeared in a forest of legs. She extended a heavy-ringed hand to him.

"And how is my poor Amatia?" she simpered. "Tell her that I am thinking of her." Pliny said that he would do so. "I am aware," she went on, "of the deaths of Pollux and the other atheists. It's just what they deserved, don't you agree with me, Vice Prefect? May we not call the case closed at this point? Lucius feels that we should."

The elapse of two days had improved her appearance and manners. She wasn't drunk, at any rate, and, perhaps, was in a mood to make peace.

"I am growing steadily less certain that Jews had anything to do with Ingentius Verpa's murder."

Her face enacted a mimicry of surprise. "Then who?"

It was far too soon for accusations. Pliny spread his hands. "The man must have had other enemies; what informer does not?"

At the word "informer" she bristled. "Just because he showed himself loyal and useful to his emperor, as every senator should do, instead of carping and caviling, and scheming behind his back, you call him that! Tell me, Gaius Plinius, if Sextus Ingentius was an informer, exactly what are you?"

"I don't understand you, woman," Pliny replied frostily.

"Don't you? You serve the same master. You come here snooping and asking questions. Your policemen spy on us. And in the end, you hope to denounce one of us and get your reward. I've lived long in this society, I know better than a small-town provincial like you how it works."

Pliny turned from her in exasperation. How dare the hag talk to him that way! He was an officer of the Prefecture, doing his duty, and not willingly either.

And yet, something of what she said lodged under his skin and stuck there.

He caught sight of Valens standing at the edge of the crowd, looking glum. "How goes it, centurion?"

The centurion was unhappy. "The lads are bored, getting into trouble. I had to cudgel two of them last night for breaking into the wine locker. Now that more slaves have arrived from Verpa's estate in Apulia, there's nothing for them to do all day. Bad for discipline, sir, and it's not likely there's going to be any more murders."

"I understand. Do the best you can. I want as many pairs of eyes and ears in this house as possible. It may still have things to tell us."

Valens cocked an eyebrow.

"While we're waiting for the will to be read, I want to talk to a couple of the slaves. Find the girl, Phyllis, and bring her into one of the vacant rooms upstairs, I'll question her there." Amatia had said that Verpa quarreled with his son over Phyllis; had actually threatened to kill the young man, which, according to law, he had the right to do, if he didn't leave the girl alone. It would not be the first time that sexual jealousy involving a slave had led to murder in a Roman household.

He didn't know what to expect from her. Some slave mistresses, sensing their power, could be bold and brassy, putting on airs as though they were the virtual mistress of the house. But Phyllis turned out to be quite different. She looked about sixteen or seventeen, was fair-haired and rather fragile. She might have been beautiful, but six days of confinement on short rations had obviously taken its toll of her. She was pale and her eyes sunk deep in their sockets. The acrid smell of sweat and unwashed bodies clung to her. Valens sat her down roughly on a stool and then left them alone. Pliny's heart went out to her.

"You shared your master's bed?"

"Yes."

"Often?"

"Yes." Her voice was barely above a whisper. She stared at the floor.

"But you weren't in his bed the night he died? Why not?"

She shrugged. "He didn't send for me."

"Did he send for any of the other girls?"

"No. Maybe one of the boys—the *cinaedi*—or maybe he slept alone. He sometimes did."

"The *cinaedi*. You mean like Ganymede?"

"Hylas, more likely. The one they killed. Master had gotten tired of Ganymede, everyone said."

Pliny had a sudden glimpse of the lives of these sex slaves. The whispered rumors, the jealous looks, the anxious observation of every clue to the master's shifting preferences. Their lives depended on it.

He cleared his throat. "I'm told that Lucius wanted your company too and the old master didn't like that."

Her hands twisted in her lap. "I never encouraged young master. It's hard for someone like me, pulled both ways. A slave can't refuse."

The girl's vulnerability reminded Pliny uncomfortably of his own wife. If life were different, if situations were reversed…He gave her a moment to compose herself. "Phyllis, who do you think killed the master?"

"Well, not old Pollux," she answered with surprising firmness. "That poor old man didn't have it in him to do such a thing. It's a shame what the others did to him and his friends, even if they were Jews and atheists."

"You know, child, I agree with you. Tell me what you think— could an assassin have climbed through the window?"

"How would I know? But it's funny then that he didn't bring his own knife with him."

"What do you say?"

"The curved dagger, sir, that was lying on the floor all bloody, it belonged to the master. I saw it when we all crowded in to see what had happened."

Pliny looked at her sternly. "Are you quite sure?"

He called for Valens, who had remained just outside the door, and ordered him to fetch the weapon.

"It's his." She studied it closely. "The red leather on the hilt. Those foreign letters scratched on the blade. See? He told me it says 'Death to Romans.' He used to make me admire it. Told me how he took it off a dead rebel in Jerusalem. I'd ooh and aah. He liked that. He kept it on the table beside the bed."

Pliny tried to force his thoughts into some order. "If you recognize it then others must have. Wouldn't Pollux have recognized it?"

"I'm sure he did," she girl answered. "But that poor man was slow-witted. Too many blows to the head."

Pliny tried to remember the details of his brief interrogation of the boxer. Had he even asked him about the weapon? He shook his head woefully. What a fool he was.

"Well, but Lucius certainly recognized it, damn him!" He hadn't meant to speak these words aloud. Now he had frightened the girl.

"I—I don't know." Her under lip quivered. "Please sir, I don't know any more. Don't make me say anything against Lucius. He's my master now."

"Yes, yes, quite. What you've told me will stay between us. You may go now, and thank you."

Valens handed her off to one of his men to return her to the guarded dormitory. He rubbed his bristly chin and looked thoughtfully at Pliny. "So young Lucius has been lying to us, sir. There was no Jewish assassin."

"Yes, but the man didn't stab himself in the back. Someone managed to climb through that window. The shutter was open, and we saw how the ivy tendrils on the column looked as if they were torn loose by someone's hands and feet."

Valens nodded.

"Get me Ganymede. He's another one who was allowed to prowl the house at night. He may, at least, have seen or heard something."

"How old are you, boy?" Pliny asked the creature who now stood, loose-limbed before him.

"Fifteen, sir."

Closer to seventeen, Pliny guessed. Almost too old for a *cinaedus*. He had seen others like this one. The boy wore a short-skirted Greek tunic, the color of crocus and diaphanous to the point of transparency. His hairless limbs glistened with oil like the limbs of finely polished furniture. But his long, scented ringlets were matted and tangled and there was a faint stubble on his cheeks; he'd had no opportunity to singe them with hot walnut shells.

"Are you home bred or bought?"

"I was purchased from the Temple of Eros, an all-boy brothel, at a high price, too. I was only nine, yet so skilled at giving old men pleasure that Sextus Verpa fell hopelessly in love with me. He came every day and would accept no one else. Finally, he made Marcus Ganeus, my owner, sell me to him. He loved me very much. He gave me presents. The slave girls hate me. He never gave them such fine stuff."

The voice was unnaturally high and wispy. He was forcing himself to speak in a falsetto so as not to betray his age. When the voice broke a boy's career was over. Ganymede fluttered his long lashes seductively and touched himself between the legs. Pliny felt a mixture of pity and revulsion. There was something that was not quite human about Ganymede. He was a work of art, the product of someone's fantasy. Every gesture practiced and studied.

"Besides giving your master pleasure, have you other duties in the house?"

"I am the principal dancer in our pantomime troupe," he answered in his light, lisping voice. "I am called 'Anguilla,' the eel, because I dance as if I haven't a bone in my body." To make his point the youth lifted his arms above his head and a ripple of motion ran through his body beginning with his ankles, rising through knees, hips, and ribs cage and ending at his fingertips which fluttered imaginary castanets. It did distinctly give the impression of an eel twisting lazily through water. Pliny noted the long muscular legs, the wasp-thin waist, the narrow shoulders and the sinuous arms. He couldn't have weighed much more than a hundred pounds. The boy flashed him a practiced smile, then let his arms drop to his sides.

This pantomime troupe of Verpa's, of Scortilla's really (she being an old trouper herself), was a bit of a scandal, hardly in keeping with the spirit of the age. A perversion, not to put too fine a point on it. Verpa and Scortilla entertained a very select group of friends of whom Pliny, happily, was not one, though he had heard things. And Martial had added other juicy details gleaned from his sources in the demimonde. Surprising, really that the emperor permitted it, since he had banned public performances of the same kind. But it seemed there were exceptions made for useful men like Verpa.

"Was that other boy, Hylas, a performer, too?"

"Hylas was a runny-nosed brat who couldn't put one foot in front of the other without tripping!" Malice glittered in Ganymede's eyes.

"Did you kill Hylas?"

"No!" Color rose from his throat to his cheeks. He sucked in his breath.

Pliny gave the boy a long, searching look. His face was haggard and there was something in the eyes that was inexpressibly tired. An old man in a boy's body. And he was frightened, but he stood his ground.

"Did you see who killed him?"

"It was dark, everyone was pushing and tumbling over each other. I didn't see anything. I tried to stay out of the way."

"Did you know he was an atheist?"

"I don't even know what that means."

"Did you kill your master?"

"Of course not."

"Were you with him that night?"

"No."

"Where were you?"

"Sleeping at the bottom of the stairs. I sleep wherever I please." Such arrogance in those words.

"Did anyone see you there?"

"I don't know. I was asleep."

"Did you see or hear anything out of the ordinary all evening?"

"No, sir." Ganymede ran his finger around the iron slave collar that circled his soft neck. Clearly, it chafed him, perhaps his pride more than his flesh. The boy had pride.

Without warning, Pliny uncovered the dagger which he had placed under a cloth on the table beside him. He kept his eyes on the Ganymede's face as he did so. The boy's eyes widened, then quickly slid away.

"You recognize this, do you?"

"No."

"What? Don't recognize an object that lay in plain sight on your master's bedside table?"

Ganymede compressed his lips into a thin line. He refused to answer. Poor Ganymede wasn't very good at thinking on his feet.

An image presented itself to Pliny's mind—of an "eel," lithe with muscular legs, shimmying up a column, negotiating the overhanging eave, somehow unlatching the shutter from the outside, and slipping in through Verpa's narrow window. But could this effeminate youth possibly have overcome Verpa, who, even if taken asleep, was a powerful and vigorous man, a fighter? Hard to imagine it. And what could the boy's motive be? These sex slaves were far more likely to kill each other out of jealousy than to kill the master upon whom they all depended. But if someone had put him up to it? Someone like Lucius? Plenty of motive there. But no, Pliny was not yet ready to charge the son of an imperial favorite with patricide—a crime punished by ancient and savage ritual—based on the innuendo of a female houseguest or the frightened look in a slave's eye. Gaius Plinius Secundus had his career to think of.

While he turned these thoughts over in his mind, Valens opened the door and admitted Lucius. The will was about to be opened. No doubt Pliny, as representative of the city prefect, might wish to be informed. Lucius was acting the gracious host this morning, confident of his new position. Pliny looked for some sign of recognition between him and Ganymede. There was none.

"Thank you, Lucius Ingentius, I had planned to stay for the reading. Centurion," turning to Valens, "I want this slave boy kept separate from the others, under twenty-four-hour guard. No one is to have access to him. No one. I've had one witness murdered already, I won't have another."

"Witness to what?" Lucius' newly-won composure was gone in an instant. "What are you insinuating? And you've no right to keep my slaves locked up any longer—especially this harmless creature. I want you and your policemen out of here, I am master here now." His voice was shrill.

"Please calm yourself," Pliny replied. "The soldiers will be here for a while longer and the slaves must remain under guard until the Games are over. Prefect's orders." Best to take shelter under his superior's authority rather than explain his own reasons.

"We'll see about that," Lucius sneered. "This family still has influence. You, your family is nothing."

"So I have already been reminded once today."

Lucius flung himself from the room. Pliny followed.

The will was to be read in the *tablinum*, the master's office, where his big iron-bound strongbox occupied one corner and cubicles containing his letters and accounts lined the walls. The death masks of his ancestors stared vacant-eyed from their niches. The room, though large, could scarcely accommodate the sweating mob of clients, relations, and cronies who were attempting to crowd into it.

Lucius sat himself in the front, next to Scortilla. Facing them sat a man at Verpa's desk. Atilius Regulus, whom he had last seen that night of the infamous "black banquet." Pliny sighed. How fitting that he should be Verpa's attorney. On the desk lay a thick leather cylinder, its clasp covered with a wax seal. Inside it was the scroll of Sextus Ingentius Verpa's last will and testament.

Seeing him standing in the back, Regulus invited Pliny, "his esteemed colleague at the bar," to come forward and join him and the heirs in examining the seal before it was broken. Pliny had examined many such seals and rather fancied himself an expert on the subject.

The seal was perfectly intact and both Lucius and Scortilla attested that the signet was undoubtedly Verpa's. Regulus, rubbing his hands together as though he were about to sit down to a good meal, broke the seal, removed and unfurled the scroll, cleared his throat importantly and began to read.

Verpa's estate was worth about eight million *sesterces*—a handsome fortune, though not as large as many had expected. It consisted mainly of valuable land near Rome and other properties in the south. Lucius was named as heir to the whole. He heard this with a smile of satisfaction. Verpa was under no obligation to name his concubina as an heir, and didn't. Pliny stole a sidelong look at her. Her face revealed nothing. According to form, the bequests must now be enumerated—subtractions from the estate which the heir was bound by law to make good on. There were several. Five hundred thousand sesterces to the emperor. Lucius winced, but said nothing. This was unavoidable: the surest way to guarantee that a will would not be challenged was to make the emperor an interested party. To Scortilla he bequeathed a half interest in their house in Rome, meaning that Lucius couldn't throw her out—a cruel trick on both of them. Then there was a bequest of a thousand sesterces to Pollux, who was granted his freedom as a reward for years of faithful service. Several other slaves were manumitted, as well, and given smaller sums. But these bequests, of course, were moot. Pollux was dead and the rest soon would be.

Regulus paused in his reading to draw a breath and unrolled some more of the scroll. As he skimmed ahead, his eyes suddenly narrowed. Lucius, seeing something in his face, leaned forward in his chair.

"And finally," Regulus read in a faltering voice, "to the temple of Queen Isis in the Campus Martius, for the purpose of founding a mortuary temple and fully-equipped embalming works where that neglected art can be practiced as in ancient days, together with perpetual stipends for the embalmers and priests who will oversee it, I give and bequeath the sum of two million sesterces; this amount to be administered at the discretion of the High Priest of Anubis, the god of embalming…"

The last words were drowned out in the uproar that filled the room.

Lucius was ashen-faced. Two million! A quarter of his estate. A senatorial fortune in itself—for Anubis, or, rather, for Alexandrinus, that charlatan! This was madness. His father would never…

"This is you, isn't it, you filthy whore!" he screamed in Scortilla's face, leaping up and knocking over his chair. He drew back his fist to hit her. But a brown, muscular shoulder came between them. It belonged to a tall man clad in white linen. Pliny had noticed him briefly when he arrived. The man had a smooth, beautifully shaped skull marked with the star-shaped scar of Isiac priests, and jet black eyes outlined with kohl. He turned them on Scortilla and a look passed between them.

Lucius rushed to the desk and snatched the scroll from Regulus' hands. "Show me. Show me where it says 'million.'" He stared at the place where the lawyer's fingertip pointed: a letter M with a line drawn under it, multiplying a thousand by a thousand. In desperation he looked around for Pliny.

Pliny bent low, until his nose almost touched the page. He shook his head. If the numeral had been altered, it had been very neat work. Whatever the original amount was, only two pen strokes perhaps would need to be pumiced out and redrawn. But he felt as strongly as Lucius that the old man was simply not capable of such profligate generosity. A hundred thousand maybe, but not this.

There was one thing he could do about it. In a loud voice he announced to the room, "I will request the city prefect to suspend payment of legacies until the question of Ingentius Verpa's death has been satisfactorily explained. Furthermore, all parties with an interest in this matter are to remain within ten miles of the city until further notice." He knew he was far exceeding his authority. Could he get away with it? The emperor would not be happy, and the city prefect was his creature. Well, it might buy a little time, at least.

◇◇◇

Pliny stood outside the front door with its load of dark foliage, Scortilla's abuse still ringing in his ears. He dabbed at the spot on his cheek where she had spat at him. But he had been adamant, and finally she had rushed from the room in tears, followed by her Egyptian. Lucius stamped off in another direction, Regulus slipped away, and the *tablinum* had disgorged its mob of disappointed sycophants with astonishing swiftness.

Pliny beckoned to his litter-bearers. There was nothing more to be accomplished here today. He had left Valens with orders to report anything he overheard between Lucius and Scortilla, and try to keep the two of them from killing each other in the meantime. He had simply no idea what else to do and found himself longing for Martial, that fount of information and excellent sounding board. He must send a slave round to invite him to dinner again tonight. In the meantime he wanted his lunch, the company of his dear wife, of clever Zosimus, perhaps of the gentle, unfortunate lady Amatia, and then a midday nap and a bath.

Just as he was about to mount his litter, however, a young slave hailed him. "Sir, are you Gaius Plinius? My master wishes you good health and begs you to come and take lunch with him today."

"And who is your master?" There was something familiar about the boy's face, but one seldom looked closely at slaves' faces.

"Quintus Corellius Rufus, sir. He hopes you won't refuse a sick old friend who has your welfare at heart."

"My welfare?"

Ever since the "black banquet," Pliny had received half a dozen dinner invitations from senators of dubious reputation, who, with their sensitive antennae attuned to every shift in the political wind, had suddenly decided that his acquaintance was worth cultivating. He had begged off all of them. But this was different. Corellius Rufus had been a trusted friend of his uncle's and a mentor to himself. He accepted gladly.

Chapter Fourteen

How is he?" Pliny whispered.

"Very bad. The gout attacks him everywhere. He can barely move without torment, but he'll never say so. You know him, he bears it like a philosopher." Rufus' wife of forty years, Hispulla, a small, white-haired woman of great sweetness, met Pliny in the vestibule of their modest house on the Quirinal. She took both his hands and squeezed them. "Come inside, he's waiting for you."

Corellius Rufus lay on a couch, his arms and legs propped on cushions. Pliny bent over to kiss the withered cheek. Hispulla, who had followed him in, fussed about her husband a bit, but he waved her off impatiently. She arranged a loaf of bread, a bowl of olives, and a plate of fried smelts on the table beside him. Then she left, taking the servants with her so that the two men could be entirely alone.

Pliny felt a deep affection for this man. He had been a consul of Rome and governor of Upper Germany before illness had forced him to withdraw from active life. Now he was beyond ambition, hope, and fear; and he made no secret of his contempt for Domitian.

The invalid regarded his protégé with watery eyes, half-hidden under brows that sprang from his forehead like white bushes. "You know I've always taken an interest in your career, dear boy." The voice was tremulous. Pliny launched into expressions of gratitude, but Corellius cut him short. "Tut. I didn't bring you here for that. I've some advice to give you; you can decide for yourself what it's worth. I've heard all about that macabre banquet at the palace last week. It was disgraceful. Exactly what I would have expected from 'Our Lord and God.'"

Pliny protested, "I was taken completely off guard! I had no intention of looking for signs of 'guilt' in anyone. You must believe me, sir."

"Of course I believe you. But there is something to be learned from this. Listen to me carefully. A tyrant always seeks to involve the innocent in his crimes, to make them sharers in his guilt. You were being tested. That's how it begins. And there will be more tests until, before you realize it, you will have become hopelessly compromised. And then you will be their creature, body and soul."

With a pang, Pliny recalled Scortilla's angry words to him: *If Verpa was an informer, what exactly are you?* He felt a sinking in the pit of his stomach.

"The banquet is over and done with," Corellius continued, "and I think not much damage was done. The noble Nerva, I understand, saved the day. But now this Verpa business worries me. Mind you, I know nothing of the details, nor do I care to. The man was a pig. Whoever killed him deserves a statue in his honor. But I see danger here for you, precisely because you are conscientious and—forgive me, dear boy—still rather innocent." Grimacing in pain, Corellius reached out a thin hand to clutch Pliny's forearm. "There may be, ah, elements to this case that should not come to light. I know nothing for certain. Perhaps Domitian is hoping you will stumble across something that he very much wants to know without yourself grasping its significance."

"What sort of something?" Pliny was half out of his chair in alarm.

"I've told you, I know nothing for certain. But Verpa had his finger in many things. Dear boy, I beg you, get out of this while you can. Drop the investigation."

"By Jupiter, I'd like nothing better! But you're wrong about this, sir. No one is using me. My instructions are merely to make a show of investigating, it being a foregone conclusion that the slaves are guilty.

"It's been my own decision to probe somewhat deeper. I'm perplexed, I admit, but I think there's nothing more mysterious here than simple domestic hatred, and I aim to prove it if I can. Anyway, I can't possibly drop the case, not when I've been given the assignment by the emperor himself. I know you dislike him, but he is the emperor and I am bound to serve him as best I can. If I don't, worse people will."

"Dislike him?" Corellius' grip tightened. "Do you know why I suffer this bodily torment? Because I want to outlive that brigand by just one day!"

Pliny froze. The old man's unblinking eyes locked with his. He had just placed his life, Hispulla's life, and perhaps many others' in the palm of Pliny's hand. If he reported that remark to the palace all of them would die very unpleasant deaths. And what reply should he make? Corellius was waiting for something. The thought flashed through Pliny's mind: was this conceivably a trap laid for *him?* No! He forced the unworthy thought away. The greatest crime a tyrant commits against his subjects is the death of trust. After a long moment, he let his breath out slowly. "I'll consider your advice, sir, as always. I'll leave you now. You're tired…" He cursed himself for his cowardice.

Corellius Rufus sank back on his cushions. "Yes, go along, now. I am tired. We'll talk again."

"Indeed, sir, I hope we will."

"Dear boy…" His hands fluttered.

Pliny stopped in the open door and turned back. "Sir?"

"Never forget that in me you have a friend, that you can confide in me—about anything, anything at all."

"Why, of course, sir. I know that." Pliny hastened out the front door, calling for his bearers. Hispulla's worried eyes watched him go.

Marcus Cocceius Nerva opened the latticed door that led from the garden to the tablinum and stepped into the room. He was angry. "That was a damned silly thing you said, my friend. And we've learned nothing by it. I, too, was at the banquet of the dead—to avert a potential disaster. Any one of those poor, frightened fools might have blurted out some scrap of rumor that could hang us. Pliny pretends to be all innocence, but I don't believe him. He was put there to spy on us, and that is what he did. You can only thank Fortune that he didn't learn anything." Corellius tried to protest, but Nerva waved him to silence. "You think a fatherly pat on the arm will keep Pliny's loyalty when Domitian tempts him with rewards beyond his dreams? You have all chosen me after being turned down by every other likely candidate. And, may Jupiter help me, I have consented. But I have the gravest doubts, my friend, the gravest doubts." He was visibly shaking, whether with anger or fear was hard to say.

"Calm yourself, Nerva," said Corellius Rufus sharply. "Sit down and have a drink. I know my man."

But to himself he thought, You old fool. Did you say too much or too little? Well, it's in the hands of the gods now. He wished he believed in them.

◇◇◇

At the same hour that Pliny was visiting his old friend, far away on the Palatine Hill, Martial was finding his way through a maze of corridors and courtyards in the domestic wing of the palace to the private apartment of the grand chamberlain.

"Aha, here you are. I'm so glad you could come at short notice." Parthenius, pressing his palms against his thighs, heaved his bulk out of a chair specially built to accommodate his girth and spread wide his fleshy arms. The cloying scent of his perfume filled the little room. He waved the poet to a chair as slaves came in bearing wine and a silver platter of honey cakes. "I always prefer to meet friends here. My office over on the other side is a madhouse. Honey cake?" He plucked one from the platter with be-ringed thumb and forefinger and held it to Martial's lips. "Wine?" A slave poured from a silver flagon. The grand chamberlain lowered his ponderous frame again onto his chair.

The poet accepted what was offered while he looked around him. The room was beautifully appointed. Exquisite pieces of Syrian glassware stood in niches, dainty ebony tables displayed old Corinthian bronzes worth a fortune. The wall panels showed sea-green vistas where pastel nymphs cavorted. Beyond a gossamer curtain, a fountain splashed in a small garden.

"I regret we've never met face to face," said the chamberlain. "I can't think why not. But, of course, I know your poetry well. Such wit, such observation! And at the same time such expressions of loyalty to our emperor. You've even been kind enough to honor my humble self with praises I scarcely deserve. But I appreciate it, my friend. I want you to know that." He favored Martial with his sleek, wet smile.

The poet mumbled his thanks, wondering why he had been summoned here at the crack of dawn by a slave in imperial livery.

"I gather that you are anxious to have your poems read by the emperor? To have the patronage of the court?"

"My new patron, the acting vice prefect, has assured me that he will introduce my poems to Our Lord and God."

"Which he can accomplish only through me." Parthenius tapped his chest with a fat forefinger. "And that will be only if you are able to perform a small service for me."

The poet was instantly cautious. "What service would that be, my lord chamberlain?"

"Your patron Gaius Plinius is a man of conspicuous rectitude and loyalty, highly regarded by our emperor. You may tell him I said so."

Martial nodded.

"You've dined with him twice since he began his investigation of the Verpa affair," Parthenius continued. "You've attended his *salutatio*. He seems to have taken quite an interest in you, and you in him. Am I correct?" Parthenius moved a finger, and instantly a slave hurried to refill the poet's wine cup.

How did the grand chamberlain know about this? But, of course, everyone was watched. As they talked, flattery and wine began to work upon the poet in spite of himself. He felt his body uncoil, heard himself babbling. He was more of a confidante, really, than an ordinary client. And Pliny had sought his advice on certain matters, he being a man of the world. Yes, they had talked about the murder. No conclusions yet, of course. His friend had some notion of exonerating the slaves. It did seem the Jews had nothing to do with it. Lucius might actually be the guilty party. No proof yet, of course…

"Interesting." Parthenius made a temple of his fingertips, wetted his thick lips with the tip of his tongue. "I would like to be kept abreast of Pliny's progress in the Verpa investigation. The next time he goes to Verpa's house, make sure you go with him. The man had certain documents in his possession, never mind what they are, but apparently they have so far not been uncovered. If that changes, I want to know it at once. I would like you to report on this and anything else of interest that you may glean from your conversation with the acting vice prefect. I want to know everything he knows, everything he suspects."

"Report?" The word stuck in Martial's throat. Fool! What had he said, what had he done? He would say no more.

"Another cake?" said the chamberlain. Martial waved it away. "I understand, moreover," Parthenius continued unperturbed, "that he has a house guest, an invalid lady who had been lodging with Verpa until the murder. I would appreciate occasional reports on the state of the lady's health and her movements."

"Amatia? Why? Who is she to you?"

The chamberlain did not answer.

"Look here, I don't know what this is about but I don't like the sound of it. I'm not a man to be bought. Good day to you…"

Parthenius checked him with a raised hand. "Sit down." The genial expression vanished as though the sun had gone behind a cloud. "It is very little I am asking of you, my dear Martial. Easy for you to do, and no danger whatever to your friend Pliny, I assure you. And the reward is very great, indeed. The emperor's patronage. It's the reason you came to Rome, isn't it? You've been here now many years? You're not getting any younger, my friend. If it doesn't happen for you soon, it never will. I can make it happen. Only I. You only have to give a little to gain so much. Now what do you say, my friend? More wine?"

Martial sat down slowly. "And what, you expect me to come to the palace every day with these reports?"

In a game like this you sense the moment of hesitation, of weakness in your opponent. You know when you have won. Parthenius smiled blandly, adjusted a lock of silver hair at his temple, waited before he spoke. "Oh, no, no. Nothing so compromising to your honor. You will make notes. When you have something to communicate you will go to a certain *popina* in the shadow of the Claudian Aquaduct, where it crosses the Via Triumphalis. You may know the place, they serve a decent stew I hear. Go there at the third hour of the night. You will see a man with his left arm in a sling. You will sit on his left side on the bench and place your note in the sling. You never have to speak a word to him. Simplicity itself."

◇◇◇

Martial sat in the corner of a smoky tavern near the Circus Maximus, hunched over a flagon of cheap wine. Somehow, he had found his way out of Parthenius' apartment, out of the palace. He didn't ordinarily drink alone, but he poured the last drops from the flagon and called for another. He stared morosely at the scarred table top. He wanted to be very, very drunk. He wanted to be away from this city—what had that Christian lunatic called it?—this *Babylon.* He wanted not to betray the trust of his friend and patron. He wanted to be a better man than he knew himself to be.

Chapter Fifteen

*The fifth day before the Ides of Germanicus. Day five of the Games.
The fourth hour of the day.*

"May I sit down? I don't mean to interrupt."

"Oh, please." Calpurnia put down the scroll she had been
studying and made room on the stone bench under the pergola.

"There's actually a breeze this morning," Amatia said, turning
her face toward it. "You have a lovely garden."

The flower beds were ablaze with color. Bumblebees buzzed
among the irises and lavender. A pair of warblers perched upon the
head of Priapus and sang their song. "What were you reading?"

"Oh," Calpurnia blushed, "just one of my husband's speeches
to the probate court. I memorize them—well, as much as I can,
it pleases him."

"Goodness, child, what a wife you are!" Amatia laughed.

"You mustn't call me 'child,' I am a married woman."

"Of course you are; forgive me, Calpurnia. Still, you are so
young. Do you have any friends your own age?"

"Not really. All the other wives in our set are much older than
me. And on their second or third husbands."

"Are you from Rome?"

"Oh, no, from the north, Comum, where my husband comes
from. Our family properties adjoin. Two years ago he went home
to visit his mother. I happened to be in the house. My grandfather, who has raised me since I was a child, had sent me there

to be a companion to the old lady. Anyway, I was there when he arrived. His own wife had recently died of a long illness. But he was sweet to me. We talked, he told me all about Rome, the baths and the theaters and the tall buildings. And, of course, all about the courts and the cases he tries there. I'm afraid I didn't understand much of that, being a country-bred girl, but it all sounded so grand. And then, before I knew it, he asked for my hand in marriage. I was speechless, terrified. What could he see in a simple girl like me? But he said it was my simplicity that he loved. That I would bring a breath of the North with me. My grandfather, of course, favored the match. And so here I am. I'm very lucky."

Amatia was silent for a while. "But are you happy? Gaius Plinius sometimes seems more like your father than your husband."

"Oh, he's husband enough!" She risked a smile. "And as for a father, well, I hardly remember mine. So, that's all right too. Oh, I know he fusses about things and some people say he's vain—I'm not deaf or stupid, I hear things—but I do love him and I want very much to please him. And so…" She tapped her forehead with the scroll.

"So you memorize his speeches and set his poems to music."

"And now, Martial's as well. I was touched by his poem, weren't you? I hope he'll like what I've done with it. I confess, he frightens me a little."

"Indeed, that man is a study in contradictions. But you, at any rate, are a good wife and a shrewd woman as well. If only Rome had more like you than of the other sort. Still, you must be bored sometimes and lonely."

Calpurnia sighed. "The hours pass somehow. I read all sorts of things, Gaius likes me to be well-informed. What else is a wife to do after all, especially one in my condition? Tell me all about your home. Of course, I've read Caesar's *Commentaries,* but I suppose Gaul is very peaceful now."

"Yes, well…" Amatia began.

"Oh!" Calpurnia touched her abdomen. "He just kicked. Do you want to feel?"

Amatia put out her hand. "I do feel it! He'll be a strong boy."

"I sacrifice everyday to Juno Lucina that he will. Sometimes I'm so afraid. My husband wants a son so badly. Soranus, my obstetrician, says I have the *pica*. I have vomiting, dizziness, headache. I must eat only soft-boiled eggs and porridge. And twice a day old Helen massages my abdomen with myrtle and oil of roses. Everything is forbidden to me—excitement, travel, crowds, and now even love-making."

"Poor Calpurnia. We're a fine pair of invalids. My births were all easy, thank the gods, but this hysteria that afflicts me now—that is something else."

"And you believe Queen Isis will truly heal you? I know almost nothing about that cult. My husband doesn't approve."

"Indeed, I do not." Pliny emerged from the tablinum, where he had spent the morning trying, without success, to draft a memorandum to the city prefect. "I have nothing against the goddess, mind you, but her rites are far too stimulating for Calpurnia in her present state. Waving those rattles around, dancing. Of course, if you want to go to the temple yourself, Amatia, my litter is at your disposal."

The woman smiled up at him. "Alas, there is no point until I receive my dream and my money. I pray for the time to be short. My dear," she turned back to Calpurnia, "do you know how to spin wool?"

The girl shook her head, her mother had died when she was a baby, no one had ever...

"I will teach you, just as I did my daughters. Pliny, be good enough to ask a slave to fetch wool and a distaff and spindle. You know, my dear, how it says on the tombstones of wives from the old republican times '*lanam fecit*—she made wool?' In those days they really did. It was the highest praise a woman could receive. I find it calms the mind. So will you, my dear."

Pliny beamed. He suddenly felt a great tenderness toward his young wife, and great gratitude toward Amatia. In just four days she seemed to have blended imperceptibly into the life of his family. She was, like himself, a provincial who valued the old

Roman traditions as few Romans of the City did. And Calpurnia clearly loved her. It bothered him a bit that a woman of such obvious good sense would want to involve herself with those Isiac charlatans, but he supposed illness makes cowards of us all. Still, he felt that if Calpurnia had a sudden emergency, he could count on Amatia to keep a level head and know what to do. He was sorry, in fact, that she must eventually leave them.

The bunch of wool was brought and teased apart, with Calpurnia's white kitten leaping up to catch the strands. Pliny turned reluctantly back to his office, leaving the two women, with their heads together, laughing.

That night Martial joined them again for dinner. He was amusing, entertaining, teasingly flirtatious with the women. He evaded Pliny's questions about where he had been yesterday. While they waited for the first course to be served, he studied Amatia, who as usual shared a couch with Calpurnia. Who was this serene, attractive woman? What was he supposed to notice about her? He told himself that he was merely satisfying his own curiosity. "You're from Gaul, madam? A part of the Empire I'm happy to say I've never visited. Do they still wear long hair and paint themselves blue?" Fishing for information.

She laughed pleasantly. "'Long-haired Gaul' is a thing of the past. We're reasonably civilized these days. Lugdunum is a good sized city nowadays. My father was a land-owner. My husband was a merchant. He died some years ago and left me well provided for. I live with my eldest daughter and her husband. But it is a rather dull place, I admit. No society that would interest a man of the world like you."

"Well, in that case, seeing as you're in Rome during the Games you should take the opportunity to see some plays. It would be my pleasure to accompany you if you don't object to being seen with such a notorious fellow as myself." He favored her with his toothiest smile.

"Thank you, but I have a horror of crowds. They bring on my attacks."

"Ah, a pity. And your illness, if you don't mind my asking? You seem well at the moment."

"Hysterical suffocation. It strikes me at odd times, whenever something happens to upset me. As I explained to Gaius Plinius, there's no medical cure. But to Isis all things are possible. Even my physician Iatrides agrees." At this she turned anxious eyes on Pliny. "I know how busy you are, but I'm so worried about him. Where can he have gone to? It's been more than a week. I'm afraid something awful has happened. Are the City Battalions searching for him? You remember—a corpulent man with a beard, about fifty years old."

"Yes, yes of course. So far no word, I'm afraid." The truth was, the matter had entirely slipped his mind. He had said nothing to the prefect, but he would do so tomorrow.

Martial gave up on the woman and turned his gaze on Pliny. "And what did you learn yesterday at Verpa's?"

"Oh, a great deal, my friend. I wish you had been there." He summarized briefly and concluded, "The difficulty is making sense of it all. Lucius is raging. He claims the legacy to the temple is a forgery, and it does seem like an extraordinary amount of money for a tight-fisted man like Verpa to donate for a mortuary, of all things. I'd like to know how much Scortilla had to do with it. She's certainly in thick with those charla—" He checked himself out of regard for his guest.

"And the two of them are still living in the house together?" Martial asked with wry amusement. "I'd like to be a fly on that wall."

"Exactly. I'm hoping the pressure will build up and one of them will say something incriminating. My men have orders to eavesdrop at every opportunity."

Martial stroked his chin. "And you say the dagger was actually Verpa's? So there was no outside assassin, despite someone's attempt to make it seem so."

"Yes, and that someone is Lucius, I'm convinced of it. Remember, he was the one who first suggested it. And having assisted his father in getting evidence against Clemens by infiltrating the God-fearers, he would know about the seven-branched candlestick that we found drawn on the wall and the significance of that dagger. But, if his plan was to incriminate Pollux, he outsmarted himself. He didn't know that Pollux had turned Christian."

"Christians," Amatia interjected. "There are said to be some even in Lugdunum. Haters of mankind who pray for the end of the world by fire. Compare that to the loving-kindness of Queen Isis."

"Indeed so," Pliny hastened to agree. Gaius Plinius wasn't much interested in the next world. His ambitions were confined to this one. Of course one paid honor to the gods of the State, while agreeing with the philosophers that the One God, if he existed, was very far away and not much concerned with mankind. What Pliny, and others of his class, objected to was *superstitio*—religious zealotry, uncontrolled passion that inevitably led to public disorder.

"Any other enemies a possibility?" Martial brought them back to the topic at hand. "There's still Scortilla and her dwarf. Perhaps the motive was money or some personal grudge we know nothing about."

"Of course I've thought of that." Pliny replied, "but I have nothing to go on."

"I suspect you'd like it to be her, wouldn't you? Something about her offends you deeply. But consider. Could a dwarf kill a man three times his size and weight? Could he have sketched the candelabrum so high above his head?"

Pliny frowned and said nothing. The poet, damn him, was right.

Sensing that he had been perhaps a little too clever and offended his patron, Martial hastened to turn the conversation in a different direction. "I suppose Verpa's papers were examined?"

Calpurnia had been about to say something to her friend, but Amatia pressed her hand over the girl's mouth; the move was sudden, swift and rude. Martial, whose place at the table was between them and Pliny, caught it out of the corner of his eye.

"Before I got there on the day after the murder," Pliny answered, "the prefect had already impounded the contents of the tablinum. I haven't heard any more about it since then. I assume they found nothing of interest."

"Then let's come back to the 'who' and the 'how,'" said Martial. The *cinaedus* Ganymede interests me. I've known plenty of boys like him." Martial suppressed a pang, thinking of his current love object, the unfaithful Diadumenus, whom he was still pursuing all over the city.

"The usual sad story," Pliny said. "Getting too old, losing his looks, and so jealous of Hylas, the other *cinaedus*, that he couldn't conceal it. It occurred to me that he might have killed his rival under cover of the other stranglings. And he might well have had reason to kill Verpa, too, if the master was getting ready to throw him out in the street to starve, which is the sort of beastliness Verpa was famous for.

"And yet plainly, he didn't act alone. It must have been Lucius who showed him how to draw the candelabrum on the wall and convinced him that, by deflecting blame onto the Jews, the other slaves, including himself, would be let off."

"Hold on, though," Martial objected, "Lucius couldn't have reckoned on you, with your rather eccentric views on slavery, taking charge of the investigation."

"That wouldn't have stopped him from lying to Ganymede. What does an ignorant slave boy know of Roman law? He'd believe whatever he was told because he'd want to believe it. No doubt Lucius promised the boy a life of ease and security for the rest of his days if they carried it off."

"All right, but could he have done it, physically?"

Pliny chewed thoughtfully on a stalk of asparagus. "Excellent point. I can scarcely imagine that sorry creature overpowering Verpa in a fight."

"Well, as to that we'll never know, but it would be something if we could prove that the boy has the ability to make that extraordinary climb."

"And just how would we do that? He'll hardly cooperate."

"No, but an idea occurs to me."

When Martial had finished laying out his plan, Pliny slapped the table with delight. "By Jupiter, we'll do it tomorrow morning—no, better tomorrow night; to be fair we must see if he could do it in the dark. You'll come with me, of course. What would I ever do without you, my friend?"

The hour was growing late. The poet yawned, stood up and called for his shoes. "Oh, by the way," he said to Pliny, his manner studiously casual, "have you, ah, spoken to Parthenius yet—I mean about my poems? An invitation to the palace?"

"Ah, well, actually no." Pliny tried and failed to cover his embarrassment. "The emperor is much preoccupied these days; they all are, in fact. Don't know why, really. Silly rumors of conspiracies. But we'll see. In a few months I'm sure I can arrange something. In the meantime, Statius—well, you know he's my friend."

"Of course, *Patrone*, don't trouble about it." Martial looked away.

"Well, see you tomorrow."

◇◇◇

The second hour of the night.

The forecourt of the temple was silent but for the susurrus of breathing, the intermittent sighs and grunts of the sleepers, the dreamers. Behind his jackal mask, Alexandrinus' eyes swept over them. Then one, a dark shadow against the wall, stirred, stood up, and came toward him, stepping carefully among the recumbent forms.

He hurried her into his private room. Her face was tear-streaked.

"I can't stay there another night, Alex. He rants, he threatens to kill me, he's going to challenge the will, he's even talking about hiring that odious Pliny for his lawyer." She clung to him.

With difficulty, the priest unlocked her arms and stepped back. "Calm yourself, my dear. Let Lucius say what he likes. The seal and the forged numeral were perfect! And the emperor will support us, if it comes to that. He's a devotee and he has a financial interest in the will going unchallenged. We've won, do you understand? Isis is with us. Feel her power."

But Turpia Scortilla would not be reasoned with. "Lucius will kill me. He's half out of his mind."

"He won't. The house is full of soldiers, isn't it? Let him threaten, he doesn't dare do anything."

"Please, let me stay here in the temple with you. I can't go back there."

"Absolutely not. We can't be seen together until all this dies down. Lucius *would* have grounds for challenging the will if he could prove something about us. We're about to inherit two million. Just be patient a little longer."

"Alex—Lord Anubis—don't forget that it was I who got it for you. You won't will you? I love you. Make love to me."

But he took off the long-snouted mask and set it aside, exposing his beautiful skull. He wouldn't play the lusty god with her tonight; he wasn't in the mood.

Soon she left, walking with her head down and moaning softly. In the stillness of the night, it was a sound that Nectanebo, working late as usual in his embalming shop, was bound to hear.

Chapter Sixteen

The fourth day before the Ides of Germanicus. Day six of the Games. The third hour of the night.

Pliny looked at him severely. "I asked you once before, boy, and I ask you again now. Did you, at the order of someone in this house, murder Sextus Verpa, your master?"

They stood in Verpa's bedroom—Pliny and Martial; Valens and three of his men; Lucius, affecting an air of unconcern which was belied by the lines of tension around his mouth; Iarbas, his monkey on his shoulder, lurking near the doorway. He was Scortilla's eyes and ears, the lady herself claiming to be indisposed. All around them on the walls, the *satyrs* and *maenads*—eerily lifelike in the glimmering light of the lamps—writhed and coupled, indifferent to the drama which was being enacted in the middle of the room.

Ganymede, his features twisted in anguish, violently shook his head no.

"Shall we put it to the test?" snapped Pliny. "We can't make you climb up to the window, but we can make you climb down… or break your neck." This had been Martial's bright idea.

"Centurion, you've stationed a man below? Good. Draw your sword and persuade this boy to show us why he is called "the eel."

Valens gripped Ganymede by his long hair, dragged him to the window, pushed his head out, and prodded him in the rump with the point of his weapon. The youth spread his arms and legs and tossed his head frantically from side to side while the centurion's blade dug deeper into his flesh.

"Save me!" he shrieked.

"Don't fear, Eros protects his own." It was Lucius who spoke, rapidly and softly. The words had an instantaneous effect. Ganymede's shoulders twisted and folded together until he seemed to have no shoulders at all. He went through the narrow window as far as his waist. Then, making a half twist with his hips, he kicked with both legs together, imitating a fish's tail, and in an instant was outside. He dropped to the overhang below, landing on all fours. Then he was hanging from the rain gutter, and then his head and fingertips disappeared.

"Here he comes," shouted the trooper down below, who held up a torch. "Scampers like a squirrel, he does. Got his legs around the column now—ooof!"

Ganymede dropped directly on the man, knocking him to the ground. The back of the garden ended in a high brick wall, thick with leafy vines. The boy went up it like a cat, leapt from the top to the street below, and bounded away into the shadows.

"Merda!" cried Pliny, using a word he never used. "Centurion, the rest of you, follow me! Bring torches!"

Moments later, they stood milling about on the street.

"It's hopeless, sir," growled Valens, "this time of night."

"Martial," Pliny confided, "when it comes to the dregs of humanity, you're my oracle. Where would you go if you were Ganymede?"

"Thank you so much. I'm afraid I agree with your centurion."

"The Circus Flaminius!" cried Pliny. "It's not far from here. Hundreds of hiding places under those arches. Come on!"

They pelted down the street toward the colonnaded supports of the grandstands. Pliny, who hated exercise of any sort, was breathless by the time they reached it. For an hour they prowled the darkened arches, but turned up no one except prostitutes and homeless beggars, who all denied having seen a running youth.

"And where to now, sir?" asked Valens, a hint of insubordination in his voice.

Pliny leaned against a wall and mopped his perspiring face.

Tight-lipped, Lucius bent over his writing desk.

To Marcus Ganeus, greetings. He scratched the words with his stylus on a pair of waxed tablets. *Ganymede will come to you tonight, seeking shelter. You will oblige me by killing him and disposing of the body. You'll be well paid. L.*

He bound the leaves together and handed the packet to a slave. "Hide this under your tunic as you go out, the soldier mustn't see it. Here's where you're to take it, listen carefully."

Suspended over the doorway of an establishment near the Laurentine Gate, half way across the city, a carved, red-painted prick and balls swung to and fro in the wind. Beneath it, a sign proclaimed this the Temple of Eros. Cleaner than most of the male brothels in Rome, it catered to a genteel clientele. A slim figure stumbled through the door.

"Who are you, then?" The shrewd-eyed man behind the desk looked up sharply.

Ganymede stopped in confusion. "Where's Marcus Ganeus?"

"Doesn't own the place any more, I do. What's your business with him?"

"I—I used to work here, I want to come back. Put me in a room, I'll make money for you."

"That good, are you? You look too old to me. Step closer. Why, you're wearing a collar! *'Fugio tene me—I'm running away, catch me.'* No, my friend, out you go. City prefect would close me down in a minute for harboring a runaway."

"Please…"

"You want me to call the Night Watch?"

The boy ran out.

Crouched in a stinking alley not far from the brothel, he twisted and tugged uselessly at the iron collar until his skin was raw and tears ran silently down his cheeks.

A quarter of an hour later, Lucius' slave knocked at the same door and asked to deliver a message to Marcus Ganeus. Now the brothel owner's curiosity was aroused. "I'm him, give it to me." He tossed the slave a copper coin.

The proprietor of the Temple of Eros wasn't much of a reader, but he got the gist of the message. His eyebrows lifted in surprise.

Hours passed, and Ganymede was hungry. He'd tried to scavenge for scraps in a heap of refuse behind a popina, but snarling, yellow-eyed dogs had driven him off. Now he shrank into the recess of a doorway, the entrance to a crumbling *insula* that rose six stories above street. He knew they would be looking for him and that he must get off the streets before daybreak. The top of this building, he reckoned, commanded a view of the brothel. Lucius would come there for him as soon as it was safe. Lucius wouldn't fail him. He must wait and watch.

He crept up the rotting stairway, intending to hide on the roof. When he reached the topmost story a better opportunity presented itself. Peering through the tattered rag that served as a door, he saw that the apartment had suffered a fire; the walls were charred and the roof was half open to the sky. There wasn't a stick of furniture in the place, but propped against the wall, scabby legs sticking out before her, sat an old crone. Her head lolled to one side, a wine jug lay in her lap.

"You come to see me, darlin'?" she croaked. "Cost you two coppers, 'at's all."

It was the work of a moment to strangle her. Then Ganymede hunkered down by the window to wait.

The search party had blundered down one dark alley after another in the neighborhood of the Circus until, at last, even Pliny was ready to give up. The night air was sultry, heavy with threatening rain. Sweat pooled in the hollows of Pliny's eyes, trickled down his neck.

"Where in Hades are we?" he demanded of no one in particular.

"As it happens," replied Martial, "we are not very far from the house of some poet friends of mine. There's always a party going on. Come along, enjoy some bad wine, good company, and better verses than Statius ever wrote. Your centurion can see you home when you've had enough."

"The last thing in the world I want to do right now is go to a soirée," said Pliny testily. "*Mehercule*, I should have been home two hours ago. Calpurnia will be worrying herself sick."

But the poet persisted and, at last, Pliny yielded. "But only for half an hour."

Valens and his men repaired to a tavern down the street to wait.

Answering to Martial's knock, the door was opened by a tipsy young man, naked to the waist, whose long hair tumbled over his face. The room behind him was dark and smoky with incense; flutes shrilled a wild melody, castanets clattered, dancers whirled in a candlelit haze.

"This isn't a poetry reading, this is a bacchanal!" Pliny sputtered. But Martial applied a firm hand to his back and propelled him inside.

"You there, boy, fill a goblet for my friend and me," Martial shouted to a slave over the commotion of voices. The poet tossed his off at a gulp. "Come meet my friends." He plunged into the crowd of revelers, holding tight to Pliny's elbow lest he escape. "Mind where you step." Tangled like crabs in a sack, bodies sprawled and writhed upon cushions—men, women, boys, creatures of ambiguous sex, sleek and oiled *cinaedi* in gaudy pantomime masks, and battle-scarred gladiators all together. A miasma of perfume, sweat, and the ranker smells of love engulfed them.

"Fancy seeing you here, old man!" An elderly senator, whose private life was said to be beyond reproach, tugged at Pliny's cloak, grinning foolishly from the floor while a naked girl tousled his white hairs.

Martial led the way through a succession of rooms until the sounds of laughter and clapping hands drew them to a small garden at the rear of the house, where torches flared amid deep shadows.

"Ho, Nepos, is that you?" cried Martial. "And Cerialis? And Priscus, too?"

The three poets occupied a bench while a clutch of admirers lay on the grass at their feet. "Glycera, Telesphorus, Hyacinthus, Thais, Thalia," Martial seemed to know them all.

"Who's your friend?"

"This is Gaius, a lover of poetry." Mercifully, Martial omitted the rest of Pliny's name. "Goblet empty already, Gaius? Here, someone fill him up."

"I'd rather he fill me up!" cackled an aging prostitute, asprawl on the ground in a pose that left nothing to the imagination.

"What, your ancient *cunnus,* Ligeia?" Martial shot back. "I don't know why you even bother to depilate it anymore—seems to me rather like plucking the beard of a dead lion!" The revelers howled with laughter.

"Bastard!" Ligeia showed him the *digitus infamis.*

"Look, my friend has come here to listen to poetry, not to be propositioned by aging *lupae.* Here, make room for him on the bench and pass the wine jug. Nepos, give us one of your epigrams."

After Nepos, they all in turn recited—wicked, cutting, scabrous verses. In the midst of the hilarity, Pliny observed a beautiful youth with hair like molten gold sit down beside Martial and put his arm around him. They kissed long and deeply. The celebrated Diadumenus, no doubt.

Meanwhile the jug went round and round, and Pliny kept finding his cup in need of refilling. Then he heard a new voice reciting—it was his own.

"Bawdy verse! Why, you old lecher!" Martial cried in delight. "Is that what's on your mind when you're looking so damned dignified?"

"I smile, I laugh like other men." Pliny was instantly defensive.

"Of course you do!" Martial thumped him on the back.

"I mean they're nothing really, mere trifles."

"You're too modest! Put a laurel wreath on his head, someone— you're one of us! You know, I always suspected there was a real poet inside there somewhere."

At that moment Flaccus, yet another poet friend, joined the circle. He was out of breath. "Have you heard the news?" he said to Martial. "Papinius Statius is dead! The old boy croaked in the middle of dinner this evening."

"Dead? Statius!" Martial kissed Flaccus, he kissed Diadumenus, he kissed Pliny. He threw his arms in the air and shouted to the heavens, "Tonight I am the happiest man on earth! Diadumenus has come back to me and Statius is dead! By the balls of Priapus, now comes my turn! I will be court poet now!"

His comrades joined in a chorus of "Hear, hear!" and "No one deserves it more than you." And Pliny found himself as merry as any of them, although he did seem vaguely to recall that he had always liked Statius.

The jug continued to go round and, as the hour grew late, amorous pairs in various combinations of sexes were seen creeping off into the shadows.

Martial roused Pliny, who had fallen into a doze, with a jab in the ribs. "There's a pretty youth over there," he whispered. "Buttocks like firm pears, balls plucked and smooth as a baby's." He's looking this way. Go on, my friend."

Pliny, in alarm, stood up on wobbly legs. "No, sorry, married man, don't you know. Look, got to be going."

Martial pulled him back onto the bench. "It's not like cheating on your wife."

"Never cared much for boy-love, to tell you the truth."

Martial looked at his friend in amazement. "Really? Why ever not? Well, have a bit of the other, then. Ye gods, man, get down off your high horse!"

This virtuous prig, Martial thought. Would it make it easier to betray his patron if he first dirtied him a little? He signaled to a girl who wore long earrings and nothing else. She swayed toward them, moving her hips to the rhythm of the flutes and cymbals.

Pliny struggled, but his legs would not obey him.

The girl knelt at Pliny's feet and looked up with liquid eyes. Her tongue darted out over her lips. Pliny trembled in every limb. He filled his hands with her thick, scented hair and drew her closer. He swelled, he grew. The music pounded in his head. The torches guttered and flared. He was a man, dammit, and it had been too long!

"Home to bed, sir?" Out on the street, Valens leered at the acting vice prefect. Enjoyable was it, sir? The poetry, I mean?" Pliny's clothes were disarranged and drenched with scent, a laurel wreath was cocked over one eye, and he steadied himself with one hand against the house wall.

"What time d'you make it, Centurion?" He tried desperately to sound in command of himself.

Valens squinted at the stars. "Dawn in about two hours, I'd say, sir."

With an inward groan, Pliny launched himself down the middle of the deserted street. Valens and his men, themselves rather the worse for drink, fell in on either side.

"Halt!" Pliny commanded, after they had gone a block or two. A street urinal stood before them. He had never deigned to use one before: common, smelly, unbecoming the dignity of a Roman senator.

"Something wrong, sir?" inquired Valens.

"Not at all, centurion, kindly wait a moment." Pliny hitched up his tunic, unlimbered, and pissed—grandly, expansively, like a mountain torrent in the Piedmont—yes, even poetically—until he could not squeeze out another drop. He gave a contented sigh.

Valens couldn't contain a furtive smile. "Feel better, sir?"

"Immensely, centurion. Let us proceed."

At his front door, Valens handed him over to his slaves, hastily roused from bed. "No *salutatio* this morning, be off with you," the centurion growled at a knot of sleepy clients, already gathered outside the door. "Have a good sleep, sir, and don't worry about that filthy little *cinaedus*. We'll find him."

Still foggy with drink, Pliny allowed himself to be undressed and put to bed. If he had been less drunk, he might have noticed Calpurnia's tear-streaked face peering from behind her bedroom door.

If he had been less drunk, he might also have noticed a man with a bandaged arm who watched from across the street as he entered his house.

Chapter Seventeen

The third day before the Ides of Germanicus. Day seven of the Games. The third hour of the day.

Gaius Plinius moaned. He had a throbbing, behind his eyes, a vile taste in his mouth, and a troubled soul. He had sent the door slave off to fetch a basin of water and, moments later, his darling Calpurnia, her under lip quivering, had appeared with it in her own hands and meekly set it down on the wash-stand. She shot him a reproachful look and fled without saying a word.

He scoured his teeth fiercely with pumice and honey, which might expunge the sour taste of cheap wine, but the taste of guilt, never. What had come over him? Drunk as an owl! Rutting with some whore in the bushes! Could a brief association with vulgarians have brought him to this! If Martial should ever, ever mention this night again, he swore to himself, he would terminate their friendship at once.

It was all Verpa's fault, of course. Damn the man for getting himself murdered! Today was almost the half-way point of the Games, time was running out, and he had accomplished nothing toward saving those sorry slaves from their fate.

He had begun to sense the tension among his own slaves too. They who had known nothing but kindness from him and who were always permitted to be lively and at ease, were now ominously silent. As always, by some mysterious telepathy, they knew what was going on and what would happen if

Ganymede were to be caught alive and made to confess. That kind of crime, inspired by a slave's sexual jealousy, allowed no appeal to extenuating circumstances. Ganymede and the whole *familia* would be hideously tortured and executed. Even Pliny's beloved Zosimus avoided his eyes now and stumbled so much in his lunchtime recitation of Greek poetry that Pliny became quite vexed and sent him away.

What did they really think of him—these men and women who made his comfortable life possible? Could one of them be planning to kill him for some slight, some grudge, without betraying the slightest sign? He was shocked to find himself entertaining the idea even for a moment. But, once thought, it could not be unthought.

To distract himself, Pliny retired to his *tablinum* and worked all morning on his accounts and correspondence, which had piled up shockingly. The tenants on his Tuscan property were in arrears again, the architect whom he had commissioned to build a temple of Ceres on one of his estates had submitted his bill. Then there were papers to be drawn up manumitting his old nurse and giving her a small piece of land where she could spend her last days.

About midday, a slave came to announce that Centurion Valens awaited him in the atrium.

"Make your report, centurion," said Pliny, as brisk and businesslike as he could manage. He would tolerate no familiarity from the man because of last night. But Valens' manner was quite correct. Standing at attention and looking straight ahead he reported no success. "That little *fellator* has gone to earth somewhere, sir."

A moment later, Martial arrived, exuding bonhomie. "Up, are we?" he called jovially. Pliny froze him with a look, which the poet understood at once. In a more subdued manner, he inquired if there was any news of Ganymede. "No? I'm not surprised. Combing the city, in my opinion, is useless even with the prefect's entire force. He's probably far from Rome by now."

"I disagree," Pliny said. *"If* he's the murderer, I'm convinced that someone—Lucius—put him up to it. Now he'll be waiting for Lucius to help him."

The poet sprawled in a chair with his chin in his hand. "So you think he's hanging about nearby?"

"I do. Where would you…?"

"I beg you, Gaius Plinius, do not ask me again to imagine myself as an ignorant adolescent male prostitute." The two men glared at each other in silence.

"Hold on!" Pliny burst out suddenly. "A male prostitute! Martial, Valens, do you recall Lucius' words to him just before he escaped?"

"'Fear nothing'—some such platitude," answered the poet.

"No, after that. Wasn't it, 'Eros protects his own?' Ganymede told me he had been purchased by Verpa from a brothel called the Temple of Eros. It fits."

"It was a signal?" said Martial, sitting up straight. "Lucius was telling the boy where to hide—in his old bordello? Pliny, permit me to say that you are a genius."

Pliny allowed himself a pained smile. "Perhaps dissipation is good for the brain, after all."

"I've always found it so," the poet agreed modestly.

"Now," said Pliny, "if we only knew where this Temple of Eros was."

"Unfortunately," replied the poet, "there are probably a dozen or more in the city, they're all named either that or the Garden of Priapus, though I reckon I know where one or two of them are."

"Martial, once again we are indebted to your peculiar expertise," said Pliny dryly.

Valens interrupted these mutual congratulations. "It'll take days to search them all with the men I've got."

"Then I'll ask the prefect to assign you more men." Pliny reached for parchment and pen and scribbled a note to Aurelius Fulvus. "Anything else now?"

Valens looked at his feet. "Well, sir, there was a personal matter, but I'll ask you another time."

"No, no go on."

"Well, sir, I want to make a will. Haven't much to leave but my family situation's a bit complex. Common-law wife, bastards, that sort of thing. I want 'em to be cared for if anything should happen to me. Wondered if you could recommend me a lawyer that won't charge too much."

"Wise man. No one should live a single day without a will. But why at this particular time?"

"I don't know, sir. Just a feeling I've got. Lot of tension in the Castra Praetoria, sir, between us and them. I mean there always is, but there's something in the air lately. The way they swagger about, like something's going to happen soon. All the lads are a bit nervous."

"You don't say." Pliny and Martial exchanged worried glances.

"Well, my dear Valens, you just find Ganymede for me and I'll write you a will free of charge such as any client of mine would be proud to have. How will that suit you?"

"Why, sir, thank you, sir."

For the first time, Valens allowed himself a smile of genuine feeling. Pliny wasn't sure how it had happened but the two men had become, if not friends, at least allies.

"Get busy then. Every bordello in Rome is registered at the Prefecture. You'll find them all there."

"Well, I'll lend our brave centurion a hand," said Martial, "just to make sure he doesn't mix business with pleasure."

"Not my idea of pleasure," growled Valens as he lumbered out of the room, followed by the poet.

But Valens paused on the threshold and came back. "I nearly forgot, I've another matter to report on, this time with a bit of success. It's about that missing doctor of the lady's. We put his description about and a sausage seller in the Forum claims to have seen him. Says he passed that way several times around midday with his doctor's kit slung over his shoulder. Says he bought hot sausages from him. But the last time he saw the fellow, three bearded men, foreigners he thinks, ran up to him and started jabbering about an accident nearby, something like that. Iatrides tried to get past them, but quick as a wink they mobbed him and hustled him into a shop. A minute later, out come our three foreigners with a rolled carpet on their shoulders, tossed it into a waiting cart and off they drove."

"The same three men, he's sure of this? And it never occurred to this damned sausage seller to report what he'd seen?"

"None of his business, says he."

"When did this happen, does he remember that?"

"It was the third day before the Nones."

"Verpa died that very night!"

"So he did, indeed, sir."

Pliny massaged his throbbing temples. This was becoming too much. The physician of Amatia, a stranger to the city, snatched off the street in broad daylight, rolled up in a carpet, taken somewhere, and almost certainly murdered. For what possible reason?

He drew a deep breath. He must inform the lady. She was taking lunch in her room, said old Helen, shaking her head. The mistress was with her, crying on her shoulder.

What a confusion of feelings assailed him! But he had been brought up in his uncle's hard school. His uncle who, setting duty before all else, had sailed into the maelstrom of an erupting volcano and lost his life. With a comparable feeling of dread, Pliny knocked upon the door.

"You have come to speak with me, Gaius Plinius?" Amatia said in her low voice. "Speak first to your wife."

Calpurnia, covering her face with her hands, tried to run past him, but he stopped her. They enacted a painful scene before their guest's steady gaze.

His story came out in halting phrases—not quite the whole truth, but enough of it—amid many endearments and promises never, never to make such an ass of himself again. At the end Calpurnia, blinking back her tears, kissed him gravely upon the cheek. A married woman learns to expect these things, she seemed to say, but from you I expect better. "We will not speak of it again, husband."

Pliny's heart overflowed with gratitude. "Thank you, my dear. And now, if you will excuse us, I need to speak with Amatia."

The lady gave him a questioning look.

"I fear I have troubling news, dear Amatia. The thing is quite baffling." He recited the few, bare facts of Iatrides' disappearance. "Can you think of any reason why someone would want to kidnap your physician? I mean murders, assaults, robberies happen every day in Rome. But this seems very odd. Where would he have been going at that hour of the day?"

"I don't know." She put her hands to her breast, her breath rattled ominously in her throat. "Oh, I wish we'd never come here!"

"My men are still working on the case, but I'm afraid I can't offer you much hope. In the meantime, may I again offer you the services of my specialist, Soranus?"

"Oh, please say yes, dear," Calpurnia urged, "he's quite a wonderful man, I'm sure he can help you."

Amatia smiled wanly and placed a finger on her lips. "Allow me awhile to think on it alone. Please leave me now, both of you."

"Will you be all right?" Calpurnia asked.

"Yes, yes, don't worry."

But they had barely closed the door when they heard a strangled scream and the thump of a body. They raced back to find Amatia on the floor. Her limbs twitched violently. Her lips were drawn back in a rictus, baring her teeth. Her eyes were wide and staring.

"Helen, quick!"

The nurse came running as fast as her short legs would carry her. She and Calpurnia between them were able to raise Amatia's head and pour spoonfuls of medicine down her throat—a preparation of hemlock, pepper, and honey, which she had brought with her. After some moments, her limbs relaxed, her eyes closed, and they were able to lift her back onto the bed.

The Roman Games consisted of ten days of stage plays followed by five of chariot races. Pliny detested chariot racing, but loved the theater. In seven days he had yet to tear himself away to see a play. And what better peace offering to Calpurnia? The poor girl hadn't been out of the house in weeks. Soranus would disapprove but he'd chance it anyway. Wall posters announced that a performance of Plautus' *The Captives*, one of his least bawdy creations, was to be performed that afternoon at the Theater of Marcellus. He would take her and Zosimus. And Amatia? She seemed to have recovered herself although she was still pale.

"I can't. As I told your friend the poet, crowds terrify me. And I've had one attack already today. But let me help Calpurnia dress."

Calpurnia was determined to plaster her face with white lead and rouge, "like a proper lady." This was a constant argument between her and Pliny.

"Your husband is quite right." Amatia touched the pouting girl's cheek. "Any dried up old matron would give a hundred gold pieces for your rosy skin. Your beauty is a gift of the gods, my dear, why ruin it with this noxious stuff. I never wear it, even at my age, and I think I'm none the worse."

Pliny was grateful to her and said so.

They sat in the section reserved for senators, front row center in the vast open-air cavern of the auditorium, facing the towering porticoed facade through whose doors the actors entered and left the stage. The singing and acting were first rate, but the play was a bad choice, Pliny soon decided. Only mildly amusing, while its theme of unjust captivity and slavery threw him back painfully on the very thoughts he had hoped to escape from. But Calpurnia seemed to enjoy herself—indeed she must have enjoyed being *anywhere* outside the confines of their house.

As they left the theater late in the day, black clouds roiled across the sky, lightning quivered on the horizon, and the heavens opened. Rain pounded on the tile roofs, gushed from Gorgon-mouthed rainspouts, and ran in rivers down the gutters. Then a sudden lightning flash close at hand and a thunderclap made Pliny jump and set his heart pounding. Where had it struck? Somewhere over toward the Capitolium he thought. An omen? A sign of Jupiter's wrath? It was said that the emperor Augustus used to cower under his bed in terror during thunderstorms. And even as rational a man as Pliny could not suppress a nervous shudder. Instinctively, he made a sign with his fingers to ward off evil—a thing which he had not done since childhood.

Ganymede, crouching by the open window, stared at the rain-swept street below and at the house fronts slowly materializing out of darkness. Water dripped steadily down between the charred roof beams of the fire-gutted flat, drumming with a hollow sound on the thin floorboards and striking with a higher, thinner sound the sodden corpse of the old woman who lay beside him.

She had haunted his dreams in the night, in those brief intervals when sleep overcame him. She had opened her eyes, crept upon him silently, he unable to move, and wrapped her bony fingers around his throat. Finally, out of desperation, he had dragged her to the window to push her out, but her arms and legs had stiffened at odd angles to her body and he couldn't manage it. He knew he would turn stark mad if he stayed there much longer.

Through veils of rain he could make out the entrance to the Temple of Eros and above it the prick and balls that banged back and forth in the wind. Lucius would come there soon, looking for him. He would make an arrangement with the new proprietor, and then, as soon as things died down, he, Ganymede, could go home again, safe and protected forever. Lucius had promised him this, if he did his part right, and he had.

It had been so easy! He had plunged the dagger again and again into Verpa's naked back, pouring out a lifetime of hate that surprised even him. The filthy old beast didn't cry out, didn't even grunt. And he had followed the rest of Lucius' instructions exactly: drawing the picture, leaving the dagger. He'd even had the pleasure of strangling that wretched little Hylas in the confusion when the other slaves were killed. Still, somehow, that vice-prefect had come to suspect him. But no matter, Lucius was too clever for them; he knew what to do. Lucius would never abandon him. But what if Lucius didn't come? No! Lucius loved him, hadn't he said so? But if Lucius changed his mind, if he were angry with him?

Ganymede was soaked to the skin and shivering. He'd eaten nothing for hours. The old crone's wine jug held only a few dregs at the bottom and if there had been any food in the cupboard, the rats had long since consumed it. Someone stirred in the apartment below. Only an inch thickness of floorboard between them! He froze, not daring to move a muscle, though his limbs ached with cold. He was trapped. If Lucius didn't come soon he would surely die! He clutched his knees and wept silently.

Chapter Eighteen

The eighth hour of the night.

"Compliments of Centurion Valens," said the breathless trooper, striding into the dining room. "We've got the pretty boy, sir! Though he ain't so pretty anymore."

Pliny was up from the table instantly, calling for his boots and cloak.

Under a dripping sky, his litter bearers set him down in front of a shabby tenement near the Laurentine Gate, where the walls were scrawled with graffiti, and the filth in the gutters was ankle-deep.

The trooper led the way up to the garret room, roughly shouldering aside curious tenants who crowded the landing. An exhalation of boiled cabbage and onions, of wood rot and stinking straw seeped from under every door. The heat was suffocating. Inside, Pliny found Martial and Valens, both looking pleased with themselves. On the puddled floor by the window lay the old woman and the boy, like two sodden rag dolls. The shards of a smashed wine jug lay between them, and one sharp-pointed fragment was in Ganymede's lifeless hand. He had used it to rip open both wrists. A pinkish pool of blood diluted with rainwater spread out around him.

"Red rain drops come through our ceiling, Your Honor, drippin' on our plates while we was eatin'. Me an' the wife." From the open doorway, an old man addressed himself to Pliny. "I come up to see what was the matter. He's a runaway, ain't he? I saw that writing on his collar but, not being a reader, you see, I didn't know where to report him. I'll wager there's a reward for him though, ain't there? You think I'll get it? Mean a lot to us. I walked all the way to the Prefecture in this rain just to report him. Be a shame not to get a reward."

"I will see to it personally," Pliny murmured.

"It took another hour for the word to get to me," added Valens.

Martial struck in, "Your excellent officer and myself were pursuing our researches into the brothels of Rome. We were visiting our, what was it, sixth or seventh Temple of Eros? The proprietors, I must say, have all been terribly obliging. They've all invited us back any time for a night on the house. Wonderful thing, being a policeman. We hadn't gotten near this neighborhood yet, but there's another Temple of Eros down there across the street. You can see it from the window. I reckon that's what our friend was doing, watching out for someone. Don't know why he would have killed himself, though."

"Don't you?" sighed Pliny wearily. "Here's matter for your pen, my friend, if you would write in a somber vein: this pathetic creature, this 'boy' who was never allowed to be a child. What happens to the pretty boys when they lose the power to please us? Whether they are house slaves like Ganymede or hustlers on the make like your Diadumenus and his little friends. What happens to them, Martial, when they no longer amuse? I think you know the answer but I imagine you've never looked at it before. Look now. Ganymede believed himself to be betrayed. What else could he do but die?"

The poet started to say something, then closed his mouth and looked away.

"You're right about him being betrayed, sir," said the centurion. "While we were waiting for you I interviewed the brothel keeper. Take a look at this." He handed Pliny the message addressed to Marcus Ganeus. "You notice it's signed 'L.'"

◇◇◇

"Patricide!" thundered Pliny, "the most hideous of all crimes!" The vice prefect, flanked by Martial and Valens, shook his fist in Lucius' face. "Oh, Ganymede wielded the dagger all right, but you, you are the murderer! Do you know the punishment for what you've done? It is as ancient as Rome itself. You will be sewn into a leather sack with a cock, a dog, and an ape and thrown into the sea. The animals will tear you to pieces while you drown!"

Seeing himself cornered, Lucius bared his teeth. "Pah! You don't scare me with your apes and sacks. You've no evidence for your ridiculous theory."

"Haven't I? Look at this." Pliny showed him the waxed tablet. "Given to my centurion by the new owner of the Temple of Eros where you told Ganymede to hide. Why arrange his death unless you feared he would incriminate you? Unfortunately for you, Ganymede isn't dead," Pliny lied, "and he's told us everything."

Lucius' eyes darted wildly to the door, his muscles tensed, but Valens' men converged on him from all sides, surrounding him with a ring of steel. His shoulders sagged. The fight drained out of him like air from a punctured bladder.

"It wasn't just the money." He spoke in a low voice full of resentment and pain. His face worked with emotion. "In return for my spying on the Jews and the God-fearers, at risk to my own life, he promised me freedom from *potestas* and money to pay my debts. Then he changed his mind! All because of that little cunt, Phyllis. On his last day alive, we quarreled again. He waved two sheets of paper under my nose and boasted he had a dozen great men by the balls and all he had to do was squeeze. I asked him who he meant but he just laughed. Said it was no business for an imbecile like me. You know what he was like. All my life he humiliated me.

"But I'd made up my mind long before that day to kill him. After all, he'd threatened to kill me, hadn't he? At first, I expected Pollux to take revenge for his Jewish compatriots and spare me the trouble. When he didn't, I decided to make it look as if he had. I knew enough about them to make a good show of it."

Pliny exchanged a look of triumph with Martial: all their guesses had turned out to be right.

"Perhaps you will enlighten us on one point," said Pliny. "Your father rarely slept alone. How did you choose the one night when he did?"

"By going around the house after everyone was asleep and counting his bed partners, male and female. I did it many times until finally that night I accounted for all of them. I wasn't surprised. He didn't like to squander his sexual energy on a night before he had important business to transact. From his wild talk that day I guessed he might have something on for tomorrow. I told Ganymede to meet me in the garden at midnight. I gave him a pouch to wear containing the dagger, which I'd taken from the *tablinum*, also a thin-bladed knife to insert in the shutter latch, and a piece of charcoal for drawing the candelabrum. I had to pour half a flagon of wine into the boy to get him to stop shaking, the little coward. Merda! I've plenty of friends who would gladly have stuck a knife into my father if I asked them to, but none who could scamper up to that window. I was forced to use Ganymede although I knew he was a weakling. When he came down again I washed the blood off him in the fountain and sent him to bed. I told him that everything would be fine if he just kept his head, and it would have been. The only thing I wasn't prepared for, vice prefect, was—you. No one else in Rome would have worried this case to death like you've done."

"You say he taunted you with some papers. What were they, where are they?"

"One looked like a letter, the other was covered with signs and symbols, a horoscope maybe. I searched the *tablinum* for them the night he died but I couldn't find them. I surprised someone else there in the dark. Scortilla, I'll bet. Why don't you ask her? Anyway, I couldn't find anything. Then early next morning, before you got here, men from the Prefecture came and carted off all his files. They probably have them."

"No one's said anything to me about it."

"Yes, well just possibly the prefect doesn't think it's any of your business!"

That stung. "Search the house," Pliny barked at Valens. From top to bottom. Search Verpa's bedroom. The *tablinum* is too accessible. If these papers were important, I'll wager he hid them some place more private."

A few minutes later, Valens reported that a locked drawer in Verpa's bedside table had been broken open with some sort of tool, leaving gouges on the wood. The drawer, however, was empty.

"Another puzzle," Pliny said glumly to Martial. "And one we'll never solve. I'll mention it to the prefect. But the main thing is that we've got our murderer, and that was all I set out to do. Centurion, place Lucius under house arrest and guard him well."

Three things remained to be done. The first was to inform the city prefect of his success. The thought of going there himself was too distasteful. He scribbled a note and handed it to one of the troopers.

The second was to inform Scortilla. He found her in her apartment. "Ganymede and Lucius?" Her voice cracked, broke into a high-pitched cackle. Her eyes glittered. With what—relief, triumph, stark madness? He asked her about the missing papers but got nothing but a blank stare. How he loathed this woman! He left quickly.

The third, was to address the slaves. He had avoided visiting them lately; their misery was more than he could bear. But now he had a purpose. As the door swung open, the stench of urine and sweat hit him like a blow to the belly. "Valens," he gasped, "this is an atrocity! I want this place cleaned up and the slaves let out in batches for a wash and some exercise."

"Yes, sir."

Watched by forty pairs of dull and sunken eyes, Pliny sucked air behind his hand and stepped into the big room. "Humble friends, hear me! The murderers have been exposed! Ganymede and Lucius conspired together to murder your master. The rest of you are entirely innocent. The Roman Games close in just eight days. This case will go to trial soon after, and I promise you that your imprisonment will end on that day. Be patient only a little longer!"

Like one writhing mass, they crawled to him on their bellies. Croaking voices cried out, "You are our god!" Filthy hands touched his feet, caught at the hem of his cloak. Overcome, Pliny fled.

At home Pliny announced his triumph to the family, sparing no detail of Lucius' diabolical ingenuity and his own clearsighted penetration. He had suspected Lucius from the start! Of course, he couldn't have solved the matter so quickly without the collaboration of his friend Martial. He threw an arm around him.

The poet, with uncharacteristic modesty, smiled but said nothing. Pliny's slaves ran to kiss his hands in gratitude for their fellows. Calpurnia sang his praises. To Amatia the news seemed like a tonic. Her pale cheeks took on color, she became positively gay and drank a glass of wine. Before dinner was served, Martial excused himself, pleading fatigue, and left them all in high spirits.

The third hour of the night.

Martial walked along the Via Triumphalis to the arch which carried the Claudian Aquaduct. The *popina* was a narrow, low-ceilinged establishment where big copper cauldrons of stews and chowders sat in holes cut in the stone counter top. The poet had no appetite, but he took a wooden bowl and spoon and was served a steaming mess of stringy meat and vegetables by a woman whose forearms were the size and color of hams. He threw a coin on the counter. He scanned the room. The place was not crowded. Some young men played a noisy game of dice in one corner. Others, a group of working men in leather aprons, sat together at a table and shoveled food mechanically into their mouths, not talking. It was a moment before he noticed the solitary figure at the back. The man sat hunched over his plate, cutting his meat clumsily with one hand, for the other was pressed to his side in a sling. Martial slid onto the bench beside him.

Who was this fellow and what had he to do with the exalted Parthenius? Martial did as he had been instructed: took from his pouch a waxed tablet on which he had scratched a few hasty lines and tucked it into the man's sling, trying to touch him as little as possible. The man never looked up. So, Parthenius would learn that Lucius was the murderer of his father; that Verpa had possessed a couple of papers, one of which might be a horoscope, but no one could find them; that Pliny was satisfied he had solved the case; and that Amatia, the lady from Lugdunum, was, as far as he could tell, in good health and good spirits. He had tried pumping her without success. If something about her bothered him it was too insubstantial to be put into words. And that was that. May the grand chamberlain be glad of it.

Martial moved the food around in his bowl. He still had no appetite. Finally, he couldn't resist the urge to speak.

"Who are you, friend?"

"No one you know." The voice, husky and barely audible.

"I know a lot of people."

"Not me."

"How did you hurt your arm? I broke my ankle once—damned long time to mend."

Silence.

"What's this all about, then? What do you do for Parthenius?"

The silence continued for several minutes. At last, the poet pushed his bowl away, got up and, in an even darker mood than when he arrived, left.

Stephanus sat and chewed his food without relish. He disliked this business as much as the poet did. But, where Martial was baffled and torn, he, Stephanus, was clear. He had once been chief steward in a great house. Born a slave, then freed by his master, he had risen to command a small army of slaves, seeing that everything was just so, that the finest wines and delicacies were always in plentiful supply, that the kitchen served dishes that were the envy of other houses. And his master and mistress knew his worth and treasured him. Those poor souls. Too late for the noble Clemens, but if he could help his mistress, at least, to regain her liberty, her house, her children—well, for that he was ready to risk his life.

That night, Gaius Plinius Secundus, acting vice prefect of Rome, composed himself for sleep with a feeling of satisfaction not to be described. Tomorrow was Verpa's funeral. He would go, and bring Martial with him. Why not witness the last chapter of this sad farce? His friend would certainly find matter in it for a wicked verse or two.

Chapter Nineteen

The day before the Ides of Germanicus. Day eight of the Games.
The third hour of the day.

The air in Verpa's atrium was heavy with incense and mystery.
Pliny mopped his face. None of the sycophants and legacy
hunters who had attended the reading of the will were present
now, and Lucius was nowhere to be seen, but the place was
filled with officiants from the temple in their tightly wound,
ankle-length linen gowns. A tall, broad-shouldered priest, his
head covered with the black and gold jackal mask of Anubis,
recited the Names and Powers of Queen Isis, Lady of the House
of Life, Daughter of Kronos, Star of the Sea, and chanted her
sacred story. How the evil Typhon had slain and dismembered
her brother-husband Osiris and scattered his limbs and how the
grieving goddess had gathered them and breathed life into them,
so guaranteeing blessed immortality to all who believed in her.

Meanwhile priestesses on either side of him stamped their
feet and jingled their bronze rattles. In an alcove, a dozen hired
female mourners, bare-breasted and disheveled, ululated around
the painted coffin. And all this to send Sextus Ingentius Verpa
into the blessed hereafter that Isis promised her initiates.

Later, a team of mules would draw the casket, followed by
this howling, chanting horde, out to the family crypt on the Via
Appia beyond the city .

Pliny found the whole thing appalling. Quite un-Roman. In the days of the old Republic the government had repressed this alien cult, tearing down Iseums as fast as they sprang up. One Roman consul took an ax in his own hands to splinter the temple's door when the workers hung back. Later, the Deified Augustus banned the cult repeatedly from Rome. It was, after all, the religion of his archenemy, Cleopatra; and Tiberius had thrown Isis' statue into the Tiber and crucified her scandalous priests. But the mad Caligula added her worship to the state cults, and subsequent emperors, even the sensible Vespasian, all paid her honor.

Domitian was especially devoted to the Queen of Heaven and had built the splendid new temple for her in the Campus Martius. So now these worshippers of the filthy animal-headed gods of subjugated Egypt paraded themselves openly and without fear.

Pliny wondered idly whether the same good fortune might befall even those world-hating Christians some day—ridiculous, of course.

Nectanebo bustled about self-importantly. Scarab bracelets decorated his thin arms, his eyes were outlined with kohl, and a gilded cobra head sat on his brow.

Martial stopped in midstride and stared hard at the embalmer. "Wait a minute," he whispered to Pliny, "I know that man from somewhere." He stepped up and laid a hairy paw on the undertaker's bare shoulder, yanking him around. "Diaulus, you bastard, is that you under all that fancy dress? By the balls of Priapus, it *is* you!" Scortilla, standing nearby, gaped in astonishment. "Woman," growled the poet, "if this man's an Egyptian then I'm a tattooed Agathyrsian!"

"What's this?" inquired Pliny, coming up.

"This is one Diaulus, a quack and a charlatan who deserves a public flogging, if nothing worse!" Martial scowled savagely at the little man. "Diaulus, this is the vice prefect of the city, who happens to be a particular friend of mine."

The undertaker knew he was trapped. With as much dignity as he could manage, he croaked, "Diaulus is my name, sir—but a quack? Never!"

The priest of Anubis stopped in mid-chant; suddenly all eyes were on them.

"Some years ago, your poetical friend came to me for medical attention," said the undertaker, glancing warily at Martial. "Some trouble with our libido, wasn't it?" To Pliny he explained in a confidential tone: "You see, sir, I am an undertaker by trade, but I aspire to the sacred calling of physician, and I've made rather a specialty of male complaints. Well, as I say, your friend came to me and I applied stinging nettles to the, ah, part in question, a remedy of my own devising, which I've had great success with, I may say. All back to normal now, I hope, sir?" There was a malicious glint in his eye.

"No thanks to you, you assassin!"

"Extraordinary," breathed Pliny.

"I fear he was dissatisfied with my treatment, and published some rather cutting verses about me."

"Diaulus buries corpses now (Martial recited).
A doctor once was he.
The patients that he used to kill,
He counts among his clients still,
And earns a double fee."

"Very witty, I am sure," Diaulus sneered. "The fact is, embalming allows me to pursue my study of anatomy. Bodies are hard to come by otherwise. I venture to say I do more dissections in a year than most physicians do in a lifetime. Your friend calls me a quack—me! But I'm a good enough doctor to have noticed something very peculiar about this particular body. Oh, I could show you something that would surprise you." Pride had gotten the better of Diaulus' discretion.

A voice screamed in Pliny's brain to ignore this little man and allow the funeral to proceed. Instead, he said, "Oh?"

Oh, yes. There was no stopping him now. When he had removed the body to his embalming shop and uncovered it, Diaulus said, the face was awful to behold: the tongue protruding, the eyes bulging, the mouth hideously twisted. "Rigor had already set in. Cadaveric spasm, we physicians call it." Here Martial made a derisive snort.

"You see, sir, it comes on quick like that sometimes; almost instantaneously when the victim is exerting himself or in a state of high emotion at the moment of death—in the act of love, for example. The gentleman's left hand was clutching his throat, the fingers really digging in. But it was his right hand, sir. His right hand was gripping his, ah, *membrum virile*—I eschew the language of the streets, sir—still in a state of tumescence. I had hard work getting him to let go of it, I can tell you. After some hours the rigor passed and things, ah, settled down, so to speak."

Pliny and Martial exchanged glances; the same thought occurred to both of them. Had Ganymede made love to his intended victim and slaughtered him at the moment of climax? Did that pathetic boy have so much nerve?

"Now, as to the stab wounds, sir," the undertaker continued, warming to his subject. "Understanding him to be a murdered gentleman, I was glad of the chance to observe the effects of the blade on the internal organs. But, to my great disappointment, there were none to be seen! Whoever wielded that knife was a weakling indeed. I would almost have said a woman. He inflicted a great many superficial cuts, but he didn't succeed in piercing a single vital organ, neither lungs, nor liver, nor kidneys, and there was no internal hemorrhaging at all, sir, I'll take my oath on that. The organs, by the way, are in those jackal-headed jars right there by the coffin, if you'd care to have a look."

"I would," replied Pliny grimly, "and more. Valens, and you men, carry the casket into that side room. We'll have it open right now. Oh, and fetch Lucius out here."

"Sacrilege!" screamed the priest of Anubis, who had been listening to this. "I forbid it!"

Martial looked at Pliny as if he'd taken leave of his senses. Their carefully constructed case was about to collapse unless he stopped now. In fact, Pliny was amazed at himself. He had never suspected he was capable of such brutal decisiveness. But there was something of his uncle, the natural historian, in him that would let nothing deter him from ascertaining a fact.

"Do as I say, centurion. And clear all these people out of here. The funeral is postponed."

The mourners, with their palm fronds, their rattles, their pitchers of Nile water, and all the rest of their paraphernalia made a hasty exit. The last to leave was the priest, who was calling down a host of barbarous demons to feast on the vice prefect's guts. He had ripped off his mask and suddenly Pliny recognized him as the man with the star-shaped mark on his shaven skull who had been present at the reading of the will. The man who was now in charge of spending an incredible two million sesterces. It wasn't hard to imagine how much of that would stick to his immaculate fingertips. Unless, of course, the will turned out to be a forgery.

Diaulus was nearly in tears. "Oh, why did I open my mouth?"

"Well, you did," said Martial, "and it's too late now."

The casket was sealed with wax. When they finally got the lid off a sweet, sickening effluvium mingled of resin and decay assailed their nostrils. Pliny felt nausea start in his throat. The wrappings were stiff and discolored with a yellowish stain. The body had leaked. "Too little time, too hot—" Diaulus mumbled.

"Cut the wrappings, undertaker," Pliny ordered with all the authority he could muster. But the little man shrank back. "I'll lose my position!" Finally, Valens drew his sword, inserted the tip at the crotch and ripped upward, laying open the cocoon of bandages. Here, at last, was the man himself. Turpia Scortilla, who had followed them in, took one look and fainted dead away. Swallowing hard, Pliny peered at Verpa's naked torso.

"That gash in his side looks fatal enough."

"That was my incision for removing the organs," Diaulus explained. "Turn him over and pull the bandages away from his back."

The back was covered with a dozen or more puckered, livid wounds. "These were the only wounds on him when I got him," said Diaulus, "and not one deeper than the tip of my little finger."

Ganymede, in an evident frenzy of hate, had rained useless, ill-aimed blows on his victim. "The veins were still full of blood when I opened him up. When a man's killed by sword or knife the blood runs copiously from him. But cut into a body which has died some hours before, as my profession requires me to do, and you notice that the blood flows sluggishly. No one knows why, sir, but it's true."

Pliny shook his head. "If I had seen the body immediately, I could have discarded the idea of a professional killer at once."

"Now, if you'll roll him back again," Diaulus continued, "and expose the throat." It was purple with bruises.

"What would make a man strangle himself?"

"Nothing in my experience, sir. But that's not what killed him either, the windpipe wasn't crushed."

Meanwhile, Martial's gaze had wandered lower. "Decent sized *mentula* on him."

"Trust you to notice that," observed Pliny with asperity.

"If you're referring to the gentleman's member, I found something rather odd there, too. Not much to look at now," wrapping his fingers in a napkin, he retracted the foreskin carefully, "but there, you see? When the body was fresh it was tumescent, quite erect. I couldn't help but notice that swollen lump on the glans." It still looked for all the world like a nasty bee sting. "I've no idea what could have made it, sir. All I do know is that this man was dead before he was murdered, so to speak."

"Dead of what?" Pliny cried in exasperation.

Diaulus pursed his lips and looked thoughtful. "We don't know what most people die from, not really, sir. We blame it on the humors, but that's just a name we give to our ignorance."

"The quack's a philosopher, too!" sneered Martial.

Meanwhile, Lucius had been brought into the room. It had taken him only a moment to digest this new development. His lips curved in a cunning smile. "Then I'm guilty of nothing, vice prefect. I can't have procured the murder of a dead man."

"Not so fast," Pliny shot back, "that's for a magistrate to decide. And when you're tried you will need a very good lawyer.

It so happens that I am a very good lawyer. I suggest you start cooperating with me if you want to avoid that leather sack. Why didn't you mention the hand on the throat and the, ah, the other detail when I first questioned you?"

Lucius gave his characteristic shrug. "I didn't mention it because I didn't know what to make of it. It was no part of my plan. I assumed that idiot Ganymede had given him a bit of fun before killing him. I threw a coverlet over him before anyone else got too close, and sent for Nectanebo, or whatever he calls himself, to get him out of the house as fast as possible. I never had a chance to question Ganymede before the soldiers arrived and locked him up."

Late in the day, Verpa's funeral was, at last, allowed to proceed. Diaulus, "Nectanebo" once again, had succeeded in rounding up his crew of hired screamers, and the cortege departed in full cry. Pliny watched them go glumly. What a day it had been; by turns, a farce, an anatomy lesson, and a new mystery. "We have a killer still to find, Martial, and damned little time left." And the slaves, always guilty until proven innocent, were once again in danger of summary execution. What was he going to do?

Martial read his friend's thoughts in his weary face. "Odious little pissant!" he said with feeling.

"Diaulus? But he knows what he's talking about. I had no choice but to hear him. Verpa died in a state of sexual arousal—can you believe it?"

They emerged from the house into the blinding light of the noonday sun.

"You look done in," Martial said. "Go home and rest, inspiration may yet strike."

"I fear I'm out of that commodity."

"Shall I come for dinner?"

Pliny pinched the bridge of his nose. He had a splitting headache. That afternoon he was invited to the coming of age ceremony of a friend's son. No getting out of it. There'd be a banquet. "Not tonight. What are you going to do with yourself?"

"Me? Just my usual haunts. You know." The poet's eyes slid away. "Shall I call on you in the morning?"

"Tomorrow morning I'm required to attend the Banquet of Jupiter at the Capitoline temple. If you've a Roman heart under that shaggy Spanish hide of yours, you'll be there too. Farewell."

That night Pliny's sleep was troubled by terrifying visions of oozing mummies and faceless figures slithering through windows. He was in Verpa's bedroom and the rutting Satyrs and their victims all around him moved and breathed and leered at him. But he was awakened at midnight to a still greater, and much more real, terror. A pounding on his front door. A stifled scream from Calpurnia. The clack of hobnail boots on the floor. In the Rome of Domitian that could mean only one thing. One winter's night they had dragged away a neighbor of his—a harmless old senator with large estates and some inconvenient friends; his corpse was "found" some days later; his widow had been afraid to put on mourning. Pliny lay rigid, his heart thumping in his chest.

Chapter Twenty

The seventh hour of the night.

Four of the emperor's lictors burst into his room and dragged him from his bed. Rough hands pinned his arms behind him. One of the men threw a traveling cloak at him. "Put it on."

"My—my shoes," he stammered. He could think of nothing else to say.

Outside, in the atrium, Calpurnia had collapsed on a couch, sobbing. Amatia had her arms around her, stroking her hair. "It will be all right, darling," she murmured, "Don't be afraid."

"Some sort of mistake," Pliny said, his voice like the croaking of a frog. He could hardly breathe. "I'll be back soon, you'll see."

Calpurnia gave him a desperate look.

In the street a covered carriage waited. Two lictors mounted the driver's box, the other two forced Pliny inside with a hand on the back of his head. They sat one on either side of him, crushing him between them. The clop of the horses' hooves echoed in the empty streets. "What is it? Why am I summoned like this?" No one answered him.

The emperor's bed chamber was ablaze with light. Tiers of lamps threw leaping shadows against the walls. The smoky air was almost unbreathable. The lictors forced Pliny to his knees, which were shaking so badly they couldn't have supported him anyway.

Like the Minotaur in his maze, the Lord of the World sat in the middle of the room, bent over his desk, all alone, except for Earinus, the little boy with the freakishly small head, who crouched at his feet.

The only sound that relieved the silence was the buzzing of bluebottles. Pliny saw the insects crawling over the inside of a glass jar. He watched as the Conqueror of the Germans pinched one large specimen between thumb and forefinger. The desk top was littered with their corpses. "You, see, how this one struggles, Earinus?" He stroked the boy's head of golden curls. "Shall I let him go? If I do, he's sure to bite me." The point of the stylus went in. He dropped the little corpse on the desk.

Minutes crept by. A wave of nausea swept over Pliny. He was afraid he would mess himself. Rivers of sweat ran down his back and sides. His knees started to ache. Still the emperor never looked up and Pliny was too terrified to speak.

Then in a sudden explosion of violence Domitian's arm lashed out, sweeping the jar off the desk. It burst on the stone floor, sending shards of glass everywhere. The flies rose up in an angry swarm. With a guttural cry, he flung himself on Pliny, brandishing the stylus in his upraised fist. With his left hand he grabbed him by the shoulder, hauled him to his feet, shoved him up against the wall. Pliny shut his eyes, he could feel the man's breath on his face. He waited, trembling, for the slashing point to rip open his cheek, tear out his eye.

Moments passed until at last he felt the grip on his shoulder relax. He dared to open his eyes. A madman's face confronted him. The eyes feverish and red-rimmed with black circles under them. The mouth twisted into something that resembled the mask of tragedy. The cheeks quivering. The fist that held the stylus shook.

Pliny slumped against the wall and struggled to breathe. "Caesar," he whispered, "there's been a mistake. Who has spoken against me?"

"The Priest of Anubis! You defiler of corpses! You jackal!" Spittle flew from his mouth. "I sent you to find a murderer, not to violate the rites of the Queen of Heaven. I'll crucify you for this." The tendons bulged in his bull's neck.

For an instant Pliny wanted to cry, to blubber, to grasp the emperor's knees, beg for his life. Instead—and he would never understand where his courage came from—he said, "Listen to me, Caesar." And without stopping to draw a breath, he laid out everything he had discovered at the funeral. The emperor's eyes narrowed.

"Two killers?"

"Yes, Caesar, and the other is still…"

"Not atheists?"

"It seems they had nothing…"

"Documents?"

"A letter, according to Lucius, possibly containing names of people Verpa was blackmailing—people close to you. And something else that might be a horoscope; whose I don't know. We haven't found them, but the prefect seized Verpa's papers before…"

"He did so at my order. One assumes the man kept papers that are best removed from prying eyes—including yours." Domitian turned to the lictors who stood at attention by the door. "You there, fetch Aurelius Fulvus here at once!" Then he staggered back to his desk and sank onto his chair with his legs splayed out. "Earinus, pour wine for me and the vice prefect."

The transformation was startling. Pliny now saw not an angry man but a man ravaged with fatigue, distracted beyond endurance. Dough-faced, dull-eyed. What was wrong with him?

"Gaius Plinius, do you believe in the stars? Don't stand there, man, sit down by me."

"Well, I suppose, I mean most people do. Of course, Cicero was a skeptic, on the other hand Nigidius Figulus…" Pliny realized he was babbling.

Domitian cut him off. "An astrologer has predicted 'blood on the moon as she enters Aquarius.'" He scratched a pimple on his forehead and drew a little blood. "I pray this is all the blood required." He gave a short, sharp laugh.

"Caesar, no two diviners ever agree about these things."

"Do they not? A soothsayer has prophesied the day, even the very hour, of my death. The fourteenth day before the next Kalends at the fifth hour. And lately another has said the same thing! That is only seven days from today! If they're right, I won't live to see the end of the Roman Games. And the day before yesterday, during the thunderstorm, they say a lightning bolt struck the temple of Capitoline Jupiter. Did you see it?"

"Why, no, Caesar, I don't believe any such thing happened."

"What, you think I'm mad?"

"No, no, Lord, of course not."

"And the wind wrenched the inscription plate from the base of a statue of mine and hurled it into a nearby tomb! One of the Praetorian Guards fetched it and showed it to me. And the cypress tree in the courtyard that flourished during the reign of my father and brother—you know the one? It was uprooted! Parthenius took me to the spot, I saw it with my own eyes!"

"Caesar, calm yourself, rest now. You're tired."

"Tired!" The Lord of the World buried his face in his hands. "I never sleep any more, Pliny, not without a strong dose of laudanum." He peered between his fingers. "I'm afraid of my dreams. Last night I dreamed that Minerva threw down her weapons, mounted a chariot drawn by black horses and plunged into an abyss. She has abandoned me."

"Sometimes opium can produce fantasies that—"

"Do you believe in the gods, Pliny? What exactly do you think they are, and where?"

This was treacherous ground. Pliny could only stammer, "You yourself, sir, being a god, must know that better than I."

"You think I'm a god, do you? You're a fool or a liar! I'm no god. If I am a god why do I fear death? If I am a god, why does my wife deceive me with actors? If I am a god, why am I despised, conspired against, lied to by my own slaves? Do people do that to gods?" His voice rose and cracked.

Domitian had always been the despised younger son; ignored, raised in squalor, unloved by the Roman populace and even by his own family. He could never compete with the memory of his brother. Titus had been handsome, generous, a great commander, and had died after only two years on the throne, too young to have developed any vicious habits. Domitian, after fifteen years of power, still seethed with resentment and quivered with insecurity.

Suddenly he was on his feet. "Come with me, I'll show you something."

Torches flared along the walls, casting puddles of yellow light in the darkness. The emperor pulled Pliny along by the arm down one echoing corridor after another. Here and there they passed a sleepy Guardsman, who straightened to attention and clapped his fist to his chest at the emperor's approach. Occasionally they saw a harried clerk bent on some late errand who cringed as they passed him. But all was stillness. They turned corners, passed through shadowed courtyards, mounted and descended flights of stairs until Pliny had no idea where he was. The Minotaur's labyrinth might have looked like this, he thought. It was not a thought to give comfort.

And at every turning, he noticed those polished disks of moonstone, as big around as shields, mounted on brackets high on the walls. He had seen them before, on the night of the "black banquet."

"You know why I'm having those things installed? I'll show you, I'll turn my back, you hold up some of your fingers." Pliny obeyed. "Three! Am I right? You see? With these mirrors everywhere, no one can sneak up behind me and..." he drew his thumb across his throat.

"But, sir, you don't really mean...?

"Don't I? But they've tried already! Why do you think I've had to execute so many? The governors of Egypt, Asia, Britannia, and Germania. Two Praetorian commandants. More senators than I can count. My cousin Clemens, and my cousin Sabinus before him!" He raked his hands through his few wisps of hair. "Do you think I *like* putting people to death? Do you think I *enjoy* scorching genitals and cutting off hands? Justice is my watchword! But I tell you, my friend, that an emperor is the unhappiest of men, for nobody believes that people are trying to kill him until someone finally succeeds! Any Roman senator with an army behind him can dream of becoming emperor. My own father did it."

This remark reminded Pliny of his schoolboy Plato: the tyrant is never happy. Here was the living illustration of that truth.

They turned another corner and, to Pliny's surprise, found themselves back at their starting point. Aurelius Fulvus was there now, quaking on his knees, surrounded by the lictors. He tried to speak but Domitian silenced him with a look.

"Verpa's papers—have you examined them yet?"

"Yes, Caesar, we've gone through everything but we've turned up nothing of interest."

"Not a horoscope or anything touching on a plot against my life?"

"Certainly not. I would have reported it at once if we had."

Domitian kicked the man in the chest and sent him sprawling. "Get out! And I command you not to sleep until you have found a letter and a horoscope. Your life depends on it, Fulvus." The lictors dragged the prefect out.

Pliny swallowed hard and felt himself swaying on his feet. He had no love for Fulvus, but violence terrified him. Domitian threw an arm around him, guided him to a chair, leaned toward him. "Plinius Secundus, I love you. You're the only honest man I know. You won't betray me, will you? I need someone I can talk to—not that reptile Parthenius. I'll have his guts out of him soon enough! Be to me as your uncle was to my father."

"Caesar, you honor me too much."

"But you went too far at the funeral." Domitian jabbed him in the chest with a blunt finger. "Your uncle wouldn't have done that."

"No, no, sir, no he wouldn't. Blame it on my inexperience, sir. I was overzealous. I will apologize to Scortilla and to the Priest."

Domitian smiled for the first time. "Don't worry about Alexandrinus. I'll settle him down. Frankly, I don't like the man myself."

"Caesar, are you aware of Verpa's legacy to the Iseum, two million sesterces for an embalming works, entrusted to Alexandrinus?"

The emperor looked at him narrowly. "Of course I've heard of it. True devotion. Admirable. Are you suggesting something? I'm a legatee in the will myself. I would not like to see it held up in probate."

"No, Caesar, of course not."

A silence fell between them. Then, "You'll be at the sacrifice tomorrow? You're a true Roman, Pliny, not like these foreigners who surround me. And I'll send for you again tomorrow night, my only friend. Now leave me, I'm tired."

Domitian enfolded Pliny in his powerful arms and kissed him on both cheeks."

The same carriage that had taken him away deposited him back on his doorstep. It was growing light in the east. How long had he been gone? As in a nightmare, time was distorted. Pliny was shaken to the depths of his being.

This talk of prophecies and assassination? What was it Verpa knew? Was there a plot against the emperor? The gods forbid it! If Domitian, bad as he was, should be assassinated, it would mean civil war, the second in a generation. The legions in Germania were loyal to him; they would exact a terrible price for his death. Legion fighting legion, blood running in the gutters of Rome, and the barbarians looking on from the sidelines, watching and calculating, just as had happened after Nero's overthrow. Could anyone, no matter how much they hated Domitian, wish to see that again?

"We pray for better emperors but we serve the one we have." Pliny repeated the well-worn line, only this time it brought him no comfort.

He found Amatia waiting up for him. "Your wife is asleep," she said. "She was half out of her mind, I feared for her and the baby. I sent a slave to fetch your doctor, Soranus. He gave her something for her nerves."

"Thank you, Amatia, I'm in your debt. You go to bed now, you must be exhausted."

But she seemed reluctant to leave him. "You're all right?"

"Oh, quite all right. Caesar, ah, wanted some information." Pliny tried to hide his agitation, but he could feel her eyes boring into him. He realized that his cheek was twitching uncontrollably. Finally, searching for something, anything, to say, he asked, "Have you received a dream from Isis yet?"

"Oh yes. It won't be long now."

He waited for her to go on, but she didn't seem inclined to say more. "Well, I congratulate you. I trust it was more pleasant than my dreams have been, or the emperor's.

She raised an eyebrow at this but said nothing. She turned and went back to her room.

And Pliny, after looking in on his wife, retired to his. He felt drained. He would have to dress for the ceremony in a couple of hours. He lay in his bed sweating, sick to his stomach, staring at the ceiling.

◇◇◇

As the sun came up, Parthenius sat in his apartment across the table from Stephanus. The former steward of Clemens and Domitilla looked thoughtfully at the grand chamberlain. He had just finished making his report on the curious outcome of Verpa's funeral, for he had met with the poet again. "May I ask what influence you have over this surly fellow who meets me at the *popina*?" he asked. "Every time he comes he looks angrier."

"Really? Oh, it's just something he wants the emperor to grant him with my help."

"But the emperor won't be with us much longer." Stephanus smiled crookedly and touched his bandaged arm.

"A pity for our friend, then."

"Another thing. I'm worried about the Purissima, sir. Why is she still there? What is she thinking of? I watch the house as often as I can. She never goes out. I was wondering if I could get in on some pretext."

"No," Parthenius replied. "Too risky—for her." He spread his plump hands. "We must trust she knows what she's doing. In fact, she may be safer there than anywhere else for the moment."

Chapter Twenty-one

The Ides of Germanicus. Day nine of the Games.
The second hour of the day.

In the temple of Vesta, little Laelia, ten years old, roused herself from a doze and felt a moment of terror. On the bench by her side, her elder "sister" Fusca nodded, too. Fusca had lectured the little novice all night long, how if the sacred flame should ever be extinguished, mighty Rome would fall. Trembling, the two girls threw sticks on the guttering flame. They had been on duty since midnight, alone in the tiny, circular temple, it being their turn to tend Vesta's hearth fire. Although tucked away in one corner of the Forum and dwarfed by loftier buildings, this spot was the sacred center of the Roman race. Their other "sisters" would be just now waking and stretching in their beds in the adjoining cloister that was their home and nearly the limit of their world.

And in this precinct, willing or not, the Vestals would draw out their days in an unceasing round of ritual duties, seldom seeing their families, never knowing the love of a man, on pain of death.

Vesta was not a goddess like Isis, who inspired ecstasy in her devotees. Vesta answered no prayers, offered no blessed afterlife. No myths were told of her. Her temple had no cult statue. But she was the living flame of the primeval kings' hearth, the heart and soul of Rome. She was tended by six virgins, the king's daughters once upon a time, who were potent with unspent fertility. Their service was not a joy but a solemn, unsought obligation.

Laelia remembered how almost a year ago the emperor, in his role of Pontifex Maximus, tall and terrifying, had come in great state to her home, spoken the ancient formula, 'I take thee, Beloved,' and pulled her roughly by the hand while her father, a Roman senator, stood by, puffed up with pride, and her mother wept.

And she remembered how she too had wept, in those first days, as though her heart would break. It was only the tenderness of her new "mother," the Vestalis Maxima, that had eased her sorrow then. Perhaps it was because the Purissima herself seemed to wear an air of perpetual sorrow that made her so gentle a friend and so patient a teacher to the young ones.

But where was she now? When would she come back to them? She had told them she was ill and must leave the cloister for awhile. But that was so many days ago, and not a word from her since. But surely, Laelia thought, she would come back today, the day of Jupiter's banquet. Hope fluttered in the little girl's breast.

The "sisters" breakfasted together, and then their serving women helped them arrange their hair in the archaic fashion: coils of hair bound with fillets of red and white wool massed on top of the head and covered with a long veil that fell over their shoulders.

Outside, Laelia heard the shuffling of many feet and the lowing of cattle. It was beginning! It was only these few grand occasions that punctuated the tedium of her life. And this time the second-oldest Vestal, who was temporarily in charge of them, had given her permission to attend the ritual banquet. With two Vestals left behind to tend the flame, there would be only three of them going. But oh, if only the Purissima could be among them!

Groggy after a sleepless night, Pliny stood atop the Capitoline Hill with a very subdued Aurelius Fulvus and other officers of the City Battalions. His bronze corselet felt noticeably less snug than it had just nine short days ago when he wore it at the opening of the Games; worry had done this to him.

At that moment silver trumpets blared, the signal for the three massive doors of the temple to swing open. The feeding of the gods was the central rite of the Roman Games. The three-chambered temple of Jupiter, Juno, and Minerva had been consecrated on this day six centuries ago, when Rome was only a collection of mean little cottages huddled on the slopes of seven low hills. Today, as on that first day, Jupiter's face was painted a fiery red, symbolic of the blood of his slaughtered enemies, and he and his two female consorts were gorgeously dressed for dinner.

Public slaves carried the massive gold and ivory statues, freshly tinted and dressed for the occasion, down the temple steps and laid them lengthwise on banqueting couches built for giants. They placed tables before them and began to carry in steaming platters of food. Other couches had been arranged for the guests, senators and magistrates, who would share this sacred meal. Truly, at times like this, Pliny thought, the gods felt very real and very close. For a little while he could imagine himself among those shaggy ancestors, who in their simplicity believed that the divine images were nourished by the same food as they themselves ate. But what should he think of these deities now after what he had been through with Domitian, Lord and God, last night?

The emperor and empress dined with the gods at their table. Pliny, sitting not far away, stole cautious glances at them. Domitia Augusta sat as still as a statue herself; her face betrayed no emotion. Very different was her husband's. His sullen, red-rimmed eyes seemed never at rest. He had gone through the long morning's ritual of sacrifice and prayer like a sleep-walker. Now his lips were moving. Was he talking to his wife—or to Minerva, who had deserted him in his dreams? Was he, perhaps, begging Jupiter for his life? Was he insane?

Pliny turned back to his food without relish. At last, the emperor and his entourage stood up. Slaves ran up to drape him in his triumphal toga, purple stitched with golden stars, and placed a laurel wreath on his head. His lictors, bearing the ceremonial bundles of rods and axes on their shoulders, shouted for the crowd to clear the way.

The emperor would mount his golden chariot now and lead a procession of chariots representing the six racing teams, each liveried in its distinctive color, to the Circus Maximus—that immense oval, nearly half a mile long, ringed by tier upon tier of stands, capable of containing a full fourth of the city's population. Today the races would begin and continue everyday until the end of the Games.

Pliny would join in the procession but then slip away as soon as possible. He regretted having missed most of the theatrical performances during the first week of the Games. He had no such regrets about missing the races. Almost unique among his countrymen, he found them inexpressibly tedious. How the Roman populace could rouse itself to a fever pitch of excitement over the Blues and the Greens, the Reds and Whites, the Golds and Purples, as if it made a particle of difference which team won, was quite beyond him.

But his musings were interrupted by a shocking occurrence. One of the Vestal Virgins, only a child, broke away from the others and streaked toward the emperor. What was she shouting? Something about her mother? The girl threw herself sobbing against Domitian's legs, holding onto his toga. He raised his hand to slap her, and would have, only the empress pulled her away just in time and handed her to an older Vestal who had raced after her.

And then it struck Pliny—the thing that had bothered him at the sacrifice on the very first day of the Games. He hadn't been able to put his finger on it then. Now there was no doubt. One of the six Vestals was missing.

He had no more time to ponder this now. To the blare of trumpets and thunder of drums, the charioteer cracked his whip and the four white horses of the imperial equipage started forward. As they turned into the avenue that led down to the Circus, an immense crowd surged forward, shouting the emperor's name in rhythmic acclamations led by trained cheerleaders. Domitian, their Lord and God, raised his right arm in salute. But, at the same time, he steadied himself, gripping the chariot's handhold with a white-knuckled fist. The rolling waves of sound made him visibly wince, so tightly-strung were his nerves. His features were frozen in a bloodless mask. He looked like a man face to face with death. If the soothsayers were right then this adoring crowd could not shelter him, the steel-clad ranks of Praetorian spearmen could not shield him. If those soothsayers were right, then in five more days, at the fifth hour of the day, his doom would find him.

The gilded chariot, flanked by twenty-four lictors passed on its way. Then followed, in turn, troops of noble youths on horseback, garlanded litters bearing statues of the gods on high, and the leaping priests of Mars, pirouetting to the music of flutes and lyres. Next, in a riot of color and noise, came the chariots of the competing teams, each charioteer pelted with flowers by women in the crowd who shouted their love. And after them the spectators formed one single mass, an immense stream of humanity surging toward the Great Circus.

Gaius Plinius, his mind sorely perplexed, signaled for his litter bearers.

Calpurnia had slept late that morning, drugged by Soranus' potion. She awoke in a panic. Where was her husband? But Helen ran into assure her that all was well. Master was attending the ceremonies on the Capitolium and would be home for lunch. Helen helped her dress and comb her hair and then walked her out in to the garden to enjoy the fresh morning air. She saw Amatia sitting on the stone bench under the pear tree, facing away from her. She called "good morning," but her friend did not seem to hear her. Calpurnia sat down beside her and touched her shoulder. Amatia turned to face her. Tears were streaming down her cheeks. "I miss my daughters," she said.

Chapter Twenty-two

The sixth hour of the day.

Before Pliny, who was longing for a bath and a long nap, reached home, one of Valens' men intercepted him in the street. "Something to do with a monkey, sir. Centurion says you should come at once."

Minutes later, Pliny and his officer knelt on the floor in Verpa's bedroom, peering at the small shape, hideously twisted in death, of Iarbas' monkey. Lucius, who had followed them upstairs, watched silently from the doorway.

"I reckon he got himself locked in here the other day, after we were here," Valens said. "A slave found him this morning. I haven't let anyone touch him. You see how he's clawed his throat."

Pliny nodded. There were bloody tufts of fur under the animal's nails.

"Now take a look at this, sir."

Pliny bent closer. There, on the wrinkled palm of one small hand was a livid welt from which protruded a bit of cork. Grasping the cork warily between his thumb and forefinger, Pliny withdrew a tiny needle from the wound. Suddenly his exhaustion was forgotten. The thing must have been shaken out of the bedclothes when the bed was stripped and lay here on the floor for days until the monkey found it. Clearly whatever killed this animal killed Verpa too. But he would want Diaulus' confirmation.

Wrapping the little corpse up in a towel and the needle separately in a napkin, and putting both in a shoulder bag, he rushed off to find the doctor. This proved to be not so easy. The embalming workshop in the temple precinct was locked and shuttered. Pliny accosted some minor priestling who was passing by and enquired after "Nectanebo." To Pliny's surprise the man dropped to his knees and begged for mercy. It was only then that Pliny, mildest of men, realized how he must look to this fellow. He was still corseleted, helmeted, and armed with his sword from the morning's ceremony. An unaccustomed sense of power suddenly welled up in him. So this was how soldiers felt when they confronted cowering civilians. Just these bits and pieces of metal made all the difference. It was a heady feeling.

Nectanebo, it seemed, had been summarily fired by Alexandrinus. Word was that he was practicing medicine again in a storefront shop in the Subura.

Feeling invincible in his breastplate and swaggering like a real trooper, Pliny made his way down into that insalubrious quarter of noisy taverns and odorous alleys that buzzed with flies and cheap commerce. After a few inquiries, one ragged inhabitant was able to point out the doctor's place of business.

He found the little man full of grievance and eager to talk. Indeed, the swelling on the monkey's paw resembled the one on Verpa's mentu—, er that is, *membrum virile*. What sort of poison produced it, he couldn't say; he was an anatomist, not a pharmacist. But Diaulus had other information to impart, and no reason now to respect the secrets of his former employer, damn him. Twice in the past few nights, both before and after the reading of Verpa's will, he had observed the Priest of Anubis together with a thin lady who walked with Scortilla's unmistakable lurching gait.

Mehercule! thought Pliny as he shouldered his way back through the crowded street. Both his concubine and his son had a crack at the old man on the same night, only she, somehow, got to him first! Still, there were pieces to be filled in. He wanted to know what sort of poison this was and where she could have obtained it. And, most perplexing of all, how she administered it. For the first of these questions anyway, he knew precisely where to look. He collared an urchin in the street and gave him directions to Martial's house with instructions to meet him without delay at the public library. It was a big job he was undertaking; he'd need the poet's help. Still carrying the monkey and the needle, he turned his steps toward the Forum of Peace.

The Deified Vespasian had built his beautiful forum after the annihilation of Jerusalem and its inhabitants and had dedicated it, appropriately, to Peace. In one angle of it he built a library, Rome's largest, where thousands of Greek and Latin manuscripts could be consulted by citizens of sufficient status. A librarian directed Pliny to the shelves which groaned under the enormous bulk of his uncle's crowning scholarly achievement, an encyclopedia of natural history.

"As a favor to the emperor," Pliny explained to Martial, who arrived soon afterwards, out of breath, "my uncle, who also became my adoptive father after my own father died, bequeathed his original manuscripts to the library. He was one of the most learned men of this or any other age." Pliny began to hunt along the honeycombed walls from which the knobs of dusty scrolls protruded. Martial watched him dubiously. "You know, he thought any moment wasted which was not devoted to work. He rose before dawn and began work by lamplight. After his mid-day rest, he would work again until dinner time, only to rise from dinner while it was still light and return to his studies."

The bookish young Pliny had grown up in the household of that extraordinary man. He began to pull out scrolls now, touching them lovingly, blowing the dust off them and heaping them on a long table while he talked over his shoulder to Martial. "Whether he was bathing, sunning himself, dining, or being carried through the streets in his litter, a secretary was always beside him, reciting from some book, while he himself jotted down excerpts. I remember how he chastised me once for wasting precious hours by walking. He was dictating notes on volcanic eruptions, you know, when Vesuvius engulfed him."

The heap of scrolls on the table grew dangerously high. "And so, I can't help smiling when people call me studious," Pliny grunted as he carried another armload to the table, "when, compared to him, I am the laziest of men. At his death he left the world over fifty volumes of history, nearly a dozen on grammar and oratory, one hundred sixty miscellaneous notebooks for which I've been offered a small fortune, and of course, the *Historia Naturalis,* in thirty-seven volumes, comprising twenty thousand facts gathered from two thousand books by one hundred forty-six Roman and three hundred twenty-seven foreign authors!"

Martial looked on, bemused, and felt that he was, at last, beginning to understand this man. How might it crush a boy's soul to have been raised in the shadow of that Titan of Tedium!

Pliny sat down and mopped the sweat from his forehead. When he recounted what Diaulus had told him, the poet's eyebrows shot up and his eyes shone with wicked glee.

"And what would your uncle have thought of your marshalling all his scholarship just to save a gang of slaves from the executioner?"

"I'm sure he would have thought I'd lost my mind. I half agree with him."

At that moment the mountain of volumes collapsed and scrolls in their cylindrical capsules rolled every-which-way across the floor.

It seemed the librarians had never gotten around to affixing labels to all the capsules. On hands and knees, the two men searched for the index volume, unwinding scroll after scroll. The poet glanced here and there among the yards of unwound papyrus that snaked across the polished floor.

>   *...contact with a menstruating woman will drive a dog mad...a statue of a woman by Praxiteles was so lifelike that a man attempted to have intercourse with it...amber is formed from the urine of lynxes...a man with eyesight so keen he could see the tiniest details at a distance of a hundred and twenty-three miles...the entire* Iliad *inscribed upon a nutshell...the Arimaspi who have only one eye in the middle*

*of their foreheads…the Megasthenes who, like serpents, have
slits in place of nostrils…*

"I've got the index," called Pliny from a far corner of the hall.
"Yes. Here we are. He treats of poisons in chapter forty-one of
Book Eight, and again in Book Twenty-seven, chapter twenty-two."

"Eight's over here," yelled Martial, catching his friend's excitement.

"Good, I just had…Where was it? Here it is, Twenty-seven."

Each of them rolled and unrolled a volume, running his finger
down the columns of crabbed writing.

"This may be something," said Martial. *"Barbarians hunt panthers by means of meat smeared with a poison called aconitum.* Goes
on to say the beasts die from almost instantaneous strangulation!"

"Here I've found it too," announced Pliny from his corner.
*"'Aconitum, panther-strangler…quickest of all poisons if the genitals
are merely touched by it…'* The genitals! That's it! We've got it!"

The poet nodded excitedly. "Poison is a woman's weapon.
And remember, Scortilla's the one who wanted the body wrapped
up like a parcel. Why else but to hide that mark! Picture it. She
enters his bedroom, rekindles the flame, arouses him, and as she
delights and distracts him, she kills him! What an epigram this
will make! Who but Scortilla could do something so shameless?
She must have held the cork end between her teeth as she bent
over him, like some fanged viper!

Scortilla, you offer to suck me—I fly!
Wise Pliny's discovered the truth.
I've no wish, Scortilla, like Verpa to die
From the bite of your venomous tooth!

Just off the top of my head, you know."

"Very droll," said Pliny. "You can recite it to the lady in person."

◇◇◇

Scortilla lay stretched on a couch in her bedroom, where she
spent most of her days now. She held a wine cup; the liquid
sloshed and spattered her gown as she stirred. She looked at

Pliny with unfocused eyes, which first showed bewilderment, then hostility, and finally fear. He remembered again his military appearance. Did she think he had come to kill her? Well, so much the better; it would loosen her tongue.

"Turpia Scortilla, I am here to charge you with suspicion of murder in the death of Sextus Ingentius Verpa." He tossed the bundle on the floor and jerked the wrapper away. Iarbas, crouched in a corner, let out a cry in his uncouth language and threw himself at his monkey's little corpse.

"You recognize him, I trust," said Pliny with his sternest expression. "We found him in Verpa's bedroom, he had punctured his hand with this." He thrust the needle in her face, observing how she flinched. "The poor creature died in agony, just as Verpa did. Diaulus—Nectanebo to you—will swear in court that the monkey's wound is identical to the one he showed us on Verpa's flesh. No doubt, you purchased the poisoned needle at some potioner's shop, we'll find it. Come now, you may as well confess."

"I know nothing of poisons!" she croaked, shrinking back on the couch.

"Oh, but Scortilla," Lucius purred from where he stood behind Pliny, "you visit the magicians and amulet sellers all the time. Don't those same shops deal in deadlier goods?"

She turned on him savagely, "You lying little shit! You'd say anything to ruin me." Her anger drove out fear. "You can't prove anything, vice-prefect. Why would I have done such a thing?"

He knew perfectly well why she had done it, but he bit his tongue and kept silent. Somehow, she and the priest had cajoled or tricked Verpa, or actually tampered with the will, so that they could spend that legacy together. But he dare not say so after the emperor's warning last night. But even if he couldn't bring the will into it, he could still prosecute her for murder.

"We'll discuss your motive later."

"I know why she did it, and I'll say so even if you won't." This was Lucius. Pliny shot him a warning look.

Scortilla smelled uncertainty. "Very well. You won't tell me why. Then *how* am I supposed to have done this deed?"

That, of course, was the question that Pliny and Martial had been debating all the way from the library.

"You may have used your wiles on Pollux to let you in."

"My 'wiles.' On that virgin! The stupid ox hated me. I tried seducing him once years ago, just for something to do. He rejected me! Me! Verpa was quite amused when Pollux confessed to him."

"Then, you entered the same way Ganymede did."

"What? Through the window!" she nearly howled.

"It's not impossible," Martial said. "Once upon a time you used to do handsprings on the back of a galloping horse. A former acrobat, one who hasn't grown fat in retirement, might have managed it. I wonder what passed through Verpa's mind when he awakened out of a deep sleep to find you poised over his privates? But I don't imagine you gave him much time to think, did you?"

Scortilla stared for a long moment in silence. And then, without warning, her shoulders heaved and tears started down her cheeks, making tracks in the dead-white powder. "So clever, aren't you, both of you? Well, I'm sorry once again to disappoint you. I did not creep through that window on these! With a swift motion she gathered her gown in both hands and pulled it up to her thighs. "Look now at what I hide even from my lovers, hide because I will not be pitied."

In spite of himself, Pliny took a step back. The woman's knees were swollen, misshapen knobs of bone. Hopelessly arthritic.

"Aren't they pretty, Vice Prefect? They're the price an athlete pays. And the pain is unbearable. No medicine, no amulet relieves it, not even the compassionate Isis to whom I pray daily. Only wine mixed with opium—which I buy from the potioners, yes—dulls it enough so that I can live my life as I wish to. And so I drink all day long, and if I stumble people like you despise me for a drunkard. Well, I prefer that. And no one, up until this moment, has ever seen me weeping for the girl I once was."

"Turpia Scortilla, you will consider yourself under house arrest and report personally to my centurion twice every day," said Pliny, grim-faced.

"Oh, spoken like a true policeman, vice-prefect! Never let mere facts get in your way!" Her voice was heavy with scorn.

"Yes, well…," murmured Martial when they were on the street again. "I think we could both do with a nice bath, don't you? Cool our heads."

But Pliny waved him off angrily.

At home, Pliny went straight to his *tablinum* and locked himself in. He was in no fit mood for company, not even his wife's. He had left the dead monkey where it lay on the floor but he had had the presence of mind to bring the needle home with him wrapped in its napkin. This he locked in a small iron casket. Then he sank onto a chair with his head in his hands. Presently, he sent for some food and wine. He drank a glass. Then another. And another. He was defeated. The Games would be over in six days. Possibly, Lucius could be charged with some sort of attempted murder. As for Scortilla—nothing. No means, no motive that he could mention without angering the emperor. But dammit the woman was guilty! And forty innocent human beings would die for her crime.

The hours wore on. Eventually, Pliny drifted off to sleep.

But not for long. He woke with a start to find the emperor's lictors standing in his doorway again. This time they treated him more respectfully, but the summons was still peremptory. Refusal was not a choice.

Five hours later he was home again. Calpurnia wept with relief. Amatia gave him a penetrating look, but said nothing.

"Just a private interview," he assured the women, smiling wanly. He would not tell them of the repetition of his previous night's bizarre conversation with Domitian, the self-pitying complaints, the dark suspicions, the wild accusations, the lavish praise of Pliny and his uncle, which turned maudlin as the emperor drank more and more; his final escape when Domitian finally passed out on the floor. Or that this time he had had a run-in with Parthenius, who seemed to be lying in wait for him as he left. The chamberlain had tried to pump him. Pliny had shoved him roughly aside.

For the second night in a row Pliny lay in the dark, desperate with exhaustion, unable to close his eyes. He could not go through this again; could not put his frail wife through any more of it. As the first rays of dawn slanted through his window, he lit a lamp and sat down at his desk to shuffle aimlessly through the correspondence that had piled up there. And so it happened that his eye fell upon a letter from Calpurnius Fabatus, his wife's grandfather. The old man wanted him to go up to Ameria to help him evaluate the condition of an estate he was thinking of buying. Since the courts and Senate weren't in session surely dear Pliny could spare him a couple of days?

"Accipio omen," Pliny murmured. "I accept the omen." He wasn't a policeman, had never claimed to be. It needed someone cleverer than him to solve this wretched case. He had done all he could. One thing he knew for certain: call it running away, call it hiding, but if he didn't get out of Rome, clear his head, calm his soul, and, above all, escape from the emperor, he would soon go mad.

Chapter Twenty-three

The eighteenth day before the Kalends of Domitianus
[formerly October].
Day ten of the Games. The first hour of the day.

Pliny emerged from his bedroom wearing a traveling cloak and broad-brimmed straw hat. "Zosimus," he called to his young freedman, "send the clients away with my apologies. You and I are going on a journey." Zosimus was on easy terms with his patron but something in the set of Pliny's mouth told him to ask no questions. "Boy," Pliny beckoned a slave, "run to the hostler's outside the Flaminian Gate and order a covered coach with a mule team and driver to be ready at once."

At the sound of her husband's voice, Calpurnia tottered into the room. Pliny spoke brusquely to her. An errand for her grandfather. Where? North. He would say no more. How long? Two or three days, he really couldn't say.

"Then I'm coming with you."

"Over miles of bumpy roads in your condition? I won't hear of it, my dear. You're best off here with Helen and Amatia to look after you. Here, I've written notes to the city prefect, the emperor, and to Martial. See that they're delivered, will you?"

"But must you go today?" she persisted. "You don't look well. You're not yourself. What is the matter, you must confide in me."

"Nonsense, I've had it in mind for some time."

"You never said..." Tears suddenly overflowed her eyes.

"Really, Calpurnia, must I announce my every move ahead of time?" He turned from her abruptly and shouted up his bearers.

Awakened by the commotion, Amatia came out of her room. She put her arms around Calpurnia and held the girl tightly. "We'll be fine on our own, won't we darling? Enjoy your trip, Gaius Plinius, I'm sure you've earned a rest. By the way, last night while you were shut up in your office I received welcome news from home. A messenger sent ahead by my son-in-law just arrived by ship from Massilia. He has gathered the money for my initiation fee and will be arriving himself in just a few days. I'll be able to make my devotions to the goddess and then I'll no longer have to impose on your hospitality. You know the old saying, 'After three days a guest and a fish begin to smell.' And I've taken advantage of your kindness far longer than that."

"Nonsense, dear lady. The advantage has been ours. You've done wonders for my wife. We will both miss you. I must say this messenger made remarkably good time."

"And," Calpurnia put in, "the poor man hurt himself on his journey, I think."

"Oh, in what way?"

"He had a broken arm."

The lumbering four-wheeler jounced over the paving stones of the Via Cassia, following the valley of the Tiber up into the Umbrian hills. Zosimus sat beside his master and unrolled a volume of Alexandrian lyrics, but before he had recited a dozen lines Pliny's eyelids drooped. He was still sleeping when the setting sun lit their way into the courtyard of an inn where they would stop for the night.

Pliny was not the only one who had felt weary and oppressed that morning. Brooding in his bed, Lucius was prey to similar feelings. He had long since given up the morning *salutatio* since no one came any more. Deserted by the family clients, who smelled better pickings elsewhere, without friends or prospects, a virtual prisoner in his own house, he had nothing much to do but drink and sleep. As for those mysterious papers that his father had taunted him with, Lucius had long since given up the search. Clearly they weren't in the house. For all his cunning, he had exactly nothing to show. The trial was not many days away and he would be lucky to escape with nothing worse than banishment for life, and that only because someone else—could it possibly have been the pitiful Scortilla?—had murdered the old bastard first.

These morose thoughts were interrupted by the knock of a trooper. Four tradesmen were at the door, dirty foreigners by the look of them. Should they be admitted? Lucius shrugged. He had nothing better to do. In an ill temper he pulled on a rumpled tunic and went out into the vestibule.

He looked sourly at the four characters, swarthy and bearded to the eyes, who loitered near the door. Three of them, he recognized. They were brothers, Syrians, whom his father had brought back with him from Judea and set up as rug dealers near the Forum. Lucius knew that his father had used these thugs to administer an occasional beating, or worse, to loosen a tongue; a regrettable, but necessary part of the informer's trade. And because they would unavoidably hear things during these inter-rogations, Verpa had warned them not to learn Latin beyond a few basic words, not that they were likely to in the immigrant ghetto where they lived.

With them was another villainous character who introduced himself as Hiram, a friend of theirs. Hiram could speak Greek.

Lucius had been an indifferent student, his schoolboy Greek was rusty, but he could get by. "What do you want of me?" he asked curtly. "What's in that box you've got with you?"

Hiram removed the soiled cloth in which it was wrapped and offered it for Lucius' inspection. It was a doctor's kit, made of sycamore wood, with a brass lock, which had been pried open, and a leather shoulder strap. Where had he seen this before?

Hiram explained: "It belonged to the man your father tor-tured to death with the help of my three mates, a job for which he agreed to pay 'em one thousand sesterces, their usual fee. I happened to make their acquaintance in a tavern last night and agreed to speak for 'em, since they're shy of you." Hiram's gold tooth gleamed when he smiled. "If they don't get their money they'll make trouble."

"Will they, indeed!" Lucius snatched the box—he expected it to be heavy, but it wasn't—and lifted the lid. "It's empty. Where are all the instruments, the drugs?"

"They sold the instruments on the street, the little bottles they threw away," answered the gold tooth. "They had nothing in 'em but colored water and sand."

"You don't say? Well, the box alone is damned near worthless and I haven't got a thousand in cash, so there!"

"The name on the bottom might mean something to you?"

Lucius turned the box over and read the inscription: *Iatrides son of Philemon,* carved in Greek letters. That gave him a start. The invalid woman's physician had some such name as this. "What did this man look like? Heavy set? Bearded?" Lucius had scarcely noticed the doctor during the brief time that he and the lady had stayed with them, but, yes, it did seem like him. But why torture him? Turning the box over again, his ear caught a little rattle within it. He peered inside more closely. A pin embedded in a bit of cork lay on the bottom. Help me Hercules! It was the twin of the one that Pliny had shown them yesterday. Trying to conceal his excitement, he scowled and said, "I'll have to know more details."

The thugs jabbered away all at once, and Hiram translated. "They were told to waylay the man at a certain street corner where he always passed. They took him by cart, rolled up in a rug, to your little farm across the Tiber, where your father met them. They all went into the woods beyond the house and worked him over. He screamed a lot, but no one lives out that way. When they got to singeing his balls, he died on 'em. Weak heart, I'd say."

"What did my father want from him? Did he say anything?"

Hiram consulted his companions. "They're not paid to listen. They don't understand much anyway. Your father wanted to know who this man was and why he was in his house. The man was harder to understand. He spoke Latin with an accent and he was, you know, screaming. He begged your father to be merciful. They understood the word '*clemens.*' And something too about clothing—they think they heard '*vestis.*' But maybe they heard wrong, these fellows ain't very smart." The three torturers, not understanding Hiram's speech, smiled hopefully at Lucius.

"After the man died," Hiram continued, "your father told 'em to bury him and the box—they can show you the spot if you like. He went back to the farmhouse for something to eat. While he was gone they hid the box under some straw in their cart, thinking it might be worth something."

Lucius wasted no time in paying the Syrians off with some silver spoons, which were worth considerably more than a thousand sesterces. He wanted no trouble from them. No, indeed. He wanted time to think. *Clemens?* Of course! Not "merciful," but Flavius Clemens, the God-fearer whom his father had denounced. *Vestis* he could make no sense of. Still, something connected this Amatia and her physician to the Clemens affair. Whoever they were, they weren't what they seemed, and Verpa had found them out.

Lucius took the kit back to his room and sent a slave to fetch one of Scortilla's cats. There were half a dozen in the house, all of them "sacred," more of her Egyptian nonsense. He picked the animal up by its neck and pressed the pin into its blue-gray flank. It twisted and made strangling sounds, and in a moment it was dead. Satisfied with his experiment, he went looking for Valens. Pliny had warned him to cooperate and cooperate he would. His life might depend on it.

He found the centurion in the garden, not alone. A bosomy, unkempt woman was seated next to him on the bench beside the pool where three sun-burned, naked little boys were engaged in pushing one another's heads under the water and shrieking at the top of their lungs.

"The family, sir," Valens explained, looking a trifle apologetic. "Been after me for days to let 'em come over for a look round. Thought it wouldn't do any harm."

Lucius suppressed an urge to swear at the man. "I want you to go to the vice-prefect's house and ask him to come here without delay. I have urgent news for him."

"Now, sir?"

"Yes, *now.* And I want this rabble out of my garden."

The centurion's face darkened, and for an awful moment Lucius feared the man might hurt him. But his woman was up at once, dragging the children out, and Valens, tight-lipped, turned smartly and marched off.

He was back in half an hour. "Vice-prefect's not at home, as it happens," he said in his surliest tone of voice. "His wife says he's left town and she doesn't know where. Didn't seem too happy about it either. Anything else you want done, you ask your own people." He returned to the garden, now emptied of his family, drew his sword and set to sharpening it with vicious strokes against the edge of a stone bench.

Chapter Twenty-four

The seventeenth day before the Kalends of Domitianus.
Day eleven of the Games.

The white napkin, released from the praetor's fingertips, fluttered down, simultaneously a horn sounded, the restraining rope dropped, and a dozen four-horse chariots shot out of the starting boxes. A roar rose from a quarter of a million throats. The drivers, distinguished by their team colors — green, blue, red, white, purple, and gold—stretched out almost horizontally over their horses' backs, cracking their whips, twisting their bodies, turning their heads for brief seconds to see who was beside or behind them, searching for an opening to the left, closer to the barrier.

As they dashed around the first turn, a Green driver tried to foul one of the Reds by crowding him but wasn't skillful enough and lost control of his own chariot, careening into the barrier. The chariot flipped up and over, throwing the driver out. His horses plunged on, dragging him, still tied to the reins, into the path of another team. The roar of the crowd redoubled. This was what they had come to see.

Martial and his four friends rose to their feet, screaming with the rest, although from high up in the cheap stands of the vast Circus Maximus it was hard to see what had happened. The surviving chariots disappeared around the turn and up the back stretch in a cloud of dust. They sat again on the benches, prodded by elbows in their ribs, knees in their backs.

"Purple's going to carry off the honors today," Priscus shouted in his ear over the rumble of voices. "The emperor's team. That's where I put my money." They could just make out the distant figure of the emperor in the imperial box, swathed in the folds of his purple toga, surrounded by his courtiers, Parthenius, no doubt, among them. "Who's your money on, then?"

But Martial wasn't listening. The momentary excitement past, he had sunk back into his own thoughts, which, like those chariots, went round and round in an endless circle. Where was Pliny? Why had he left the city yesterday morning without warning, telling no one where he was going? He would have to meet Stephanus tonight at the *popina*, but what could he tell him? Stephanus. That man gave him the shudders with his cold eyes and sallow cheeks and that perpetually bandaged arm. And what if Parthenius refused to believe that Pliny hadn't confided his plans to him? What if Parthenius dropped him after all this? He doubted that anything he had reported so far had really been of much interest to the grand chamberlain. It was that woman Amatia he seemed most interested in.

And there, Martial had simply drawn a blank. An ordinary and harmless provincial matron was all he saw. Rather reserved, rather sad, a bit foolish on the subject of religion. None of the gossip-mongers knew anything about her, naturally, since she hadn't been in Rome more than a couple of weeks. But in that case, why did Parthenius care? And yet he did care. Which must mean that there was more to Amatia than he had guessed. The thought pounced on him like a cat leaping from cover upon an astonished mouse. Amidst the din of a mindless crowd, Martial's mind suddenly gained clarity. The woman was lying to them. As simple as that. But what was he to do with this new idea? Martial, who had always thought himself so clever, so knowing, suddenly felt out of his depth, baited and hooked like a fish into betraying his friend and patron for reasons he couldn't fathom.

He must tell Pliny, as he should have done in the first place. But how could he do so without confessing to his deal with Parthenius and all of his small betrayals over the past days? No, he couldn't afford that. He would lose both Pliny *and* Parthenius as patrons.

Thirty years in Rome, grasping for a fame always just out of reach, had changed him into a man that he didn't like any more. But "the die was cast," as the Deified Julius had once famously said. There was no alternative now. He would go back to Pliny's house tonight, play the dutiful client, make himself agreeable to the little wife, and see whether he could pry any information loose from the mysterious Amatia.

The chariots thundered past and Diadumenus, sitting beside him, clutched his arm and screamed, "On, the Greens!" in a transport of excitement, Martial tried hard to look attentive.

A second day's journey by coach brought Pliny and Zosimus to the lovely hill town of Ameria, where they were met by the bailiff of the farm, who had brought saddle horses for them. The farm lay about four miles west of the town.

At a walking pace, they took their way through the rolling country, thick with oak and poplar. Away on their right, Mt. Soracte, a towering wedge of granite, soared above the hills; behind them on the distant horizon stretched the folded masses of the Apennines. In the deep shade of leafy trees the air was autumn crisp, while Rome, sixty miles below, still sweltered through the last days of summer. Rome. Pliny shook himself to drive the image from his mind; he would not think of Rome, not today. Though his purpose was "business," he savored his illicit freedom like a truant schoolboy. How good it was just to have a horse between his legs again! He breathed deeply—more deeply, he felt, than he had in weeks.

They reached the farm toward evening. Pliny was ravenously hungry. The food was plain, but satisfying. After dinner he dictated a note to Calpurnia to tell her that he had arrived safely, though being careful not to say where. Then he went to bed and slept more soundly than he had in days, lulled by the croaking of the frogs.

The next morning he was up with the sun. He spent an hour with the bailiff, a good-natured and capable man, going over accounts and the rest of the day riding with him round the property. The farm pleased him; it was well worth the asking price—and Pliny was canny about such things. Barley and wheat stood high in the well-watered fields and the tenants were already at work with their sickles getting in the harvest. He stopped and talked with some, though he could barely understand their Umbrian patois. But they seemed to be prospering. What a delight to be here, rubbing soil between his fingertips, slapping a cow's backside. Weren't all Romans farmers at heart, born for this life!

But the next morning Pliny—Roman senator, respected lawyer, acting vice prefect, loving husband, expectant father—awoke feeling ill at ease. How long could he prolong this holiday? There was really nothing more to be done here. He had written his report to Fabatus, urging him to buy. What now? Must he return to Rome today? The thought depressed him.

But the bailiff, who was a repository of local lore, had thought of a small diversion for him. He described a certain lake in the neighborhood, sacred to the local folk. "Lake Vadimon it's called, on t'other side Tiber and worth the seeing, your honor. Funny things happen in that lake. I'll say no more," he winked mysteriously, "but ye ought visit it before ye go."

Pliny was happy to comply. Was not investigating marvels in his blood, after all? His uncle had, of course, been a prodigious collector of them, though he had never heard him speak of this one as far as he could recall. With directions from the bailiff, he and Zosimus mounted up, carrying a picnic lunch and a jar of the local wine in their saddle bags.

They struck off toward the Tiber, across fields and through dripping woods. Where the ground fell away sharply, they put their horses down the slope and splashed across the river, surprising an ox who had come down for its morning drink. A raw chill was in the air, making their horses' nostrils steam. Here Father Tiber wound between high, narrow banks, overhung with willows, honeysuckle, and wild vine. They followed its twisting course downstream about five miles, then stopped in a clearing and ate their lunch. After resting, they continued on their way, took a wrong turning and got lost for a time.

But toward evening, at last, they came upon the lake. In fact, they smelled it before they saw it, so strong was the stench of its sulfurous water. Lake Vadimon was of moderate size and perfectly even all around, like a wheel lying on its side. Pliny and his young companion pushed through bulrushes waist-high down to the water's edge, and Pliny knelt and cupped the water in his hand. It was whitish and thick to the touch, and tasted like medicine. And yet the cows drank it; he could see six or seven of them crowding down to the shore on the farther side.

"Patrone," said Zosimus, "it's a marvelously nasty place." He batted at a cloud of gnats that hung about their heads. "But I can see no other marvels hereabouts."

They were just turning to go. The air had been dead still, but suddenly a breeze sprang up, ruffling the water.

"Patrone!"

Pliny turned back and stared, rubbed his eyes and stared again. "Yes, I see! Extraordinary!"

As they watched in astonishment, a floating island of reeds sailed toward them across the lake. Upon it one of the cows, sensing itself adrift, lifted its head and bellowed in fright. Then more islands detached themselves from the shore and, driven before the breeze, glided here and there across the water. Wherever an island came to rest against the shore, it seemed to add to the solid land on that side, until it separated again and drifted on. What a trick was played upon their eyes! Solid land not solid at all. Whatever the explanation of this wonder, and Pliny could imagine none, it showed how easily the eye could be fooled.

And then, in a swift instant, as though the solution had been there all along, just waiting for this key to unlock it, the thought flashed like an arrow through his mind. "*Mehercule, that's* how she did it!"

"Who, Patrone?" asked Zosimus, startled.

"Scortilla, of course!"

His inner eye saw the form of a murderess, not creeping through Verpa's window; rather someone there all along, in plain view but unseen because she was a part of the background, just like these little islands. Amazing how Fate arranged things! He had come here to escape from the investigation and, by doing so, he had stumbled on the solution. Oh, but really! Could it be so? This notion, when you really thought about it, was even more outlandish than his earlier one. Pliny was quite surprised at himself. To have lived thirty-five years untroubled by an imagination, then suddenly to find himself embarrassed by one that flourished exuberantly like some strange, unwholesome plant! Is this what police work did to one? But everything fit. Scortilla and Lucius were accomplices. Their mutual hatred was all an act. One murder was used to conceal the other. And now he saw how it was done. All that remained was to prove it and the slaves would be saved.

As they left the lake, he knew already how he would put his theory to the test, and he was certain—his heart beating fast as he thought of it—certain that this time he could make Scortilla convict herself, because she was, though full of cunning, really quite a stupid woman. "And I will play her a trick that'll drag the truth out of her lying throat!" He laughed aloud.

There was no time to lose. "Mount up," he cried to Zosimus. "It's back to the town to hire a fast two-wheeler and then to Rome! If we ride through the night, we'll arrive before tomorrow's dawn—just the right moment for what I have in mind."

Chapter Twenty-five

The fifteenth day before the Kalends of Domitianus.
Day thirteen of the Games. Night.

Under a bright harvest moon a team of tired horses galloped along the Via Cassia between rows of tall poplars, drawing the light, two-wheeled gig toward Rome. Zosimus held the reins and urged the team on, while Pliny, beside him on the seat, fretted and devoured the road with his eyes. They would change the horses for fresh ones two or three more times before reaching the city. It was impossible to know the hour with any certainty. He could only pray they would be in time.

The eleventh hour of the night.

"I think we are all here. Anyone who is not we must treat as an enemy from this hour on. There's no time now for second thoughts. Are we agreed?" Parthenius, all smiling blandness, looked from face to face, allowing none of them to avoid his eyes.

Here, in Corellius Rufus' house, some of the conspirators were seeing others for the first time, astonished to find themselves together in the same room, and some of them secretly wishing they were somewhere, anywhere, else: Corellius himself, prostrate on his couch, his face etched with pain, his mouth set in a grim line; Titus Petronius, the Praetorian commandant, a big blustering man, but subdued now, cracking his knuckles to release tension; sleek Entellus, the emperor's secretary for petitions, with two other imperial freedmen, the three of them sitting close together and trying not to look intimidated by the company they were in; Cocceius Nerva, his handsome, long-nosed face pale and drawn, drumming his fingers on the tabletop and exchanging worried looks with two other senators who were as nervous as he was; and finally the empress, Domitia Augusta, looking more manly than any of them, her large hands resting motionless on the arms of her chair and not a muscle in her body betraying the strain she must be feeling. She was dressed in a plain stola, without jewelry. She had arrived in a long, hooded cloak, and when she removed it, the bruises on her face were unmistakable even through her face powder.

All of them seemed to be waiting for Parthenius to speak again. This son of a Levantine slave, who had devoted his whole life to intrigue, was their unquestioned leader—and he knew it.

Inclining his head to the empress, he said, "I did not dare ask the Augusta to risk coming here tonight, but she insisted. Your Highness, please tell the women of your bedchamber how grateful we are for their help in smuggling you out of the palace. And now, let us begin." He swallowed the bile that rose in his throat. His stomach was torturing him but he wouldn't allow it to show. "Our fortunes are at a crisis. Tomorrow is the fourteenth before the Kalends. By mid-day either the tyrant will be dead or we will. We have much to discuss, and little time, it will soon be sunup. For the benefit of some of you, let me review the sequence of events that has brought us to this point."

"Wait!" the Praetorian commandant lurched to his feet, crossed the tablinum and ripped back the curtain that gave onto the garden. Half a dozen of his Guardsmen in civilian clothes had taken up positions there. There were still more at the front of the house.

"All quiet, Sir," their officer reported. The commandant went back to his seat. He had already taken the precaution of cancelling all leaves, and his officers had been alerted to attack the City Battalions if they rallied to the emperor.

Parthenius drew a breath and began again. Over the past months, he explained, he had orchestrated the tyrant's mounting terror. "We wanted to drive him mad, encourage him to even greater outrages which would eat away at his still considerable support in some quarters. I have sent people to report lightning strikes in every part of Italy. With the help of my colleagues in the palace, we arranged a series of parlor tricks all designed to unnerve him. His morbid imagination did the rest. Not long ago I procured a soothsayer to prophesy the date of his death: tomorrow at the fifth hour of the morning. The unfortunate man paid with his life, but that is no matter. And our campaign of terror has succeeded. Don't be fooled by the image he displays at the Games. I happen to know that he has scarcely slept in days.

"When I and the empress first combined to plot his overthrow, we knew the importance of horoscopes in molding public opinion and lending nerve to a potential replacement. The empress wished Clemens to succeed, and so we prepared a horoscope predicting his imperial destiny. We gave it to him so that he could produce it at the crucial moment. This was a calamitous mistake. The horoscope can be traced to us. In fact, I composed it myself in my own hand. Foolish, I admit. Two months ago our plans came crashing down. Out of the blue, that snake Verpa astonished everyone by accusing Clemens and his wife of atheism and Jewish practices. We had known nothing of this mania of theirs. We were completely routed, terrified that the conspiracy would come to light. We held our breath and waited for the ax to fall, but it didn't. Clemens went quietly to his death, his wife was banished to a desolate island, and the incriminating horoscope seemed to have vanished.

"After a time, we gathered our courage once more. We had to begin again to recruit someone to take Clemens' place. The noble Nerva has courageously accepted our offer." Parthenius nodded in the man's direction and favored him with a tight smile. Nerva looked around as though he wanted to bolt for the door and only shame kept him in his place.

"It was during this tense period," Parthenius continued, "that the Vestalis Maxima, the Purissima, came to our aid. I think most of you know, without my going into the details, the reason for her hatred of the tyrant." Several heads nodded. "The Cloister of Vesta would be our center of communication. The wives of senators and other allies of ours could go there to leave messages and receive instructions, and the empress' loyal women would serve as a link between the Cloister and ourselves. This way no senator would ever be seen in a compromising conversation with someone like me or with the empress. This is what we proposed and she undertook it eagerly on behalf of her Order.

"Several weeks went by in this way while we bided our time. Then, just a little more than three weeks ago, Verpa struck at us. It seems Domitilla had managed to get a letter to him revealing the conspiracy and telling where they had hidden her husband's horoscope. We learned this both from Stephanus, her steward, a most useful man in many ways, who came directly and reported to me, and also from Verpa himself. He wrote a letter to the emperor, well knowing that Entellus here would intercept it. It was his way of announcing himself to us. Over the next days, I bargained with him, but the price of his silence was astronomical, and finally he had the audacity to propose himself as emperor! He wouldn't tell me what the letter said, but he hinted that he held all our lives in his fist. Maybe he exaggerated, but who could be sure?

"Somehow he had to be stopped. We decided that, while we continued to negotiate with him, we needed a spy in his house. Someone who might be able to find and destroy the horoscope and the letter. Again the Vestalis Maxima came to our rescue. As you know she proposed herself for this mission. We men were reluctant to allow this absolutely unprecedented act by one so holy, but she had her reasons, and our empress seconded her. She is the only one among us whom Verpa and Scortilla would not know by sight or by name. The Vestals are never seen in public without their veils and no one dares to stare at them or enquire too closely about them. We might have sent some low-born person, but the spy, to be effective, had to be someone with breeding and manners, someone who would have the freedom of a guest, sit with them at dinner, befriend them, listen and observe. Her idea was to pose as a devotee of Isis with some story of coming to Rome on a pilgrimage and being robbed. We thought an appeal to Scortilla's piety and vanity would be most effective, and we were right.

"She took with her one of Corellius' freedmen, a philosopher, one of the few to escape the recent purge. The man wanted vengeance for many a dead friend. He said he had a smattering of knowledge in the sciences, enough to pass himself off as her physician under the name of Iatrides. And he would be her courier. If she learned anything, he would carry a message to the Cloister and drop it just outside the gate, where one of the Vestals would retrieve it and pass it on to me or the empress."

Here one of the senators interrupted. "How was a Vestal able to be away from the Cloister for so long? As Pontifex Maximus, the emperor is their religious superior. They can't just come and go as they please."

"Quite so. I told him about her hysteria, that it had suddenly become more serious and that she needed medical attention that she could not get in the Cloister. This does happen from time to time. The fact is, she has no living family, I'm told they all perished in the eruption of Vesuvius, so I invented a sister for her in Capua, a woman of impeccable reputation. Oh, believe me, Domitian actually pretends to care about such niceties. He might have looked more closely into the matter except that he has been so distracted with fear. He told me to handle the arrangements. So the tyrant never knew where she was—or is."

"And where exactly *is* the woman?" This was Nerva, whose nerves made him petulant.

"She had not been at Verpa's more than three days," Parthenius replied, "when the man was killed, under what circumstances we don't yet know. The information that Pliny has seen fit to release is extremely confusing, and she is now at his house—has been for the past twelve days, apparently without Iatrides, who disappeared around the time of Verpa's murder."

"Then how do you know she's there?" asked a senator.

"The resourceful Stephanus, against my advice, I may say, talked his way inside and got a look at her. He couldn't speak freely to her, the silly little wife was around, but he tried to convey to her in guarded language that, one way or another, this will all be over soon. That was three days ago. Since then we've had no communication with her. The truth of the matter is, I am very concerned.

"I also have an informant, a certain ambitious, foul-mouthed poet, who has attached himself to Pliny like a barnacle and tells me the man is convinced that Verpa's murder was a family affair, as it very well may be, knowing that family. But Verpa's son said something about papers—surely our letter and horoscope—and my fear is that Pliny may yet find them or that the Purissima will make some slip. We know she suffers from a weakness of the nerves that could overcome her at any moment, with the anxiety she must be feeling. The fact that nothing has happened to us so far eases my mind only a little. Gaius Plinius is, by all appearances, a loyal soldier of the regime."

"Chamberlain, I protest!" Corellius quavered, raising himself painfully on one elbow. "I've known Pliny all his life. I can vouch for his good character. He will do the right thing."

Parthenius frowned patiently. "Forgive me, sir, I know he is your protégé, but while others spoke out against tyranny and paid with their lives, his career has flourished under the emperor's patronage. Now he has been given this extraordinary police job under the city prefect, who we all know is the tyrant's creature. Why?"

Corellius looked about him helplessly. "I yield to no one in my hatred of Domitian, but Pliny must have a career, mustn't he? He still has years of service ahead of him. It isn't his fault if he has had to serve a bad master; he's guilty of no evil himself. I defy you to prove otherwise."

"Then how do you account for his nocturnal meetings with the tyrant?"

Suddenly everyone looked sharply at the grand chamberlain. Even in the empress' eyes there was a flicker of what might be fear. "What nocturnal meetings are these, chamberlain?"

Parthenius was never a man to conceal his air of superior knowledge, and he didn't now. "I have not told you the worst. They have met twice in the emperor's private rooms until the small hours of the night. No one has overheard them except little Earinus, who is, of course, feeble-minded and incapable of understanding anything. Believe me, I tried. I had thought at first that Pliny was going to be punished for the way he behaved at Verpa's funeral. But on the contrary, the emperor seems to dote on him. And now Pliny has suddenly left the city, pretending, according to my informant, that he is going "north" on some undisclosed business. He was seen leaving by the Flaminian Gate."

"North," said the Praetorian commandant. "North." Then he slapped his palm with a heavy fist. "I'll tell you what's north of here, the town of Reate! The home of the Flavian clan, where the family estate and all their clients are! The townsfolk there are fanatically loyal to the Flavian name! Domitian knows what's coming, and he's preparing a bolt hole. A place where he can defend himself until the German legions can come to his support. And this Pliny, whom no one suspects, is preparing the way for him! What else can it be?"

Suddenly everyone was speaking at once. Parthenius with difficulty brought them back to order.

"Titus Petronius, I think you may be right. But that only means that we must be resolute. I have my poet friend in Pliny's house and the reliable Stephanus is watching at the Flaminian Gate. If Pliny doesn't return before tomorrow then there is nothing we can do.

"If he does return…" Parthenius let the sentence hang in midair.

◇◇◇

Half an hour before dawn, the pair of spent horses trotted through the Flaminian Gate. Zosimus steered for Verpa's house.

As they turned off the Via Flaminia onto the Vicus Pallacinae, Pliny ordered him to pull up. He saw leaning wearily against a wall what he had been looking out for. She wasn't very pretty, but she was young and slim.

She yawned, almost ready to go home and sleep after a night that had brought her little profit. But then it seemed her luck had turned. When a couple of well-dressed fellows invite you into their coach and wave a coin under your nose, even at this ungodly hour, a working girl doesn't have to think twice.

Chapter Twenty-six

The fourteenth day before the Kalends of Domitianus.
Day fourteen of the Games. The first hour of the day.

"Wait with the carriage, Zosimus. What I have to do here is not for your chaste eyes." The sun was not yet a hand's breadth above the housetops, a pink smear on the horizon; the street still in deep shadow, exactly as it had been on the morning Verpa's body was discovered. Pliny knocked on the door. No answer. He pounded harder, using his fist, and shouted at the window. If the sun rose higher, his experiment would be ruined. At last, a tousle-haired slave opened the door a crack, recognized the familiar face of the vice prefect, and admitted him.

"Wake my centurion and tell him to meet me upstairs with the lady Scortilla—but she is to wait outside the bedroom until I call her." Pliny raced up the stairs with the prostitute in tow.

Valens, his face creased with sleep, came grumbling into the bedroom and stopped abruptly. He broke into a gap-toothed smile.

"Eyes front, centurion," said Pliny. "You're not here to gawk. Be good enough to light the lamp on that stand next to the bed." Pliny moved back and forth across the room while he examined the shadowy figures that populated the walls. "Now girl," he addressed the prostitute, "no one's going to touch you, that's not what we're here for. Undress. Yes, and now go and stand in that corner—yes, that's right, flat up against the wall. No, not her, I think. The one to your right. Yes. Now, on your knees, fit yourself to her form, head a little up. Yes, you understand what I mean, don't you? And now I'm going to turn down the lamp a little. Yes—remarkable, remarkable." The girl vanished, perfectly fitted to the painted figure behind her. In the feeble penumbra of the single lamp, unless you put out your hand and touched her, you could not have told she was there in the flesh.

"And now we are ready for the lady!"

Scortilla was ushered into the room by two troopers, who shut the door behind her. She was in her nightdress. Without her wig, sparse tufts of graying hair stuck out from her head. And she was very, very angry. "You!" she snarled. "Again! Haven't you played the fool enough already? This is harassment. I warned you, I will complain to the emperor personally. He will have you crucified!"

"Do you find it dark in here, Scortilla?"

"What?"

"Valens, open the shutters, will you?"

The open window was a pale rectangle of light that left the room still in deep shadow.

"Would you say, lady, that we are alone here—you, me, and the centurion?"

Her eyes were suddenly wary. Her head swiveled in quick jerks like a bird's. She took a step toward the bed, back again, looked behind her.

"Answer me, woman. Are we alone?"

"Yes, damn you!" What else could she say?

"Girl, show yourself!"

Like one of those islands in the lake, detaching itself from shore and swimming into view, the naked girl emerged from the wall. Scortilla clapped her fist to her mouth to stifle a scream. It was as though the mural had come to life.

"'Ere, this is going to cost you, whatever this is," the girl complained. "I ain't used to being made a show of in front a' ladies. And my neck is stiff besides."

"Centurion, give her a silver *denarius*, more than she earns in a week. Thank you. You may go now."

Pliny bent his brows on the speechless Scortilla. "Woman, I charge you with the murder of your husband by poisoning. And I will tell you how you did it. You and Lucius planned this together, one murder concealing another."

"Centurion, go and get Lucius out of bed and bring him here." He turned to Scortilla. "Your mutual hatred is all a charade, isn't it? You both wanted Verpa dead. You, Scortilla, had the poison and knew how to administer it, but Lucius contributed the idea of using Ganymede and the dagger and candelabrum to make it look like a political assassination. You could easily make Pollux, the Jew, out to be an accomplice. You went to Verpa's room before he went to bed and before Pollux came on duty on a pretext of wanting a private word with him or something. You must have enticed him sexually and poisoned him with that needle, just as I thought. Then Lucius sent Ganymede in to stab him. You didn't expect much from that nerveless youth, it only had to look like a fatal stabbing, but he was even more inept than you expected; he managed to not inflict a single fatal wound. But you, because of your arthritic knees, couldn't escape through the window the way he did. Instead, you hid yourself against the wall and slipped out in the confusion when everyone ran in—you obviously practiced this ahead of time when the room was empty and chose your spot carefully. As for your motive, perhaps you would like to tell me about your nocturnal meetings with Alexandrinus, the Egyptian priest. No doubt Lucius never dreamed that you and that priest planned to take a full two million out of the estate."

He was being reckless, he knew, but he was willing to risk everything on this throw of the dice. Scortilla didn't know that Domitian had warned him off from challenging the will. He had to extract a confession from her by overwhelming her with the evidence.

And it seemed to work. The woman was thoroughly frightened. She sank down on the bed; when she spoke her voice was so low he could scarcely hear her. "I never planned anything with Lucius and I didn't poison Verpa. I never saw that needle before you showed it to me. To put an end to this, I will confess to what I did do. I cursed him. The tablet is still buried in the garden. I'll show you, if you don't believe me. I know you can prosecute me for it—but it didn't work! I thought at first that it had—that a demon flew in the window and slaughtered him and left some unholy symbol scratched on the wall to mark its passing. It seemed so real."

Pliny recalled seeing her the morning the body was discovered; the glassy-eyed shock in her expression like someone who had played at black magic and found, terrifyingly, that the spell had worked. The stupid woman!

"Now I know it was only Ganymede—and that is all I know. I swear it. I will swear by our Lord and God, by any god you like." Suddenly her thin shoulders shook with sobs. Pliny just stared. He'd been so sure!

At that moment, Lucius was brought in. He looked from Pliny to the weeping Scortilla. What was happening here, and what did it have to do with him? Pliny explained, tight-lipped.

Lucius knew at once what he needed to do. "Vice prefect, you said you'd help me if I cooperated with you. I hope you're a man of your word. As much as I would like this filthy witch to be guilty of murder," he jerked his head toward Scortilla, "there have been some developments while you were away that put things in a different light. The centurion can back me up. Ask him to go fetch the medical kit from my room."

While they waited for Valens to return with the box, Lucius described his visit from the Syrians. "I went with Valens to our farm across the Tiber and it didn't take us long to find the grave. Nasty sight. Poor fellow had been dead two weeks or more but you could see what they'd done to him. And it was him all right. The one calling himself Iatrides. My father must have wanted something out of him very badly indeed. Apparently he said the word 'clemens' and, as the Syrian understood it, 'vestis,' whatever sense that makes.

Valens returned with the box and handed it to his chief. "You'll find his name on the bottom, sir. And you'll find something interesting inside."

Pliny reached in and brought out the bit of cork with its deadly needle.

"It works," said Lucius, "I tried it on a cat. I suppose Iatrides planned to use it on himself if it came to that, but he didn't get the chance." Pliny let the object fall back into the box. A cold sweat had broken out on his body.

Scortilla looked up and wiped her paint-smudged face with the back of a bony wrist. There was anger again—even triumph—in her voice. "You officious dunce! Don't forget that there was another woman in this house the night Verpa died— but, of course, she's above suspicion, so endearing, so helpless. Not like me."

Pliny's leaving, like his arrival, was quick and unceremonious. He glowered at Zosimus and repulsed the young man's questions as they rode through the dawn-lit streets toward his home. Vestis? He thought. Or Vestalis? No. He recoiled from the thought. But a tightness gripped his chest.

Chapter Twenty-seven

He was met at the door by Martial. "You're back! Just thought I would come by in case—"

"Yes, well, go home now. State business, not for your ears." Pliny brushed past the poet, almost knocking him over. He was about to call for Amatia when, instead, Soranus emerged from his wife's room, closing the door behind him.

The physician was a young Greek, not yet thirty years old, with a brisk, confident manner. He wasn't well known in Rome, though he had come highly recommended from his native Ephesus. His face was half hidden behind a massive black beard, which he hoped added authority to his youthful face. He had a pair of intelligent, owlish eyes. He blinked them at Pliny. "Not to worry," he said. "Bit of an emergency last night—bleeding and pain. I trust you had a good reason for leaving her alone." There was an edge to his voice. "The fetus is alive, I can detect its heartbeat through this little tube of mine. You owe a debt of gratitude to your house guest, Amatia. While I was attending another case, she stayed with your wife, comforted her, wouldn't let anyone else touch her, so say the servants."

Pliny felt his conviction ebbing away. He pursed his lips. This was going to make what he had to do even harder. He looked into Calpurnia's bedroom. She was very pale. Her eyes fluttered open, and she smiled wanly at him. If there was reproach in her eyes, he could not afford to think about that now.

"We rejoice at your return." Amatia approached him from the far side of the atrium. Her hair was disheveled and the circles under her eyes were darker than ever, the skin around them finely wrinkled. "Your trip was a success?"

Pliny knew it was no idle question, but she didn't dare press him. "A success? Yes, madam, in ways I wouldn't have wished for."

"Madam?" She measured him with her eyes. "We're not usually so formal, are we?"

If he prolonged this he would lose his courage entirely.

"Thank you for attending my wife, I'm very grateful. We have something to discuss. Come with me into the *tablinum* and shut the door." He turned and she followed him. When they were alone, he said, "Lady, do you recognize this?" He produced the medical kit from under his traveling cloak. She shook her head, no. He turned the box over, exposing Iatrides' name inscribed on the bottom. He didn't have to ask again; her face told him everything. She groped behind her for a chair and sat down heavily.

"Your friend was murdered, I regret to say, quite brutally. Tortured to death by Ingentius Verpa. Now I ask you, why would Verpa do that?" Amatia sucked in her breath; it made a high-pitched wheezing sound like a child with pneumonia. But Pliny was relentless. "Forgive me, lady. I must play the role of policeman, not friend, although I hope I am your friend." He went to his desk, opened the small strongbox and brought out the needle that had killed Iarbas' monkey. He held it in front of her face. "Do you recognize this? We found it in Verpa's room. It's what killed him. There's its twin in Iatrides' box. Now, madam, what do you have to say to me?"

Before he could put out a hand to catch her, she was on the floor, her arms and legs thrashing violently, her teeth clenched, sweat pouring out of every pore, the veins at her temples bulging.

"Soranus!"

The physician had been about to take his leave. He rushed in, tossing his cloak aside. "By Apollo!" He fumbled in his kit and produced a bottle of some liquid. "Help me force her jaws open." This was no easy thing but at last they were able to get a few drops down her throat. "A mild sedative," the doctor explained. Gradually, the convulsions subsided and her body grew limp. They carried her to her room and laid her on the bed. Pliny had never seen her as bad as this. But there was no pretending here.

"She suffers from hysteria," he told Soranus. "We must find something with a stink for her to inhale."

"Nonsense." The physician frowned with authority. "Even the great Hippocrates could talk rubbish sometimes. The womb scampers around like a kitten chasing a ball? I don't believe it. Some day I shall write a treatise on the subject."

"Have you seen many cases, then?"

"Well, actually, no. One doesn't come across these things every day. And so I would be most grateful, sir, if you would permit me to examine the lady while she is at rest."

"Saving her modesty, of course," Pliny warned.

"Oh, absolutely. I will avert my eyes; I can tell a great deal by touch alone. I'll just get my kit and then if you'll leave us for a few minutes?"

A quarter of an hour later, the doctor emerged, frowning in puzzlement. In his hand he held a contraption such as Pliny had never seen before. It was made of bronze and comprised four prongs whose distance from each other could be adjusted by means of a screw-threaded handle and crossbar mechanism. Soranus set it on the table between them. "A speculum of my own design," he explained. "I call it the dioptra. It allows me to look through the cervix."

To Pliny's eye it looked like some dreadful instrument of torture. "You examined her with that thing!"

The physician looked a bit sheepish. "Well, just a peek, sir. I mean, in the interests of science. And I can state with confidence that the lady's womb is precisely where it should be. In one way, however, the traditional wisdom has proven to be true. It's no wonder she suffers from hysteria. It's a very common effect of sexual deprivation in a passionate woman. It is, in short, a virgin's disease. And this lady, sir, is a virgin, astonishing as that sounds."

Pliny felt his heart flutter. But hadn't he already guessed?

"Well, ah, I mean, was a virgin," the doctor blinked rapidly, "that is, I fear I inadvertently did her a little damage. I mean, how was I to know?"

"You what? Out! Out of my house, you butcher!"

Pliny, on his feet, his hands balled into fists, watched the physician's disappearing back. He felt as though all the air had suddenly been let out of him.

"Husband, I heard you shouting." Calpurnia tottered unsteadily toward him. "How can our dear Amatia be a virgin if she is the mother of five daughters?"

Pliny could only shake his head silently. The implications were just beginning to sink in. Amatia and Verpa. He tried to erase the picture from his mind but couldn't. A shudder of dread —something from deep in the racial memory—ran through him. A Vestal Virgin polluted by man's touch and by death.

"Go back to bed, dear."

"But—"

"Go back to bed!"

Calpurnia's door had hardly closed when Amatia's opened. She held on to the doorposts, her face drained of blood, her hair down across her face, and gazed at him with eyes of stone. "What—have—you—done to—me?"

There was no turning back now.

Pliny swallowed hard. "I know who you are, Purissima. I know what you did. With a heavy heart, I charge you with the murder of Sextus Ingentius Verpa. If it were up to me, I would award you the Civic Crown for patriotism, but the Law thinks otherwise. It's all been a pack of lies, hasn't it? The family in Lugdunum, the pilgrimage to Isis…I am an officer of the State. I must go to the Prefecture and tell the prefect what I know. He will report to the emperor."

She took a step forward, swaying on her feet, and clutched his arm. "Wait, please!"

He pulled away from her. "I warn you, you're playing a dangerous game. I'm not a fool."

"No indeed. You're much cleverer than I thought. Too clever for me.

"Before Iatrides died, he spoke the name of Clemens. This touches on the emperor's family—on the emperor himself. What is it all about? Why have you been hiding in my house? You have lied to me and my wife, who adores you. I have never been more angry than at this moment."

"*You* are angry?" she shot back. "Your anger is a small thing compared to mine! I have nothing to say to you—and very soon it won't matter anyway."

"Then I will go to the Prefecture at once." He turned from her.

"No, stay a minute! Whatever you do, you mustn't hate me. I—I want to tell you something about myself. Perhaps it will answer one of your questions." She was playing for time. Surely, by now the final steps were in motion. She would say anything to keep him here. She sat down and motioned him to sit beside her.

Pliny hesitated.

"I was six years old when I was taken. Without spot or blemish, as sacral law demands. It was in the first year of Nero's reign. He must have been no more than seventeen. I can still remember that pudgy face and those insolent eyes. He thought the whole thing was a huge joke. When he called me 'Beloved' according to the ritual formula, he licked his lips and smirked at me. I was too young to understand.

"The Vestalis Maxima in those days was a horrid, shriveled old woman who smelled of decay. But there was another Vestal there, only a few years older than me and she became like an older sister to me. Her name was Cornelia. I loved her from the first and, in time, we became everything to each other. Everything. The years passed happily for us. I never missed the "world." I had everything I wanted within the small round world of the temple. And then six years ago catastrophe struck us. The tyrant Domitian conceived a hatred for our Order. Three Vestals were falsely charged with unchastity and forced to commit suicide.

I never dreamed it could happen to Cornelia, who by then was the Vestalis Maxima—a woman of nearly fifty, who had not known a man in her whole life, who had never loved anyone but me..." She turned away, her shoulders working with grief.

Pliny said nothing. He knew all about the Chief Vestal, Cornelia—or, at least, what the Senate had been told: how she had been caught *in flagrante* with her lover. Pliny had stayed away from the execution, but everyone in Rome knew what had happened. Cornelia was bound and gagged and carried in a closed litter through the Forum to the Colline Gate. The crowd drew back from the cortege in shocked silence. Since a Vestal's blood could not be shed, she would die by suffocation in an airless underground chamber with a bed, a loaf of bread, and a jug of water. Rome hadn't seen this ancient penalty exacted in generations.

"We were made to watch," Amatia continued. "While the other pontiffs turned away, the tyrant dragged her to the lip of the chamber. She cried out and prayed to Vesta although her head was muffled with a cloth. The public executioner set her foot on the ladder and forced her down. Her dress caught and she tried to free it. The executioner reached out his hand to help her but she shrank back. She would not let her chaste body be touched by the foulness of death. Then they pulled up the ladder and shoveled earth over the opening until it was level with the ground. I felt my throat constrict as hers must have, felt black death cover my eyes. They say I fainted and began to thrash. My hysteria dates from that moment.

"The night she died I tried to hang myself. My faithful Virgins prevented me—and they were right, my life was not mine to throw away. As the next oldest I, Amatia, was forced to take her place as Vestalis Maxima. And I have tried to be everything to my girls, my daughters, as much as if they sprang from my own womb. Just as she was to me.

"But from that day on I swore vengeance on Domitian, and I have waited for the moment of my revenge. Waited six years while I stood beside him at all our holy rites, while I smiled and bowed my head to him, deferred to him and praised him—that murderer of all I loved! The effort of dissembling has worn me down to nearly nothing. We Vestals could do nothing by ourselves, but when we learned that others were leading the way and invited us to help them, we—I—eagerly accepted. The younger Vestals know nothing about this, and I have no living family; they all died in the ruins of Pompeii, where I was born. And that, Gaius Plinius, is all I will tell you."

"*Mehercule*, Purissima, I—" But Pliny didn't finish his thought because at that moment he heard a noise behind him. He spun around and saw Martial making for the door.

Chapter Twenty-eight

The second hour of the day.

A breathless Stephanus was ushered quickly into Corellius Rufus' *tablinum* where the others still sat in tense conversation. He addressed himself to Parthenius. "I've just seen your poet outside Pliny's house. Pliny knows who she is, claims that she murdered Verpa. What else he guesses isn't certain, but if he takes her in to the Prefecture and they torture her we're all done for. Even now she may be telling him everything."

There was tight-lipped silence around the table. Suddenly Nerva leapt up. "This has gone far enough. I must have been out of my mind to listen to you, Parthenius. It's time to abandon this whole mad scheme."

"Senator, you surprise me. You were brave enough at our little charade two weeks ago. What has happened to you?" The chamberlain's voice was silky, although his stomach was shot through with arrows of pain. "I'm afraid things have progressed beyond the point of turning back."

"Not for me! Domitilla was banished before you approached me. She can't give them my name."

"No, but I could," Parthenius said softly, "and, though I admire the Stoical virtues, I fear they will desert me in the face of torture. No, Nerva, there is no going back now. You are our choice for emperor, suited to the job in every way: respected, uncorrupted, known as a friend of ancient Roman liberty." Nerva had not been their first choice, but he was definitely their last; it had to be him. What was there to recommend him? Old age and ill health. He would die soon and then the real search for a successor could begin.

"Guttersnipe," Nerva snarled, "you talk to me of Roman liberty! You care for nothing but your own well-barbered neck."

"All our necks at this point." Parthenius voice got lower as Nerva's grew shriller. "Please sit down, senator. You're not going anywhere until the Praetorian Guard proclaims you and then you will go to the palace and be hailed as Caesar. And I will be there applauding with the rest."

The grand chamberlain turned back to the others. "This man Pliny needs to be dealt with now. He is too dangerous. Even if we called off the assassination, he would still live to denounce us. We need to get the Purissima out of that house at once and Pliny cannot be allowed to live. Are we agreed? I want each of you to cast his vote in the presence of us all." Parthenius looked at each one in turn. "Cocceius Nerva Caesar, if I may call you so. As our future sovereign, I defer to you. How do you vote?"

Nerva composed his face with an effort, made an angry gesture with his hand. "Death by all means!"

"Thank you. And you, Empress?"

"This man, Pliny. Who is he?"

"A lawyer, a quite junior senator."

"How long has the family been senatorial?"

"He is the first to reach that rank."

"He has powerful protectors?" At this, Corellius looked away in shame. He had been powerful once. No more.

"No, Empress," Parthenius answered. "No. His uncle had some influence with Vespasian."

"Vespasian has been dead a long time."

"May I compliment your majesty on your understanding of affairs."

She ignored the compliment. Her dark, deep set eyes were as hard as a gladiator's at the moment of the kill. "Death, then."

"And the rest of you?" The chamberlain's gaze swept the room. "Petronius?"

"I will drive the sword in with this hand!" The Praetorian commandant made an upward stabbing motion with his fist.

"Thank you. Entellus?"

"Death."

And so on as he proceeded around the room until he came finally to Corellius Rufus. "Senator?"

A red spot burned in each of his withered cheeks. "He's a good man. His only crime is obedience to orders. Perhaps if I speak to him…"

"Yes, you tried that already," Nerva sneered. "It was not a success."

"Sir, I ask you again. There is no more time for talk. Your vote. We are waiting."

The invalid's face twisted in anguish. "Death."

"Sir, I could not hear you."

"Death!"

"Thank you, sir."

"He won't outlive the hour," Petronius growled, jumping to his feet. "And I'll bring the Purissima back here to wait until it's over. I've already given sealed orders to my tribunes to neutralize the City Battalions when the hour comes."

"And we," Parthenius said, nodding to Stephanus and Entellus, "must be back at the palace before we're missed. The emperor will be calling for me soon. Is everyone clear about the plan?"

They nodded.

"Then may Fortune favor the brave!"

Chapter Twenty-nine

Pliny drew a long, deep breath and shook his head. What a story she had told, and he didn't doubt the truth of it for an instant. Knowing what he knew, how could he hand this woman over to certain death? Before he decided what to do, he needed to know more. "What were you doing in Verpa's house?"

She shook her head, her lips a tight white line.

"Purissima, you would do better to tell me than to have to tell it to the emperor."

"He won't be emperor much longer if the gods favor us. And if not, I am content to die. I am already polluted by a man's touch, I can never return to the service of the goddess."

Pliny raised his hands, then let them drop in his lap. "You leave me no choice then, Purissima." Now was the moment to stand up and call for his litter. But somehow he didn't move. They continued to stare at each other.

"Very well," she said finally. Anything to keep him here while the others did their work. "I will answer your question, vice prefect, and then I beg you not to oppose us but to join us."

"Join you in precisely what, madam? Treason?"

Her eyebrows drew down sharply. "Liberation!" She leaned close to his face and began to tell him, though without naming names, how their plan to put Clemens on the throne had been thwarted by Verpa's denunciation. Then, how weeks later Verpa had contacted them, claiming to have an incriminating letter from Domitilla as well as her husband Clemens' imperial horoscope. "We had to know how much she had told him, or if it was all bluff. And so Iatrides and I talked our way into his house and spent four days with that vulgar, vicious family." Her lip curled. "All the while, as I smiled and made myself agreeable, I listened as hard as I could. Whenever they questioned me too closely I became faint, and not all pretense either, the strain was nearly unbearable. During those days I tried to be wherever I could overhear Verpa talking. That was my plan, and it bore fruit.

"As I have already told you, on the third evening I was sitting in the garden and overheard Verpa and his son arguing; Lucius demanding to be free of *potestas* and live on his own, Verpa threatening to kill him if the boy tampered with any more of his bedmates. What I didn't tell you is that I also heard Verpa boasting about the letter and horoscope. I decided right there that I would steal them if my courage didn't fail me. The next morning I wrote a message and gave it to poor Iatrides to carry to the cloister.

"Late that afternoon, I was in my room resting when Verpa burst in. He showed me Iatrides' severed finger with his signet ring on it. He said he had mistrusted both of us right from the start, that he wasn't as gullible as Scortilla. It was plain that I was no devotee of Isis. He had questioned me at dinner about some detail of the goddess' liturgy. I had tried to learn something about that filthy foreign cult before I entered his house, but I was quickly out of my depth. And he had discovered that Iatrides was a fraud too. He'd asked him for a dose of some Isiac remedy for headache and, of course, the poor man had no such thing. 'So I followed your physician,' Verpa said, 'and we got him before he could deliver your message, took him to a very private place, and oh, the things he told us when we applied fire to his genitals. I've just come back from there.' He laughed at me. 'Really, Purissima, what a dishonorable trick you've played me! I expected better than this from a priestess of Vesta. I am through wasting time with you and your friends. Tomorrow, I go to the emperor. At one stroke I can give him the documents and another deceitful Vestalis Maxima to bury alive. That is, unless you do exactly as I tell you. I can keep your name out of it if I choose to. I have done everything in a long and interesting life but debauch a Vestal Virgin.'"

"Then he dragged me to his room. This was before Pollux came on duty at the second hour of the night. He told me to stay there and make no sound. He would be back for me later. 'In the meanwhile,' he said, 'you will have time to study my murals. They'll instruct you in the arts of Venus, a far more endearing goddess than Vesta.'

"He went away then, and in the interval before he returned I tried to make ready the poisoned needle. I intended to kill myself."

"Whose idea were these needles?" Pliny asked.

"One of us—I'll tell you no names—knew someone who could prepare them and we all agreed to carry them. In case the worst happened, none of us could denounce the others."

"It didn't work for Iatrides, though."

"No, sadly. I kept mine knotted in a corner of my *palla*. But when the time came, my hands shook so badly I couldn't untie it. What I suffered that night was horrible enough. And now I must tell it to you—a policeman, a *man*."

Pliny held up his hands. "Not all of it, lady. I've already guessed a good deal."

"Have you. How very clever. But you can't know what it was like. I was so frightened I couldn't even scream. I knew I couldn't resist his strength. When he returned, I wept and pleaded with him. He laughed and kissed me with his obscene mouth and stripped me of my clothes…" Her words came in little gasps, in a voice so low that Pliny had to strain to hear her. He couldn't take his eyes from her face which was flushed and beaded with sweat.

"He made me drink wine with him. Then, holding a lamp in one hand and gripping my wrist with the other, he took me around the room to look at his filthy pictures. Things I never imagined people did! Meanwhile I heard Pollux outside taking up his post, rocking his chair back against the door. Verpa said he would do me the favor of saving my virginity technically—he had that much fear of the gods in him—but he would use me in every other way…" Amatia's breath began to come hard, her hand went to her throat and Pliny was afraid she was going to have another attack, but with a violent shake she mastered herself.

Listening to her relive this horror, Pliny gripped the arms of his chair until his knuckles turned white. As bad as he knew Verpa to be, this was almost inconceivable. A Vestal abused like this! He was shocked down to the soles of his feet.

"He mounted me from behind, like an animal, but while he couldn't see my hands I got hold of my palla where it lay on the bed, put the knotted corner in my teeth and freed the pin at last. I kept the cork between my teeth, careful not to let my lips touch the poisoned tip. Somehow I must kill him and then myself. After he had finished, he turned me toward him and poured a goblet of wine for us. I kept my head lowered so he couldn't see my face.

"You admire it, eh?" He thought I was staring at his thing, still swollen with lust. "Well, now, I'll teach you a whore's trick. Kiss, it, darling." He thrust it up in my face—and I struck like a viper!

"He let out a yelp, jerked away, looked at his thing with disbelieving eyes, the needle still stuck in the flesh. Faster than I could have imagined, he doubled up in pain and clutched at his throat. I think he tried to scream but only a gurgling noise came out, not loud enough for Pollux to hear through the door. As he fell back on the bed I pried myself loose from his grip. With a final spasm he rolled over on his stomach, covering the needle with his body. I couldn't bring myself to touch him. He was still alive but unable to move—I don't know for how long. Only his nostrils moved in and out with his breathing. I remember that."

Pliny felt humbled by this woman's strength. She was like some heroine of ancient days, a modern Lucretia.

"Then it seemed like only a moment later that I heard a noise outside the window. I only had time to roll off the bed onto the floor. I heard the shutters swing open. A figure slithered through."

"And that was Ganymede," said Pliny. "There is no coincidence. Lucius chose that night because, by counting the slave

girls and finding them all in their own beds, he naturally concluded that his father was sleeping alone, as he occasionally did.
In fact, he had you there with him."

"I couldn't imagine what this marauder's purpose was, but he
crept toward the bed and I saw in the lamplight that he carried
a dagger. Still naked, I scuttled back into the farthest, darkest
corner of the room and crouched in front of one of the figures
on the wall. From there I watched the intruder throw himself
on Verpa, hacking and slashing until his breath came like sobs.
He seemed not to notice that Verpa never stirred, never let out
a sound. And he didn't see me! Finally, he tossed the dagger on
the floor beside the bed and, with a piece of charcoal that he
had with him, sketched some sort of figure on the wall. Then
out he went again through the window. I could hear him drop
to the garden pavement below.

"As soon as he was gone, I dressed again. I can't describe the
thoughts that whirled through my brain after that. Somehow
I must get out without being seen. But how? The window—
impossible! I looked down at that two-story drop and my head
swam. After that, the hours dragged by. The oil lamp guttered
and went out. I was in despair.

"And then, as it was growing light, I heard muffled voices
outside. Verpa's servants coming to wake him. They knocked on
the door, waited, knocked louder. I did the only thing I could;
realizing how I'd escaped assassin's notice, I thought maybe it
would work a second time. I undressed again and matched
myself to the figure of the woman on her hands and knees being
mounted by the Satyr—"

Pliny stopped her with a gesture. He didn't need her to
describe the trick, he had seen it. "No more, please, I know how
it was done. Only I thought it was Scortilla!"

Amatia answered with a bleak smile. "I wish it had been. I
could hear them talking outside the door though I couldn't make
out the words. For a while nothing, then the voice of Lucius
calling out Verpa's name. My clothes! I had left them in the
middle of the floor. I raced to get them and stuffed them under

the bed, then back to the wall again. My heart was pounding so, it nearly broke my ribs. Then the door burst open and they all tumbled in, Lucius in the lead, holding a lamp. They saw the body tangled in the sheets. For an age, it seemed, they milled around the bed, while I, only a few steps away, pressed myself against the painted figure, trembling, and praying with all my might to Vesta to help me. 'Bring more light,' one said. 'No carry him outside.' Then, all shouting and gesticulating, they carried his body out and left me there alone.

"I threw my clothes on again. But still, how could I leave? The atrium below was full of people. If someone were to look up and see me sneaking away…I did the only thing I could think of, gave a loud scream and backed out of the room. Of course, everyone looked up: and all they saw was the invalid guest who must have been roused by the commotion, entered the room, saw the blood and become hysterical; she was known to be suffering from weak nerves anyway. And that is all that happened."

Martial runs down the Via Sacra, his heart pounding in his shaggy breast. His knees are aching and his chest is on fire. How much farther to Verpa's house? Up the Citadel steps and down the other side, not the easiest route but the most direct. He doesn't think he can make it. But he must!

He hadn't meant to tell Stephanus so much—not about Amatia! But the man had threatened to knife him right there in the street and, after wringing everything out of him, had dashed off somewhere. Parthenius' creature!

At last! He stumbles against Verpa's door. A trooper opens the door cautiously, recognizes him, and pulls him inside. In the atrium the others are sitting about, grim-visaged and talking in low voices.

"Valens!" The poet is panting so hard he can barely speak. "Gaius Plinius—needs you—at once! What? What are you saying?"

"I'm saying that we've been ordered to return to barracks and surrender our arms to the fucking Praetorians. If we're seen in the city we'll be treated as rebels. We've just been talking about what to do."

"What you must do is come with me, now! I'll explain on the way."

"Your pink-cheeked senator friend has gotten himself in trouble? How is that our problem?"

Assenting grunts from the men.

"Valens, that will he was going to write for you? You may need it sooner than you think!"

◇◇◇

"And why, madam, are you here in my house?" Pliny challenged.

"You invited me," Amatia said simply. "And there was no more to be done at Verpa's house. Without Iatrides I had no way of communicating with the others. So, on my own, I decided to spy on you, I confess it gladly. You insisted on investigating the case, day after day, with your obnoxious friend, as if it actually mattered whether a few slaves were executed or not! What if you somehow stumbled on the truth? I had to steer you away from that."

It dawned on Pliny then how easily he had let himself be fooled by this woman. There were a dozen ways he could have checked her story, but it had simply never occurred to him. Why should it have? He was so bent on exposing Lucius and Scortilla, and Amatia was so good to his wife. Was that only a charade too?

"Now, I have told you everything," she said, "I appeal to you. If you simply do nothing, all of this will be over in a matter of hours. Today is the appointed day."

Do nothing? His anger flared. "You speak so contemptuously of the slaves, lady. Does justice mean nothing to you? You are willing to sacrifice the lives of forty innocent human beings who will be punished for murdering their master when it was *you* who committed the crime?"

She rounded on him, matching her anger against his. "You expect me to risk all our lives for slaves! Tell me, Pliny, aren't we all slaves? Slaves to the tyrant? Have you no tears for us? Or for yourself? For you are as much a slave as any of us. You know what kind of man he is, don't deny it. I studied your face when you returned from those midnight visits with him. I saw the fear in your eyes. You know what that monster will do to us and to our families and friends if we fail. We've suffered him for fifteen years. He could live for another twenty or thirty. The fate of Rome is more important than your wretched handful of slaves!"

"No, madam. I sympathize, I understand, but I do not agree. The Deified Julius was murdered, Claudius murdered, Caligula murdered, Galba and Vitellius murdered amid the horrors of civil war when blood ran in our streets. And now Domitian, too? Do you want that again? He's popular with the legions in Germania. They'll demand blood for blood. We have been lucky in Vespasian and Titus, not so lucky in Domitian. But we must endure him. Otherwise it is back to the old ways where everything is decided by the knife. Are we a great and noble people or are we a pack of savages?"

"You little prig!" She was on her feet, her small fists clenched. "Don't talk to me of nobility. My family was noble when yours was still hoeing turnips. You have the soul of a subordinate, you will always have a master, if not Domitian, then someone even worse. You were the emperor's praetor three years ago, weren't you, when the philosophers were purged. On your watch, good men like Rusticus and Senecio and their noble wives were executed or deported to prison islands. These men were your friends, your mentors. Was one word heard from you?"

He looked away. He remembered that Scortilla, on the day of the funeral, had called him an informer. Then it had merely exasperated him. But coming from this brave woman, the words cut like a knife. "I loved them, I admired their courage. Secretly, I wept for them."

"Secretly," she sneered.

"Dammit, they went too far. They would have plunged us into civil war!"

"For the last time," she demanded, "what will you do? There is no more room for excuses. Are you going straight to denounce me? If you don't then you are one of us."

The room seemed to contract around him. Suddenly he couldn't breathe. How easy it would be to do nothing…But no. His duty was clear. Not even for Amatia—and his heart ached for her—could he allow this reckless attempt to go forward.

"Zosimus," he called out, "come here."

The young man appeared in the doorway. "Patrone?"

"You will prevent the Lady Amatia from leaving until I return. I'm going to the palace. I'll knock Parthenius down if I have to, but I'll get to the emperor's ear."

"So he can reward you yet again?" Her lip curled. "And just what will you tell your precious Lord and God? That Verpa raped me and I killed him? Go ahead then. But I'll deny everything else. I don't fear torture or death. And you have no proof, no evidence of any conspiracy."

"Oh, but there is evidence, madam. The horoscope and Domitilla's letter, naming all of you. Where are they?"

"I told you I couldn't find them. The night Verpa died, I searched the *tablinum* in vain. So did Lucius—I nearly collided with him in the dark. The next morning men from the Prefecture came and carted everything away."

"But the prefect couldn't find them either. I suspect they never were in the *tablinum*. Come now, you haven't told me quite the whole story of that night in Verpa's bedroom, have you? What did you do during those long hours alone with his corpse. Merely tremble? No. You noticed his bedside table with its locked drawer, the only place in the house where neither you, nor Lucius, nor the prefect's men had looked. You had the dagger that Ganymede dropped and you had plenty of time. You pried open the drawer—we've seen the gouges in the wood—you found those dangerous papers there and you took them out with you. When I brought you here you wouldn't have left them behind and, since you haven't left my house since you came here you have them still. I ask you again, where are they?"

"And I tell you again, I don't have them!"

"I don't believe you. They're here and I will find them. Zosimus, keep an eye on her."

The room he had given Amatia for her bed chamber was small and uncluttered. It had hardly a place to hide anything. She had brought with her a bag containing some belongings. Pliny dumped it out on the bed. There wasn't much—combs, a few pieces of jewelry, some coins, an amulet. He tossed them on the floor and ripped off the bedclothes. He shook the sheets and coverlet, tore open her pillow. Nothing. He flung it away from him. He got on his knees and looked under the bed, he peered into her chamber pot, felt along the top of the doorjamb. His eyes darted everywhere. Where had the damned woman put them? He felt no pity at all for her now. Anger had driven pity out.

He ran back to where he had left her. "Give them to me!"

Young Zosimus blinked, he had never seen his master in a rage before. But Amatia did not flinch and, after a moment, Pliny sank into his chair, baffled, not knowing what to do next. He had been so sure. Just then a slave appeared in the doorway. "Master, that doctor, the one you just chased away—he's back. He begs to see you."

"Send him away, I've no time for him."

"Yes, master."

But Soranus pushed past the slave. Pliny glowered at him.

"Look, sir, I am sorry. You're quite right to be angry with me." He avoided looking at Amatia. "I wouldn't trouble you further but for this." He held out a small roll of papyrus, tied with a string. "When I loosened the lady's girdle, it fell from her underclothes."

Amatia drew a sharp breath. Her hand went to her waist.

"I tucked it in my belt," he explained, "meaning to give it back to her later. But then you, ah, requested me to leave your house. On my way home, I realized I still had it. Allow me to return it to her now together with my apologies."

"I will take charge of it, doctor. Thank you for your trouble. I was too hasty with you. Good night."

Pliny undid the string and spread the two sheets out on his knees. The horoscope, the letter. He felt Amatia's eyes on him as he read. Then he let the papers fall and buried his face in his hands. Amatia retrieved them.

"Does this change anything for you, Gaius Plinius?" Her voice was almost gentle; there was no mockery in it, and no triumph. "You know these names, don't you? The empress, the senators, your friend Corellius Rufus—I've heard you mention him. Will you send them all to their deaths? You can't do it, can you?" When he made no reply, she stood beside him and touched his arm. "I was wrong to hide this from you. I should have shown it to you straightaway. I should have trusted you. In a little less than three hours the deed will be done. You only need to wait…"

Her words were cut short by a commotion outside. Then the front door opened with a crash and the atrium filled with armed men. At their head was the Praetorian commandant. "Purissima, you're coming with us to Corellius' house!" Petronius shouted. "And him, kill him!" Rough hands seized Pliny, twisting his arms behind him. He felt a blade pressed against his throat. Felt it begin to cut.

Then, from somewhere a body hurtled toward him, grabbed his assailant by the throat and right arm and flung him away. Valens! Swords flashed out of scabbards, the clang of steel on steel filled the house. Years of hatred boiled up between these two forces. Here was a chance to even scores. Insults flew back and forth. "Cocksucker!" "Faggot!" The City Troopers formed a ring around Pliny. But they were outnumbered by the Praetorians and were no match for them in fighting skills. One went down, then another, while the house slaves and freedmen ran back and forth screaming. In a moment the polished floor was slick with blood. Valens, his cloak wrapped around his left arm, was doing his best to shield Pliny.

"How…?" Pliny managed to gasp.

"Your friend the—" Valens started to answer just as he received a sword thrust in the belly and went down.

It was over in minutes. "Go out and clear the street," Petronius ordered his men.

Drawn by the sound of fighting, a crowd of passers-by had gathered at the front door. Blood-spattered Guardsmen ran out shouting and slashing at them. They fled, Martial among them.

"Purissima, are you ready?"

Pliny cowered on the floor. Petronius seized him by his hair and raised his sword to hack off his head…

Then came the piercing shriek of some tortured animal. But no, not an animal. Calpurnia was dragging herself along the floor toward her husband. Ashen-faced, clutching her abdomen, her shift soaked with blood.

Chapter Thirty

The fourteenth day before the Kalends of Domitianus.
Day fourteen of the Games. The fifth hour of the day.

Earinus, dressed in the red silk tunic that he always wore, stood in an alcove of the emperor's bedroom, pouring a libation of wine to the household gods. It was one of his duties and he performed it proudly. The brain in his little head didn't retain much, but he knew the ritual words by heart. Elsewhere in the room, slaves were dusting, polishing, changing the bedclothes, plumping the pillows. Usually, they chattered to each other while they worked. This morning they seemed unusually quiet.

Earinus ignored them and they him. They didn't like him, he knew that; knew that they made fun of him behind his back. Let them laugh. Caesar loved him, told him how beautiful he was—especially his small, yellow-curled head. Like the head of a golden doll. Caesar loved to touch it for luck.

He had been the emperor's favorite bedmate for three years, ever since he was brought to the palace at the age of ten as a newly cut eunuch. He had nearly forgotten the pain and terror of the operation. But now he would be a boy forever, they told him, and so Caesar would love him forever.

One of the slaves, with his back turned to the boy, busied himself with the big water clock that stood against one wall of the room. Water flowing into a silver cylinder raised a float that lifted the tiny figure of a man. The figure held an arrow in its hand with which it pointed to the hours that were inscribed on a column. As the day proceeded, the figure rose until the arrow pointed to the twelfth hour at the very top. Then it had to be reset. There were complicated gears at the base of the clock which rotated the column with imperceptible slowness throughout the year in order to make the hours longer or shorter depending upon the season. Earinus loved to watch this mechanism during the long hours when he had nothing better to do. When the slave moved out of the way, Earinus was surprised. Where had the time gone? Could it be the sixth hour already? Well, his mind did play tricks sometimes. Even Caesar, who loved him, called him a silly, slow-witted child.

As Earinus was puzzling about the clock, the big double-doors opened and in bustled Parthenius. His gaze swept the room. "Out," he ordered the slaves, "Caesar is coming." His eye lit on Earinus. "You too, little girl."

Earinus didn't like Parthenius, who always called him "freak" and "little girl" and sometimes pinched him when no one was looking. But he was not to be bullied. He stood his ground. After a moment the fat man shrugged. "Suit yourself, then."

There was the scrape of many feet out in the corridor. The emperor approached, trailed by a retinue of courtiers and guards.

Earinus had seen his lord and master grow more haggard and ill day by day. He looked like an old man now, shuffling instead of striding as he used to do. Often at night he would pace the room for hours, or kill flies, or call him to his couch and fondle and kiss him until finally sinking into a labored sleep.

The emperor spoke wearily to the grand chamberlain. "I've spent all morning with Entellus trying to dictate letters but I can't make my brain work any more. He finally ordered me to take some rest. Good man, Entellus. Cares for me."

"Quite right, too, Caesar." Parthenius pulled a sympathetic face.

Some of Domitian's retinue were trying to follow him into the room, but the chamberlain blocked the doorway with his great bulk. "Please, gentlemen, Caesar wants to be alone." He shut the double door in their faces.

To Earinus' eye the grand chamberlain was sweating more than usual this morning and breathing heavily. The emperor noticed it too.

"What's the matter with you, then," he said irritably. "You're too damned fat is what you are. I order you to go on a slimming diet."

"Yes, Caesar."

"What time is it now? It's the fifth hour, isn't it? The hour that soothsayer foretold for my death this day."

But Parthenius only smiled and pointed to the clock. "You are mistaken, Caesar. Look, why it's already the sixth hour. The fifth hour has come and gone, and nothing at all has happened, you see? He was lying, there is nothing to fear."

"What do you say?" Domitian crossed the room in two strides, bent over the clock. When he turned back, his eyes were suddenly alive and a slow disbelieving smile uncovered his teeth—the smile of a wolf, if wolves smiled. "By thundering Jupiter, you're right, Parthenius! The man lied! I'm all right then? The nightmare is over! Earinus, you hear that? The danger is past. Come here, boy, let me kiss you! By the gods, I feel like a new man. Bring me wine." Earinus fetched the flagon and a goblet. Domitian tipped the flagon down his throat and drained it. He wiped his mouth, took a deep breath and expelled it slowly. The weariness seemed to drop away from he him. He did a little dance step and laughed like a boy. "Well that's that. All this worry, all these precautions for nothing. For nothing! Do you delight at my good fortune, Parthenius?"

"Of course, Caesar. How should I not? Soon the whole world will delight at it. And I myself will build a temple to your good fortune at my own expense."

Domitian held the chamberlain by his shoulders, pulled him close and kissed both his fat cheeks. "Thank you, my loyal friend, thank you. And now, by Jupiter, I'd like my bath!"

"Excellent idea, my lord. Shall I summon the guards to go with you?"

"Eh? No need for that today. I'm a free man!"

"As you say, lord."

Domitian strode out followed by the chamberlain who, with a last malignant glance at Earinus, shut the doors behind him.

Alone in the room, Earinus went over to the clock and watched the water dripping from its pipe into the cylinder. Presently, it struck him that the gears which turned the column had not moved even a little in all the time he'd been staring at them. It was water from the outflow pipe that operated them. He looked more closely and saw that there was no water running from it. Someone had stuck a plug of wool into the pipe so that water couldn't escape from the cylinder. The float and the little man with his pointer were rising too fast! Earinus scratched his small head and worked his small brain and wondered. What could it mean? He must tell his master.

As he stood pondering this discovery, he heard the sound of footsteps and whispered words outside the door. The door opened, admitting a dark-haired man with an injured arm. "Wait for him here," he heard the sentry say. But it was more of a whisper than the sentry's usual bark. Something about this made Earinus take fright and he ran to hide himself in the alcove before he was seen. From his hiding place he could not see the man directly but by looking up at one of the polished moonstone mirrors that were fixed near the ceiling in each corner of the room he saw his reflection.

He watched as the man sat down on a nearby chair and felt along his bandaged left arm with the fingertips of his right hand. Earinus held his breath.

Minutes passed and then again the door opened. And this time it was the emperor, wearing a loose bathing robe and sandals, dripping water on the marble floor.

"What is this about?" he demanded. "Why have I been dragged from my bath?"

The man with the injured arm jumped to his feet. "Caesar, I have an urgent message for you. The Praetorian commandant has uncovered a new conspiracy against your sacred person. Read this." He held out a pair of wax tablets.

The emperor tried to laugh. "Another conspiracy? There can't be another one. I've escaped my fate, don't you see." He looked the messenger up and down. "Who are you? Haven't I seen you around here before?"

"Yes, Caesar," the man replied. "I am called Stephanus. I make myself useful here in small ways."

"I see. What's wrong with that arm of yours? It's been bandaged for some time, hasn't it?"

"An infection, sir. It's healing slowly."

"Well, have it looked at by a competent man. You can't be too careful with those things."

"I will, Caesar. Thank you."

Earinus crept from his hiding place. He pulled at the emperor's sleeve. "Master?"

"What, you still here?"

"Master, the water…broken…"

"Can't you see I'm busy? Get away with you now."

The boy was desperate, his throat constricted. Why couldn't he make his words come out?

Stephanus put the tablet in Domitian's hands. "Please, Caesar, there's no time to lose!"

Again Earinus tugged at the emperor's sleeve but he cuffed him on the side of the head and sent him sprawling. "Later, I said. Stupid boy!"

Earinus watched in silence as the emperor unwound the cord that bound the two leaves of the tablet together and lowered his eyes to read. Then, in a movement so fast that the boy couldn't follow it, there was a dagger in the messenger's hand. The blade flashed upward, piercing the emperor in the groin. Domitian groaned and doubled over. The blade came out followed by a gush of blood from between his legs. Stephanus stepped back but Domitian, crouching, flung himself at him with a scream of rage, grappling him around the knees and throwing him down. Stephanus' arm was tangled in his sling and he couldn't free it. He struck the emperor a glancing blow in the side but then Domitian was on top of him holding his right wrist. Earinus, petrified but desperate for his master, ran from his hiding place. "Boy!" Domitian gasped, "my sword under the pillow!" Earinus ran to the bed while the two men, both smeared with blood, thrashed and grunted on the floor. He reached for the sword and pulled out—a hilt with no blade!

The two men, rolled over and over, Domitian gripping the dagger blade with bloody fingers, while with the other hand he clawed at his assassin's eyes. Even mortally wounded, he was stronger than his attacker. Stephanus shouted for help and now the sentry was running in followed by one of the imperial gladiators with their swords drawn. They dragged Domitian off and stabbed him again and again until he stopped moving. A moment later Parthenius and two of his assistants appeared. Stephanus struggled to his feet, breathing heavily, and for a brief moment the vision of rich rewards from his grateful compatriots danced before his eyes. But only for a moment. The gladiator ran him through, as he had been instructed to do by Parthenius. One less mouth to tell the tale. The steward had never been one of their kind anyway.

"Send for the empress," Parthenius ordered and one of his men dashed off.

Domitia Longina Augusta looked down at her husband's corpse. Her lips twisted in contempt. "All those polished mirrors, all the guards and watchmen. Useless." She spat on him.

No one paid any attention to the small-headed boy who lay in the corner sobbing, his red tunic pulled up over his eyes to keep out the horror.

The eighth hour of the day.

The streets were filled with Praetorians in full battle gear. The City Battalions had been disarmed, and their prefect, Aurelius Fulvus, arrested. At a hastily convened session in the Senate House with as many senators and magistrates as could be rounded up, Pliny not among them, Marcus Cocceius Nerva was unanimously voted the collection of titles and powers which gave a gloss of civil legality to his usurpation. A noisy delegation marched to his house to hail him. Unfortunately, he was too indisposed to welcome them. He had spent the whole morning throwing up.

Chapter Thirty-one

That evening.

The tumult outside penetrated even to the innermost rooms of the house. Romans marching, dancing and singing in the streets—still celebrating the overthrow of the tyrant. On every corner, his gilded statues were being pulled down with ropes amid the cheers of the populace and the shrilling of flutes.

Pliny sat by his wife's bed, holding her bone-white hand while she slept, watching the slight rise and fall of her breast. The floor was still littered with bloody cloths.

"I'll be going then," the midwife said. "Have your people change the poultice every hour regular and feed her only a little broth. Make a vow to Aesculapius. I can't do more. Goodbye, sir. And I'm truly sorry."

He barely nodded as the woman left.

Zosimus tapped on the door and came in. "You must come away and sleep, Patrone. I'll keep watch. And…Patrone, I want to beg your forgiveness."

Pliny looked up in surprise. "What on earth for?"

"For being useless, scared out of my wits. I failed in my duty."

"Nonsense, what could you or anyone have done? We owe our lives to the Purissima."

"You still call her that, even though—"

"Of course I do. What else?"

At that moment, Calpurnia sighed, and her eyelids fluttered open; she moved her lips. "Gaius? How…?"

"Hush." He lifted her to him, kissing her forehead, murmuring thanks to every deity he could name.

"Have I been sick?"

"The gods have given you back to me, that's all that matters. We…we despaired. So much blood. Hush now."

"No, but tell me what has happened. What are they shouting outside?" She gripped his hand and tried to struggle up on an elbow. He felt her trembling.

"Yes, yes, all right. The emperor has been assassinated. Before that, the Praetorian commandant and his men came here to take Amatia away and to, well, to deal with me." She needn't know every detail. "Then you went into labor and Amatia took command. I confess I've never seen anyone so magnificent. She refused to leave us. She sent a slave running for the midwife. And she convinced Petronius that I had joined their conspiracy to overthrow the emperor. Yes, that's what it was all about. I don't know if he believed her, but such force leapt from that woman's eyes…Short and stout she may be, but at that moment, she seemed to tower over him like the great statue of Minerva come to life. Anyway he backed down."

"And had you? Joined them?"

Pliny shook his head wearily. "At that moment I honestly don't know."

For a while they were both silent. Then Calpurnia whispered, "And now, husband, I want to see my baby."

He covered his eyes with his hand.

Chapter Thirty-two

A week later.

Domitian's corpse had been carted away on a common litter by the public undertakers, as they did with paupers. His old nurse saw to his burial in an inconspicuous spot. The elderly Nerva, looking shrunken inside the voluminous folds of Domitian's triumphal toga, had presided as emperor over the final day of the Roman Games. In the city, people waited nervously for the tramp of approaching legions, but, as it became clear that there would be no civil war, rejoicing broke out anew and continued for days.

A communiqué had been promptly released from the palace announcing that the tyrant had been killed. No names were named but the text underlined that his death had occurred at the fifth hour on the fourteenth day before the Kalends, the precise day and hour that had been widely prophesied. Plainly, Fate, or the stars, or call it what you will, had spoken. There was no gainsaying it. And Parthenius had even found the time, during those last hectic days, to throw together an imperial horoscope for Nerva. So that clinched the matter.

The dead emperor's memory was formally damned by the Senate. In an orgy of hate, his arches and monuments were demolished, his name obliterated from inscriptions. The months Germanicus and Domitianus reverted to their old names, September and October.

The Deified Julius and Augustus had named the months Quinctilis and Sextilis respectively after themselves, but they had died with honors and the changes seemed likely to last; not so Domitian. It would be as if he had never existed. The following day Aurelius Fulvus, the city prefect, who had been a regime stalwart to the end, was removed from office, and Pliny was politely relieved of his post as vice-prefect, although with a commendation from Nerva for good work and a hint that, having shown such a talent for detection, there might be further assignments of a confidential nature. Pliny devoutly hoped there would not be. He had sunk into a deep funk, crushed by the double loss of his stillborn son and Verpa's slaves. Apart from unavoidable duties, he hadn't left the house in a week.

All that drew him out today was a desperate message from Hispulla. Corellius Rufus, her husband, had resolved to starve himself to death; she begged Pliny to come and reason with him. He approached this meeting with a heavy heart.

When he arrived he was dismayed to find Amatia there too. How should he feel about this woman who had saved his and Calpurnia's lives while coolly condemning forty innocent human beings to death? Now, unexpectedly he was face to face with her one last time. Though he scarcely recognized her. She lay stretched on a couch beside the old man, looking nearly as ill as he did. Her hair hung limp around her drawn face. She too had decided to end her life.

Pliny went swiftly to his mentor, knelt beside the couch and took his hand. "Sir, I have lost much, am I now to lose you?"

The old man dismissed this with a stern look. "I told you once, my boy, that I only wanted to outlive that monster by a day, and I have done so, thanks to the bravery of Amatia and Iatrides and, though I hate to say it, the odious Parthenius— perhaps him most of all. Domitian could kill any number of us senators with impunity. His great mistake was in frightening the creature who put him to bed every night."

"Sir, I know your part in all this. Why couldn't you have confided in me?"

"And forced a role on you that you mightn't have chosen for yourself? And a reputation for conspiracy that could follow you the rest of your days? No. It was better this way. You will be a valued senator and a trusted adviser. You have a distinguished career before you. Accept it and put this past unpleasantness out of your mind; that is what a philosopher would do. It's all over and done with." He smiled benignly and patted him on the shoulder. And as for that meeting where he himself had voted for his protégé's death? Well, what good would it do to confess that now?

All over and done with, Pliny thought ruefully. For the slaves certainly. He had forced himself to go to the Colosseum to view their charred remains, still smoking on the embers of the pyre where they had been burned alive. He regarded it as his punishment.

There had been no trial in the Senate; Nerva Caesar heard the case in private. Pliny laid out the facts and pleaded for the slaves—he had spent all night preparing his oration. But the emperor stopped him in mid-flight with a peremptory wave of his arm. The transformation of man into monarch, Pliny noted, had taken place with remarkable swiftness.

"Enough! I will not inaugurate my reign by involving a Vestal Virgin in scandal as Domitian would have done. You tell me the slave Ganymede attacked his master with a dagger. The fact that the man was already dead is a detail. No one wants to know that the Vestalis Maxima has committed a sordid murder. They want to hear that slaves are guilty and will get the punishment they deserve. If I let them off, not a senator in Rome will feel safe in his bed at night and it is crucial that I keep the Senate on my side in these early days."

"But in the name of justice, sir…"

"Senator, justice and the law are rather different things—a lesson you should have learned by now. I will be as just as I can afford to be, no more and no less."

Amatia interrupted his reverie. Raising herself on an elbow, she ventured a smile at him. "You were wrong, you know, Gaius Plinius. There is no civil war, no blood in the streets."

Pliny inclined his head. "We have been luckier than we deserved. Perhaps the gods have pitied us."

"Don't thank the gods," Corellius broke in, "thank Trajan, the governor of Upper Germany. He is content to hold his legions in check and wait for Nerva to die a natural death. He knows it won't be long. I had his word on it."

Pliny sighed. How much else was there that he hadn't known?

For a long moment a silence hung between the three of them. Then Amatia spoke. "You may ask yourself, Gaius Plinius, why I didn't destroy the letter and horoscope once I possessed them."

He raised an eyebrow. He had wondered.

"I had a reason. I vowed to burn them at the underground chamber where my darling Cornelia lies buried, as an offering to her shade, so that she would know how I took vengeance for her. And a few nights ago, in secret, that is what I did. And the next day I petitioned Nerva to release me from my service to the goddess—which he has done. I am no longer the Purissima, but only a woman, alone. Nothing remains for me now but to die and, if the poets speak truly, my shade and Cornelia's will soon be together again."

"Hades, they say, is a gloomy place."

"It won't matter."

"Even if you encounter the mournful shades of forty slaves there?"

She stiffened at that. "For what it's worth, I regret their deaths. Don't think unkindly of me, my friend. We're all a mixture of elements, aren't we?"

As she spoke, a light burned in her eyes like the last flare of a dying flame. Then she sank back again on the cushions.

"Madam—Amatia—if I may, I have one question to ask you and then I will leave you in peace. *Why* did you stop Petronius from cutting off my head?"

"Ah." She made a little smile. "Because Rome needs principled, decent men like you. The things I said to you that day—I spoke in anger. You aren't a bad man. You deserved a better master. And there was another reason too. Childless as I am, I seem to have the soul of a mother. Calpurnia is dear to me, I could not abandon her. What do the doctors say?"

"She is still very weak."

"But she has the resilience of youth. She will live to bear you more sons. And now I have a favor to ask of you. I'm told you are something of a writer, that you record your thoughts and observations of life in the form of letters, which, from time to time, you publish. You will oblige me by omitting me from your reminiscences and leave me to a welcome oblivion. I ask it not for my sake but for the Order."

"I assure you both," Pliny replied with feeling, "that I have no wish to revisit these past two weeks. They have left a bitter taste on my tongue. The world will not learn of it from me."

No, the world would not learn of it, but what had *he* learned? He felt he had grown older, as if those fifteen days had been as many years. Most Romans drank in cynicism with their mother's milk. He somehow never had. But now he no longer felt the comfort of his old certainties. At the crucial moment, they had turned to water and trickled through his fingers. Would he ever again find firm ground to stand on? He suspected he would be a long time looking.

Epilogue

One year later.

Seagulls swooped and cried in the salt-sharp morning air. Martial leaned on the railing of the *Amphitryon* and watched the dock-hands as they trundled the last of the cargo up the gangplank. The harbor of Ostia rang with seamen's shouts and the creak of ropes as yardarms were hoisted up masts. The morning tide would soon be running, and a score of ships would depart from the busy port of Rome to every corner of the Empire. This one would take him home to Spain. Forever.

He was past fifty and felt his years heavy on him. He had spent half his life in Rome without ever achieving the success he dreamed of. He could no longer afford the expense of living in the city and, truthfully, he had begun to miss the hills and woods and rivers of his youth.

Domitian's victims were heroes now. In his inaugural address, Nerva had promised to repress the informers and respect the freedom of the Senate. Of course, Domitian had said the identical words when he came to the throne. So had Caligula, so had Nero. Hearing this, Pliny and his ilk wept tears of joy and rushed to heap flatteries upon their new master. Some months afterwards, though, the Praetorians, instigated by their new commandant, Aelianus, rioted and besieged the palace, demanding that Nerva execute the murderers of Domitian.

The frightened emperor reluctantly handed over Petronius, whom he had already removed from his post as Praetorian commandant, and Parthenius. The former was dispatched mercifully with a single stroke of the sword, but the grand chamberlain had his private parts cut off and stuffed into his mouth before being strangled. Domitian's empress withdrew to her country estate to lead a quiet life of retirement.

Pliny had come out of it very well, Martial reflected. He had joined the ranks of the new majority, applauded Nerva, and was now fulsome in his praise of those senatorial martyrs who had died for their republican ideals under Domitian. If he felt any lingering bitterness over the fate of the slaves, he was careful not to let it show.

But no, this was too harsh. Pliny wasn't as cynical or as opportunistic as many others. He was a trimmer, but which of us, Martial told himself, is innocent of the charge of flattery and trimming—certainly not I. The age we live in has shriveled our spirits.

Some things that seemed important at the time now seemed trivial in retrospect. No more had been heard of the Christians, for one thing. As is generally the case with these hole-in-the-corner fanatics, they had dissolved back into the general muck, leaving the field to some other gang of lunatics.

As for Verpa's charming family, the old man's will was never challenged since the complainant, Lucius, had absconded. Left unguarded by Valens and his troopers, and with the city in turmoil, he had simply disappeared, taking with him whatever loose money was in the house. By now he could be in Egypt or Britain or anywhere in between. Regulus, Verpa's lawyer, acted as executor of the estate and, in due course, the legacy to the Temple of Isis was paid. Soon after that Turpia Scortilla disappeared. One night, she attended a nocturnal ceremony at the temple. She was seen entering the private chapel with the priest of Anubis. She was never seen leaving it. Odd. But no one cared to pursue the matter.

Without much delay, Alexandrinus too left town to pursue his priestly vocation in other climes. How much money he took with him no one knew. The Isiac clergy were grimly silent on the subject.

Verpa's mansion was soon sold off to some businessman who converted part of it into a fuller's works. The odor of piss now made the whole street quite unlivable.

Martial scanned the waterfront. Pliny had promised to come down from Rome to see him off. Since the day of Domitian's death they had never discussed the Verpa case and, in fact, the two men had rather avoided each other; there was no open breach, but a coolness grew up between them. Martial felt ashamed of his part in the affair. How much of that Pliny suspected, he preferred not to know. On the other hand, his erstwhile patron had never succeeded in gaining for him his heart's desire, the position of court poet and, when Martial had, at last, asked him for a gift of money to pay his way home, Pliny had seemed to leap at the chance—though with many expressions of regret—to perform this small service.

And here he came now, bustling among the bales heaped at the water's edge and up the gangplank. All smiles.

The farewell was brief and awkward enough. Martial recited a poem he had written in his honor; Pliny had the good manners to praise it. He overflowed with best wishes and lamented that life in Rome kept him too busy to travel. He promised to write. Of course, he wouldn't. They bade each other farewell with a feeling of mutual relief.

And then the *Amphitryon* cast off and set sail. Toward evening they dropped anchor in the Bay of Naples to take on a consignment of wine before standing across to Sicily. A blood-red sun was setting behind the barren speck of Pandateria. Martial leaned out over the railing and squinted. He thought he could make out a lone figure walking slowly along the shoreline, gazing out to sea. It piqued his poet's imagination. Could it be Domitilla—she whose letter to Verpa had set in motion all that followed? Still there? Conveniently forgotten and likely to remain so forever. Did she miss her old life or was she content to remain alone with her strange god, the one who forbade his worshippers to make images of him? This made Martial think fleetingly of the familiar Roman gods, nourished with the blood and smoke of sacrificial meat. And that made him think of the Roman Games, although he would rather not have. They had been enacted once again since the fall of Domitian. He had done his best to ignore them; they left a bad taste in his mouth. The Roman Games, he thought morosely: lies, murder, hypocrisy, betrayal. These are the games we Romans play best.

The wind was turning cold. He shook himself and went below.

Appendix

The Roman Calendar

In the Roman calendar, each month contained three "signpost" days: the Kalends (the first day of the month), the Nones (either the fifth or the seventh), and the Ides (the thirteenth or fifteenth). After the Kalends was past, the days were counted as so-and-so many days before the Nones, then before the Ides, and then before the Kalends of the following month.

The story takes place during the first part of September (which Domitian had renamed *Germanicus* in honor of his victories in Germany.) The modern dates with their Roman equivalents are as follows:

The Kalends of Germanicus	September 1
The 4th day before the Nones	September 2
The 3rd day before the Nones	September 3
The day before the Nones	September 4
The Nones of Germanicus	September 5
The 8th day before the Ides	September 6
The 7th day before the Ides	September 7
The 6th day before the Ides	September 8
The 5th day before the Ides	September 9
The 4th day before the Ides	September 10
The 3rd day before the Ides	September 11
The day before the Ides	September 12

The Ides of Germanicus	September 13
The 18th day before the Kalends of Domitian	September 14
The 17th day before the Kalends	September 15
The 16th day before the Kalends	September 16
The 15th day before the Kalends	September 17
The 14th day before the Kalends	September 18

Roman Time-Keeping

Romans divided the day, from sunup to sundown, and the night from sundown to dawn into twelve *horae*. As the length of the day and night varied throughout the year, one of these "hours" could be as short as forty-five minutes or as long as seventy-five. In September, when the days and nights are of about equal length, the hora came closest to our standard sixty-minute hour. The first hour of the day in September was about 6:00 a.m. The sixth hour was noon; the twelfth hour, sundown. And similarly, the first hour of the night was about 6:00 p.m., the sixth hour was midnight, and the twelfth hour was the hour just before dawn.

Emperors from Augustus to Trajan

The Julio-Claudian Dynasty

Augustus, 27 B.C. – 14 A.D.

Tiberius, 14 – 37

Caligula, 37 – 41

Claudius, 41 – 54

Nero, 54 – 68

The Year of Three Emperors

Galba, Otho, Vitellius, 69

The Flavian Dynasty

Vespasian, 69 – 79

Titus, 79 – 81

Domitian, 81 – 96

The Adoptive Emperors

Nerva, 96 – 98

Trajan, 98 – 117

Glossary

Atrium: The central room in a Roman house, lying on an axis between the vestibule and the *tablinum*

Caldarium: The hot water pool in a Roman bathhouse

Capitolium: The Capitoline Hill; site of the temple of Jupiter, Juno, and Minerva

Cinaedus: A lewd male dancer in the pantomime

Clemens: Merciful

Concubina: A concubine. Unlike a casual sex-slave, the concubine had certain legally defined rights. Senators were not permitted to form legal marriages with women from degrading occupations such as actresses, prostitutes, or circus performers and so took them as concubines.

Culus: Asshole

Cunnus: Cunt

Denarius: A Roman silver coin equal to four sesterces (See below.)

Digitus infamis: The extended middle finger

Dignitas: Status, standing

Domus Augustana: The private apartments of Domitian's palace

Domus Flavia: The portion of Domitian's palace reserved for public business and state banquets

Familia: Not only 'family' in our sense but the slaves and freedmen of a household. Freed slaves continued to maintain close ties with their former master, who became their patron.

Fasces: Bundles of rods and axes, representing the magistrate's power to punish and execute.

Fellator: Cocksucker

Filius familias: The son and heir

Frigidarium: The cold water pool in a Roman bath

Fututor: Fucker

Gravitas: Authority, serious demeanor

Honoris causa: Honorary

Impluvium: The shallow catch-pool in the center of the atrium beneath the open roof

Insula: A multistory apartment building, often in ruinous condition

Lares and *Penates:* The household gods

Lictor: An attendant of a senior magistrate or the emperor

Lupa: Prostitute (literally, she-wolf)

Maenad: A frenzied female devotee of the god Bacchus

Mehercule (may-HAIR-coo-lay): So help me Hercules!

Mentula: Prick

Merda: Shit

Mos maiorum: The way of the ancestors, tradition

Palla: A woman's cloak

Paterfamilias: The oldest living male in a family, even if unmarried or childless (He had *patria potestas* over his *familia*, and only he could legally own anything.)

Patria potestas: The father's power of life and death over his children and slaves

Pica: In ancient medicine, a morbid condition thought to accompany pregnancy

Pontifex maximus: The chief priest of Rome. (In the imperial age this post was always held by the emperor.)

Popina: A fast-food restaurant

Praetor: A Roman magistrate with judicial functions

Quirites: A ritual term for Roman citizens

Salutatio: The morning ceremony in which clients paid court to their patron in return for a handout of food or money

Salve: "Greetings"

Sestertius (in English, sesterce): A silver coin equal to a quarter of a *denarius* used to count small or large sums of money.

Sica: A curved dagger

Sistrum: A rattle made of bronze or other metal used in ritual performances by priests and priestesses of Isis

Stola: A woman's dress

Tablinum: The master's office in a Roman house

Tepidarium: The warm water pool in a Roman bath

Thermae: Large public baths

Triclinium: The dining room (specifically, the dining table with couches on three sides, each couch holding three diners)

Tullianum: Rome's prison. Located in the Forum, it was quite
  small and used as a holding cell for political prisoners,
  generally of high status, awaiting trial or execution.

Vale: 'Goodbye'

Vestis: Clothing

Victimarius: An attendant at a sacrifice who slaughters the animal

Author's Note

The Roman historian Dio Cassius writes: At this time [the 90s A.D.] some people made a practice of smearing needles with poison and pricking with them whomever they pleased. From this sprang the idea for my story. From Dio also comes the description of the bizarre "black banquet" that the emperor hosted, although I have put my own interpretation on his motive.

Sextus Ingentius Verpa and his family are fictitious. However, the conspiracy to assassinate Domitian is historical and well documented by both Dio and by Suetonius, in his biography of the emperor.

The most valuable source for the social background of the period are the letters of my protagonist, Pliny the Younger (as he is called in English to distinguish him from his uncle, the author of the *Natural History*). I have made use of numerous events described in the *Letters* (though without regard to their chronology). Perhaps most curious to the reader will be Pliny's observation of the floating islands (actually dense mats of reeds) in Lake Vadimon. I have followed his description exactly. He himself could offer no explanation for this startling *trompe-l'oeil*.

A different slant on the mores of the age is provided by the poet Martial, whose *Epigrams* can be read in countless English translations—some bawdier than others. The translations in the novel (plus one poem that Martial never wrote) are my own.

Martial had several literary patrons, but Pliny is not known to have been one of them. Nevertheless, the two men did know each other and Pliny did, in fact, pay Martial's passage back to Spain and see him off. Based on this I have ventured to imagine a patron-client bond between them.

This is a work of fiction and I have taken a few liberties with history. I have coined the title "Purissima" for the *vestalis maxima*. Pliny never held the office of vice-prefect of Rome and is not known to have investigated a murder. I have predated his marriage to Calpurnia by several years. But, of his three wives, she was the last and the only one that he ever mentions. She was, in fact, less than half his age when they married and, she did suffer a miscarriage. They never succeeded in having children.

Concerning the religion of Clemens and Domitilla, there continues to be debate as to whether their "atheism" took the form of Judaism or Christianity—they are claimed as martyrs by both faiths. I have chosen to follow Dio, who says they were accused of "atheism and Jewish practices." The so-called God-fearers (Romans and Greeks who were attracted to Jewish monotheism and morality) are authentic. Christianity was still in its infancy, especially in the Latin-speaking half of the Empire. (Some years after the date of our story, Pliny, as governor of Bithynia, had occasion to investigate accusations of Christianity.) Isis worship, on the other hand, was enormously popular.

The gouty old senator, Corellius Rufus (of whose death Pliny writes a moving account in the *Letters),* was a fierce critic of Domitian, but there is no evidence that he participated in the conspiracy to assassinate him. Soranus of Ephesus is not known to have been Pliny's physician, but he was beginning his career in Rome at about this time. His *Gynecology* makes fascinating reading.

Finally, the execution of the Chief Vestal Cornelia by suffocation in an underground chamber actually happened and is described in detail in our sources.

Bibliography

For readers interested in learning more about Pliny's Rome and the background to this story, I suggest the following as a good starting point:

Primary sources:

Dio Cassius. *Roman History.* Translated by Earnest Cary. Harvard University Press (The Loeb Classical Library), 1925.

Martial. *Epigrams.* An excellent recent translation of a selection of the poems by Garry Wills is both skillful and properly racy.

Pliny the Younger. *The Complete Letters.* Translated by P. G. Walsh. Oxford University Press, 2006.

Suetonius. *The Twelve Caesars.* Translated by Robert Graves. Penguin Books, 1957.

Secondary works:

Balsdon, J. P. V. D. *Life and Leisure in Ancient Rome.* McGraw-Hill, 1969.

Beard, Mary; John North, and Simon Price. *Religions of Rome.* Cambridge University Press, 1998.

Clauss, Manfred. *The Roman Cult of Mithras.* Routledge, 2001.

Crook, J. A. *Law and Life of Rome.* Cornell University Press, 1967.

Hopkins, Keith. *A World Full of Gods: The Strange Triumph of Christianity.* Plume, 1999.

Shelton, Jo-Ann, ed. *As the Romans Did: A Sourcebook in Roman Social History,* 2nd ed. Oxford University Press, 1997.

Witt, R. E. *Isis in the Ancient World.* Johns Hopkins University Press, 1971.

THE BULL SLAYER

REVIEW

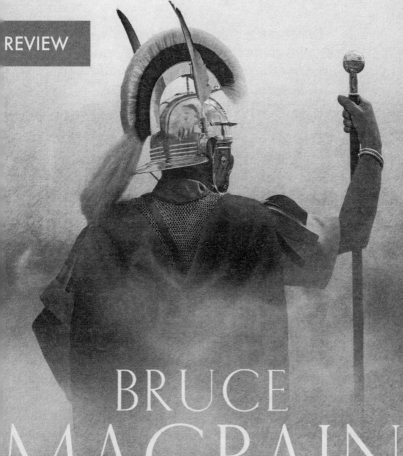

BRUCE
MACBAIN

Chapter One

THE TENTH REGNAL YEAR OF THE EMPEROR
TRAJANUS AUGUSTUS, CONQUEROR OF GERMANY,
CONQUEROR OF DACIA, PONTIFEX MAXIMUS,
HOLDING THE TRIBUNICIAN POWER,
CONSUL FOR THE FIFTH TIME, FATHER OF HIS
COUNTRY, BEST OF EMPERORS

The province of Bithynia-Pontus

Through long weeks of instruction, the Father had taught him the rituals, the star-lore, and the incantations that he must pronounce when the moment came. All that study had made his head hurt; but he had a purpose that drove him. For the past week he had abstained from sex, meat, and bathing. And now at last he was drawing near to the cosmic cave, to a confrontation with the beautiful young god in his fiery splendor. He would see the mystery of the bull's death, he would be baptized with water from a living spring, his soul would soar up through the seven planetary spheres to the starry firmament where one day it would dwell forever. He would share bread and wine—the flesh and life-giving blood of the bull—with his brethren and be born again for eternity.

They emerged finally from the dark woods at the foot of a craggy upthrust of bare rock and, just as they did so, the sun broke over its top and bathed them in its rays. The Unconquered Sun. All-powerful Mithras. Lord and Savior.

No casual traveler could have stumbled upon the entrance to the cave; it was low and only some six paces wide and well concealed by brush. While the *mystae* busied themselves clearing this away, the Father, a frail old man with infinitely wrinkled skin, turned to him, grasped his hand in fellowship, and smiled at him. "Are you ready, my son?"

Following the Father, he ducked under the rocky overhang and descended the seven stone steps, worn smooth by the feet of the blessed, down into the earth's dark womb. The damp subterranean chill made him shiver. The stale air smelled of dripping stone and burnt pine. Now the *mystae* moved here and there in the cave, igniting incense and lighting the pine torches that stood in niches along the walls. He gazed around him in the guttering light. The cave was no ordinary one; it had been reshaped by men's hands. It wasn't large—forty paces long, fifteen across. Twenty men filled it full. A narrow nave ran the length of it with stone benches along each side where they would recline for their meal. The low ceiling was arched, painted midnight blue, and sprinkled with golden stars; the signs of the zodiac ran around the walls. The nave ended in an apse where curtains hung before the altar. The crash of a bronze thunder sheet shattered the silence and unseen hands drew the curtains back. Then he gazed for the first time upon the mystery of his new faith. Suddenly he thought his heart would burst—the intensity of his feeling took him by surprise. Sculpted in high relief from the living rock, the figure of Mithras, a serene and handsome youth dressed in a billowing blue cloak and red Phrygian cap, straddled a kneeling bull, holding it down with his knee, pulling its head backward with one hand, and plunging his dagger into its throat. A dog and a serpent licked the bloody wound, a scorpion attacked the bull's testicles, and from the bull's tail sprouted ears of wheat.

Bells chimed and the hollow eyes of the god blazed with sudden fire. The *mystae* began to chant the *Nama Mithras*. They raised their hands, each one holding the emblems of his rank—cup, spear, sickle, whip, thunderbolt. The torchlight threw their shadows huge against the wall.

Now hands removed his clothes, blindfolded him, and guided him down the nave toward the altar. Hands on his shoulders forced him down, pressing his forehead painfully against the cold stone. Other hands pulled his arms behind him and bound them with the hot guts of a chicken. The sharp point of an arrow pricked his neck.

"Take three deep breaths," spoke the Father close to his face. "You will rise into the air, you will look upon the face of our god, you will taste immortality."

And so he did, or thought he did at any rate, for a brief moment. And then it was over. His new brothers raised him up, removed his blindfold, clothed him. They pressed around him, shaking his hand. The Father beamed. The Sun-Runner, second in rank to the Father, hailed him in his rich baritone.

"You're a Raven now, my good friend, and soon to rise still higher in our ranks. You honor us with your patronage, a man of your rank and power. And now let us eat and drink to your good fortune. I should say to *our* good fortune."

The new-made Raven looked from face to face and was answered with smiles all around. Indeed, *fortune* was the word.

Chapter Two

Nicomedia, capital of Bithynia-Pontus. Two years later.
The 13th day before the Kalends of October

Clerks bustled back and forth in the great hall, carrying armloads of scrolls, making a great to-do of hunting for the missing documents, accomplishing very little. Gaius Plinius watched them with growing exasperation. The chaos of the archives, the slovenly habits of the staff he had inherited from his predecessor, the ruinous state of the old royal palace in which they were housed. Day three in his new post. He had expected bad: this was worse.

"Patrone." His freedman Zosimus touched his shoulder. "It's past midday. You'll want to eat something and then rest for a bit. Doctor's orders."

"What? It can't be so late already. No, just have a tray brought in." Zosimus frowned. "It's all right, my boy. I'll rest later, I promise."

What would he do without Zosimus? Secretary, companion, nursemaid at times. Friend. He had a head of yellow hair like an untidy haystack and the innocent, earnest face of a fool—but he was far from being a fool.

"See if you can't find Suetonius out there somewhere and ask him to step in. And stop looking so worried." Pliny waved him off. While confusion reigned around him, he busied himself arranging the objects on his desk—ink stand, styluses, sheaves of parchment, a carafe of watered wine, a bronze bust of Epicurus the philosopher inherited from his learned uncle, a cameo of his darling Calpurnia painted by her own hand. There was comfort in orderliness, even in small things. His passion for order amused his more exuberant friends.

Lately he had begun to be aware of his own mortality. He was nearing a half century of life—more than three-quarters of his allotted span. A half century that had seen the enlargement of the empire while rot set in at the center. By the grace of the gods they had survived Caligula, Nero, and Domitian and come at last to the present happy state of affairs—the reign of a sane and benevolent emperor who respected their liberty. He prayed it would endure at least as long as he did.

Pliny knew that others saw in him only a rather plump, rather domesticated, rather fussy man. He made no apologies. It was a lifetime of hard work, reliability, attention to detail that had won him, at long last, this extraordinary appointment: Governor of Bithynia-Pontus with overriding authority to clean up the most corrupt, mismanaged, seditious, and turbulent province in the Empire. The province had been a backwater for too long; a place for second-raters, governors from whom little was expected. That would all change now. Only a few people knew it, but Bithynia was to be the staging area for an invasion of the Persian empire. Restoring order and sound finances was now a top priority. Trajan, Best of Emperors, had entrusted this to him. And he would not fail him. Bithynia was a graveyard of governors. Pliny knew he had enemies who would relish his downfall. What man of importance didn't? He was determined not to give them the chance.

"There's a line of people out into the street waiting to see you. All clutching petitions in their sweaty hands." Suetonius, pink-cheeked and pink-scalped—at forty he was already losing his hair—edged through the mob of clerks, accountants, and messengers, and dropped into an armchair beside Pliny's desk. "Shall I send them all away?"

"On the contrary, I want you to interview them—unless you're otherwise engaged?"

"I was about to be. Research, you know. But it can wait."

"Ah, and which of your many works-in-progress are you researching today? Greek Terms of Abuse? Famous Whores? Physical Defects of Mankind?"

"Well, one never knows what will turn up, does one?"

They laughed easily together. Gaius Suetonius Tranquillus was one of Pliny's literary protégés: a talented writer, a man of restless curiosity, a bottomless repository of rude anecdotes, a tireless collector of backstairs gossip, a lover of the odd fact, fascinated by the grotesque—in short, an extremely useful man to have along in this hellhole of sedition. He was vain, too, and combatted his baldness with concoctions of horseradish, cumin, and worse things—all to little avail. No sooner had he arrived in the province than he'd exchanged his white Roman tunic with an *eques'* purple stripes for a colorful Greek outfit of sheer linen. *The better to blend in—you learn more.* He had jumped at the chance to come to Bithynia on Pliny's staff.

"Have you found what you wanted in the files?"

Pliny pressed his fingers to his temples and rubbed, feeling the skin move on his skull—for an awful instant imagining the skull bare of flesh as it might look ten, fifteen years from now if he lasted that long, if he husbanded his strength. He drove the image from his mind. "Beyond belief, the mess he's left us with! Six former governors of this province have been prosecuted and our friend Anicius is likely to be the seventh, for sheer incompetence, if nothing worse. Transcripts of trials, minutes of meetings with the local grandees—all missing. He's taken them home with him or more likely burned them. And the people he's left behind, this lot." His glance took in the room. They come in late, they leave early, they give you sour looks when you speak to them. I'm putting you in charge of the secretariat. Whip them into shape."

Suetonius winced. "Not really my—"

Pliny held up a finger. "What on earth is that racket?"

Through the open second-story window, carried on a soft September breeze, came a sudden shriek of flutes and a crash of cymbals. A parading army couldn't have made more noise. Pliny and Suetonius looked out and, as they watched, a mob turned the corner, marching along the avenue below them, men and women together, dancing, leaping, shouting something—a word, a name? Pliny strained to make it out but in the general din it was impossible. But there was no doubting who the focus of this adulation was. On a litter that swayed above the heads of the crowd, rode a handsome man whose hair hung down his back in long curls. He stared straight ahead, looking neither left nor right, motionless as a statue while eager hands reached out to touch his long, white garment as he passed. In his right hand he held a glittering scimitar, but what held everyone's eye was the giant python that draped itself around his chest and over his shoulder, its head swinging to and fro.

Pliny felt a stab of anxiety. Somewhere out there in this alien city was his wife.

◇◇◇

"'Purnia, don't let go of me!"

"Hold tight, Ione!"

Calpurnia, the taller and sturdier of the two women, gripped her maid's hand as they struggled to keep their footing in this crowd of madmen that surged outside the temple of Asclepius and filled the whole marketplace alongside it. Elegant matrons pressed against greasy-aproned shopkeepers, beggars contested with merchants for a glimpse of the holy man who rode above them in his litter like a raft tossed upon a sea of eager faces and outstretched arms.

A sharp elbow hit Calpurnia in the side, knocking the breath out of her. Her knees buckled and she thought for an instant she would fall and be crushed under the stamping feet.

"Pancrates! The god returns!" The shout rose up from five hundred throats, mingling with the din of cymbals, flutes, and drums.

Calpurnia and Ione had spent the morning going round the shops and stalls and ateliers of the unfamiliar city, escorted by a retinue of slaves and local guides—all of them now lost somewhere in this seething confusion of color and noise. The palace in which she and Pliny and all their staff were housed had once belonged to the ancient kings of Bithynia. Mithridates the Great—a name that could still strike fear in Roman hearts even after a century and a half—had ruled his bloody empire from here; and so had Pompey the Great, who defeated him and made the kingdom a Roman province.

The palace, which sat on a high hill overlooking the harbor, was vast: more than a hundred rooms grouped around two great peristyle halls. Impressive in size but disappointing in detail. All the portable works of art, all the splendidly wrought furnishings had long since been looted, first by Mithridates and then by a succession of Roman governors, culminating with the wretched Anicius, who had filled a whole ship with whatever was still worth stealing. The mosaic floors were original and fine, but the statues that populated the courtyards were now mere copies of copies. The tapestries and draperies were shabby, the brass work tarnished, the frescoed walls black with soot, the rooms littered with trash, the smell of mildew heavy in the air. Calpurnia sighed for her Italian villa, swallowed hard, and determined to turn the place into a home worthy of her husband. Worthy of Rome. The last governor, who had no wife, was so parsimonious that tradesmen had stopped coming to the palace, so she must seek them out herself. In a single day she had examined fabrics, contracted with cabinetmakers and painters and silversmiths. Thank the gods she had Ione with her. Her freedwoman spoke fluent Greek, while Calpurnia's halting kitchen Greek was not up to haggling in the marketplace. That was another thing she was determined to rectify.

It was the end of a long and productive morning. Hunger and the hot sun overhead urged that they return to the palace for a bath—at least the plumbing worked—and a meal with their overworked husbands, Pliny and Zosimus. And then suddenly they had found themselves swamped in this sea of frenzied celebrants.

"Long life to Pancrates! Oracle of Asclepius!"

The crowd surged forward as the object of their adulation was helped down from his litter—he and the astonishing snake. At that point she lost sight of him as he passed within the bronze doors of the temple. But a herald stood on the topmost step and cried out, "The god has returned to his house. Present your questions and they will be answered to your heart's desire for the fee of one drachma."

The crowd was mostly male but there were women too, Greek women modestly veiled as their custom was. But then, to her surprise, Calpurnia saw Roman faces too, unveiled and elaborately coifed like herself. One towering hairdo atop a whitened face and fat neck forced its way toward her through the press of bodies.

"You remember me, Lady Calpurnia? Last night—the reception—such an honor…"

"Yes, of course," Calpurnia murmured. *What was the woman's name?* "So many new faces—Atilia, isn't it?"

"Philomela, you stupid little bitch, where are you?" The woman looked around angrily as a little slave girl, who couldn't have been more than ten, struggled after her, fighting with both hands to hold up a large parasol.

The woman turned back to Calpurnia. "Impossible to find decent slaves in this country. But isn't it wonderful, he's returned at last!"

Calpurnia looked at her blankly.

"Pancrates, of course. Our oracle."

Chapter Three

That night. The villa of Marcus Vibius Balbus

Balbus snapped his fingers. Thick fingers covered with coarse hairs. Fingers that in their day had gripped a centurion's *vitis*, bringing it down hard across the shoulders of any legionary who didn't jump to attention quick enough. Fingers that lately wielded nothing heavier than a stylus—but even a stylus was a weapon in those fingers. Marcus Balbus snapped his fingers and a young slave boy ran up to refill his goblet.

"More wine, Governor?"

Pliny, reclining beside him in the place of honor, hastily covered his cup with his hand. He'd drunk too much already. Balbus preferred his wine unwatered and forced his guests to do the same.

"Another bite of turbot?" He held out the morsel dripping with sauce on the point of his knife. Eat." It was very nearly a command. Balbus' face, square, brown, and hatched as a chopping block, leaned close, smiling unpleasantly. He was a man made entirely of bone and gristle, a man who kept himself fit, with big-knuckled hands and a shock of stiff red hair speckled grey. Gaulish blood there somewhere, Pliny imagined, or even German.

Pliny waved the food away. The dishes were all too sauced and spiced for his frugal tastes. And he would not allow this man to bully him. After a long moment, Balbus withdrew his hand and shrugged.

Conversation, which had died momentarily, resumed with pretended gaiety. There were nine of them at table, the usual number for a *triclinium*. In addition to Pliny and Calpurnia, the guests included Suetonius, who was always reliably entertaining at affairs like this; two wealthy Roman merchants, one accompanied by his wife, and a man named Silvanus, who was Balbus' chief accountant. The merchant's wife seemed to know Calpurnia and conversed with her throughout the evening with great animation. "Thrilled to see you again…this morning…a god…miraculous man…you must ask him…yes, a snake…" Calpurnia had that fixed smile on her face that meant she was bored to tears.

Again Balbus brought his battered face close to Pliny and said in a whisper that was meant to be heard around the table, "We've met before, you know, you and I."

"Have we? I'm afraid I—"

"Don't remember my face? Well, I was younger and handsomer then, and I was only one of many. The night before Emperor Domitian was murdered. I was a Praetorian Guardsman then. We paid you a little visit, didn't we? Almost cost you your life, didn't it? And your charming wife's." He smiled at Calpurnia the way a crocodile smiles.

Pliny felt the blood drain from his face. That was a night that still, after fourteen years, haunted his dreams. And Calpurnia's. And why was Balbus mentioning it now? To make him squirm, why else? Suetonius shot Pliny a worried look. Calpurnia felt for his hand.

Pliny drew a long breath. "Those were difficult days, my friend. Thank the gods we live in happier times."

Eager noises of assent around the table. Then Fabia, Balbus' wife, a big-boned woman all bosom and jewels, hastily changed the subject to her favorite, her only, topic of conversation.

"These Greeklings," she said, "scoundrels every one of them. They don't love us." She spoke in a fluting, gentrified Latin that didn't quite disguise something foreign in the accent—Thracian, it was rumored. Pliny had heard that she concealed barbarian tattoos under her clothing. He could almost believe it.

"No reason why they should," he answered mildly.

"We've brought them peace, haven't we?"

"Peace, lady Fabia, has never been what they wanted. If the Empire were to disappear tomorrow they would all be fighting each other again and loving it."

"Strange words for a governor," Balbus struck in.

"I'm a realist. They pay a high price for Roman peace as you, of course, would know, Procurator."

Balbus eyed him suspiciously. "Is there a question buried in that remark, Governor?"

Marcus Vibius Balbus was not accustomed to being questioned. Trajan had appointed him Fiscal Procurator of the province. For over two years now he had wielded absolute authority to raise taxes and pay the soldiers, answerable to no one but the Emperor. He had his own office and staff and lived lavishly with his family in a spacious seaside villa south of the city, while Pliny and Calpurnia camped out in the shambles of their ruinous palace. Balbus' power had equaled that of the governor himself. Not bad for a man who had started life as a common soldier, and clawed his way up the ranks: Chief Centurion of a legion, then a stint in the Night Watch, the City Battalions, and the Praetorian Guard, and finally a succession of civil posts in every corner of the world. The typical procurator's career, it produced the tough, experienced men who made the Empire run.

Balbus was a man whom no governor questioned. Until now. Pliny's extraordinary commission from the emperor overrode his authority. Balbus knew it. Pliny knew that he knew it. How long would it be before they had to confront it?

The procurator pulled in his horns just a little. "You have questions about the taxes, Gaius Plinius, speak to my man Silvanus. You there, Silvanus, are you still sober enough to speak? Introduce yourself. Where're your manners, you ugly fellow? This is our new governor, come all the way from Rome to help us count our pennies. Show him some respect. Perhaps you've brought your abacus with you, show him how well you do sums."

The man addressed was short-necked, beak-faced, and bald but for a few sparse hairs combed ear to ear; he resembled, Pliny thought, nothing so much as a tortoise. His eyes were narrow and nearly without lashes. He blinked them myopically. He stared at his food, his jaws working, and said nothing.

"The man's as dumb as he is ugly," Balbus said in a loud voice and laughed.

But Fabia, Pliny noticed, did not laugh. What was it that crossed her face for an instant? A tightening of the jaw muscles, the eyes moving to Silvanus and then sliding quickly away. Perhaps it was only his imagination.

"But he's loyal," Balbus continued. "Loyalty's the great thing. Been with me for years."

Another uncomfortable silence. Broken by Suetonius, who asked, "What can you tell us about the former governor?"

"Anicius?" Balbus answered. "Excellent man. Excellent. Miss him already."

Pliny and Suetonius had met Anicius Maximus at the harbor where he was waiting, amidst a mountain of luggage, to sail back to Italy on their ship's return voyage. He had seemed almost pathetically eager to be on his way. The emperor had nothing against the man, or at least nothing he had shared with Pliny, and yet Anicius' jumping eyebrows, his fluttering hands, his muttered apologies for his hasty departure all seemed to signal some consciousness of guilt. Would he be the seventh governor of Bithynia to be indicted on his return for crimes real or contrived?

"We got along like brothers, each to his own sphere, no conflicts, no ruction." Balbus seemed to feel the point needed underlining.

"We're having trouble finding a number of documents in the—"

"Took 'em with him," Balbus cut him off. "Perfect right to. Governor's papers are his own, you know that. Mine too."

Pliny decided for the moment to let that pass. This was not the time or place.

Balbus swung his legs off the dining couch, stood and stretched. "Show you around the place." Dinner, it seemed, was over.

The villa and grounds were spectacular, crammed with first-rate statues and objects, although jumbled together and poorly displayed as though the mere having of them was all that mattered to the procurator and his wife. Calpurnia, who was an artist herself, made appreciative comments to her hostess and asked where they had acquired this bust, that vase. Fabia glowered and answered her with curt monosyllables.

It was growing dark now and they were returning from the garden, Pliny and Calpurnia walking ahead, followed by Balbus and his wife and the others, when a slender figure, half-hidden in the shadow of the doorway, suddenly bolted across their path and vanished into the dim recesses of the house. It was so unexpected Calpurnia gasped and grabbed Pliny's arm. "What on earth was that?"

Instantly, Balbus and Fabia were on either side of them, shouldering them back. "One of the slaves," said Fabia too loudly, "pay no attention." But her eyes said something else. For an instant, Calpurnia could have sworn, those agate eyes turned liquid.

It was all over in a moment and Balbus was eager to see his guests to their carriages.

◇◇◇

"Delightful couple," said Suetonius with a twinkle in his eye. He, Pliny, and Calpurnia had stepped down from their carriages and stood together at the palace gate. "You're going to have your hands full with Balbus."

"Balbus will open his books for me or find himself back in Rome explaining himself to Trajan. The emperor was very clear. There is too much money sloshing about in this province, misspent, unaccounted for, squandered on projects that never seem to be completed. Whether our friend Balbus has his fingers in any of that I do not know. But I plan to find out."

"Do they have children?" Calpurnia asked.

"Why do you ask?" said Pliny.

"I just thought—no reason, really."

"You, by the way, were wonderful, my dear as always. Putting up with that dragon."

"Fabia doesn't like me."

"Not surprising. She's enjoyed the highest rank among the Roman wives up until now. I know that doesn't matter to you but it does to a woman like her. You now hold that place, like it or not, 'Purnia."

If it had not been so dark Pliny would have seen the anxious look that crossed her face. Suetonius, with sharper eyes, perhaps did see it.

"Well," said Pliny. "Let's make an early night. Busy day tomorrow. We meet the Greeks."

"Just one thing more, Gaius Plinius," Suetonius said. "If you don't mind. What Balbus said earlier, something about the Praetorians visiting you the night before the unlamented Domitian died. Some danger to yourselves? Happens I'm gathering material for another project of mine, biographies of the Caesars from Julius to Domitian. I'd be grateful for anything you might…"

Pliny froze him with a look.

"Well, I mean, that is…" Suetonius looked from Pliny to Calpurnia, who gazed at him steadily.

"We don't speak of that night," she said.

"Yes, well—sorry," he stammered, "please forget I asked."

"Already forgotten, my friend." Pliny smiled and clapped him on the shoulder. "Sleep well."

Not everyone slept that night.

In the temple of Asclepius, in a secret chamber beneath the great gold and ivory statue of the god, lamps burned late and a dozen sweating figures bent to their work: *Shall I receive the allowance? Will I be sold? Am I to be reconciled with my father? Will I get a furlough? Is he who is away from home alive? Is my partner cheating me? Am I to become a beggar? Will I become a fugitive? Will my son waste my property? Am I to be divorced from my husband? Will I get my money back? Is someone diddling my wife?*

Lads with nimble fingers inserted hot needles under the wax seals of the *tabellae*, opened them, and read out the questions. This was accompanied by a good deal of laughter. ("Yes, you old fool, half the town's diddling her!")

Pancrates permitted this. He paid them little enough, let them enjoy themselves. Better paid and more serious were his oracle writers, men with a smattering of literary education who composed the answers in crabbed poetic verses that could mean anything. The written replies were attached to the *tabellae*, which were then resealed so deftly that no one would suspect they had been opened. Often though, if the hour grew late and they were tired, they would simply attach stock answers without bothering even to read the questions. In any case, the next day the questioners would receive their responses for the price of a silver drachma. Hundreds of drachmas a day.

But that was for the common run of questioners. Seekers of higher status were vouchsafed an oracle from the mouth of the sacred python itself. Pancrates was careful to do this only rarely so as not to dilute the effect by overexposure. It was a complicated and tiring performance. He would sit in the doorway of the temple, the snake, asleep with drugged milk, hanging like a dead weight from his shoulders, its head under his arm, while he opened and closed the mouth of a canvas snake head by pulling invisible strands of horsehair. A confederate hidden behind him spoke through a tube made of cranes' windpipes.

For still more important clients—the Romans and their foolish wives—Pancrates would grant personal visitations: drawing out their secrets so subtly that he seemed, to their amazement, to read their unspoken thoughts. It was a talent he had perfected over years.

For the past six months he had toured the provinces of Greece and Asia, drawing immense crowds everywhere he went and putting to shame those shabby Christian proselytizers whom he encountered at every turn. Now he had returned in triumph to Nicomedia, all the more sought after because of his absence. It was time now to reactivate his network of informants. For in every great house there was some servant, some lowly hanger-on, who was on Pancrates' payroll. They sent him people's characters, forecasts of their questions, and hints of their ambitions, so that he had his answers ready. And sometimes the questions revealed that the writers were up to illegal activities. In these cases he didn't return the tablet with an answer but held on to it and used it to blackmail the sender. Here was where the real money was made.